The Intimate Memoir of
Dame Jenny Everleigh

Book One

In which an eager young miss learns the virtues of vice

Also in the Dame Jenny Everleigh Series in Sphere Books:

THE INTIMATE MEMOIR OF DAME JENNY EVERLEIGH VOLUME 2
THE INTIMATE MEMOIR OF DAME JENNY EVERLEIGH VOLUME 3
THE INTIMATE MEMOIR OF DAME JENNY EVERLEIGH VOLUME 4
THE INTIMATE MEMOIR OF DAME JENNY EVERLEIGH VOLUME 5

The Intimate Memoir of Dame Jenny Everleigh

Book One

Sphere Books Limited

SPHERE BOOKS LTD

Published by the Penguin Group
27 Wrights Lane, London W8 5TZ, England
Viking Penguin Inc., 40 West 23rd Street, New York, New York 10010, USA
Penguin Books Australia Ltd, Ringwood, Victoria, Australia
Penguin Books Canada Ltd, 2801 John Street, Markham, Ontario, Canada L3R 1B4
Penguin Books (NZ) Ltd, 182–190 Wairau Road, Auckland 10, New Zealand

Penguin Books Ltd, Registered Offices: Harmondsworth, Middlesex, England

First published in the United States of America by Pocket Books, 1986
Published by Sphere Books Ltd 1987
3 5 7 9 10 8 6 4

This novel is a work of fiction. Names, characters, places and incidents
are either the product of the author's imagination or are used fictitiously.
Any resemblance to actual events or locales or persons,
living or dead, is entirely coincidental.

Printed and bound in Great Britain by
Cox & Wyman Ltd, Reading
Set in Sabon

Being the personal recollections of one Jenny Everleigh and her life of devotion to Queen, Country and Pleasure amongst the gentlemen and the fools of Merry England and the heroes, rogues and the wogs of its Empire, on which the sun has never yet set, nor shall it.

Prologue

What you have before you, gentle reader, is a romance, to be read in a time when the only romance is one of nostalgia. I am qualified to speak of such things as I am fifty years older than this horrid century, the twentieth. (I have lived in it roughly as long as I lived in what I consider my own, the nineteenth.) In short, as I write this, it is 1947 and I am 95 years old. I have survived everyone.

My time, the years of the Queen and her son Edward, was bracketed by two inventions that changed the face of the globe and man's attitude toward it forever—*the railroad and the machine gun*. The period between the introduction of these two inventions was a time of innocence we shall never again experience.

The young girl I had once been still resides in this antique hulk. If given the privilege to live it all again, she would change nothing, not a single adventure, neither action nor spoken word. Ahh, how sweet it was! How marvelous to be sought after, to be fashionable, to be a cultured and glamorous figure of the demimonde known for her beauty, her charm, her wit. (Surely at this age I can be forgiven a certain lack of modesty.) And how satisfying to know that I stood at what was then the center of the universe—Britannia at the height of her glory! It was a glory in which I shared and to which I contributed.

There is not enough space on my ample bosom for the international honors and decoration bestowed on me. Amongst them; The Order of the Golden Fleece, The Order of Annunziata, The Order of the Red Eagle, The

Order of the Golden Spur, The Order of Palonia Restituta, The Legion of Honor.

I was confidante to kings, soldiers, poets, adventurers, explorers, sheiks, and other architects of history. Yes, dear reader, I have within me the seeds of greatness, deposited at one time or another into an hospitable quim that played hostess to the most imposing pricks of an exciting, but piquantly innocent, time.

Côte d'Azur, 1947

ONE

Virginity is a disease, easily cured between the ages of eighteen and twenty-three. After that, it is liable to become chronic. [J.E., 1892]

Travelling on the railway wasn't half the fright I thought it would be. Trains had seemed such noisy, smoking brutes all those times I lay on the embankment with my brother Sean, watching them huff and puff up Bainbridge Hill belching fire and brimstone like diabolical dragons up to no good.

But here I sat in a kind of cosy parlour on wheels, my bottom comforted by real leather as were the bottoms of the three other ladies sharing the compartment with me. Out the window, the countryside sped by at a fearsome pace. I was pleased that the sight of it didn't make me dizzy. Meanwhile, I felt every bit the lady ensconced snugly in a place of polished wood and leather and fine carpeting. It was all far more elegant than any house in which I'd ever been. (And one could even sleep on the railway!) I sat back, rested my head on the crisp linen antimacassar and, mesmerized by the regular clacking of the iron wheels, closed my eyes. What more, I wondered, could the first class have to offer? Little did I realize that before the day was over, I was to find out.

It was the summer of 1871. I was on my way to London to live with my Aunt Portia whom I dimly recalled from my childhood as being the beautiful, red-headed younger sister of my now dear departed mother. Aunt Portia, widowed at the age of nineteen, had many years before moved to London as the mistress of a Mr Pflumshawe, a well-to-do tea merchant. After the death of his wife, Mr Pflumshawe had married my aunt and she moved from the small flat she occupied as his mistress into the big house in Knightsbridge. Now once again a widow (Mr Pflumshawe having gone down just north of the Maldives with the steamship carrying him home after a visit to his holdings in Ceylon), Aunt Portia had agreed to accept me, her only living blood relative, into her home. It was hoped I could there be educated in the ways of a lady.

The three women sharing my compartment were foreigners. They jibbered and jabbered in a language I had never heard. Despite that, I soon found the conversation intriguing. It was as if they were discussing intimate secrets to which I was not privy.

But at eighteen I barely spoke my own tongue and had little inkling of anything outside my hitherto limited province. Even love was a mystery, hinted at by little more than an occasional wet spasming of my undeveloped quim, which from time to time I attempted to quiet with awkward fingers. Such fumblings accomplished little. I was still uneducated as to my secret geography.

Then the woman next to me was speaking a charmingly accented English. In my half-wakened state it did not occur to me that I was the object of her words until I felt the light touch of her hand on my knee. 'My dear,' she was saying, 'would you care to share some wine?'

I opened my eyes on her smiling face. 'Please, ma'am,' said I, hardly knowing whether I meant yes or no. I had never imbibed – either in wine or anything else. (And in Liverpool only whisky and beer were drunk by men and women alike.)

One of the other ladies handed her a glass from an open basket resting on a folding sideboard under the window. Hardly bothering to take her eyes from mine, she poured from a bottle she held in her other hand. 'I am,' she said, 'Madame Kooshay.' Handing me the glass, she reached into a small, ornate, beaded purse to pass me a calling card. It was printed simply, in eloquent gothic letters.

Female Equestrian Society

For recommended gentlemen sportsmen of
the highest calibre

22 Highcastle Road   Madame Kooshay, Prop.

'Equestrian?' asked I, in my ignorance.

'Yes, my dear. We are what you delightful English call riding instructors.' Then, gesturing about the compartment, she said, 'And this is Yvette and Yvonne, each of us horsewomen extraordinaire.' She spoke with a heavy but, at the same time, peculiarly soft accent which made every word seem like a kiss. 'And you, my dear?'

'Jenny,' said I, my voice cracking halfway through.

'Charming name for a charming girl.' She smiled.

'Thank you, ma'am.' Not knowing quite what else to do, I gulped the wine as she poured for the two others and herself. By the time Madame Kooshay had filled the three glasses, I had finished mine. She emptied the bottle graciously into my glass.

'A toast,' she said. The ladies raised their glasses. 'To Jenny.' Blushing, I raised mine. 'Prosit!' said she and this time, aping the others, I sipped rather than gulped.

In a matter of minutes I was feeling quite fuddled. The compartment rotated slowly on its axis. At first this illusory motion was unsettling. But by the time I had emptied my second glass, I rather enjoyed it. As the compartment melted around me, I relaxed into a deeply luxurious ennui. All of the straight lines and hard angles had vanished from my giddy world. Everything about me had softened, the walls, the ladies, the murmur of voices, the sound of our speeding train. . . .

Then quite suddenly, with a startling *woosh*, it all went pitch black! Feeling a dim panic, I assumed that also to be a function of unaccustomed wine. But we had merely entered a tunnel.

I lay back against the seat and closed my eyes to keep out the dark. I no sooner had done so when I felt a presence just inches from my face. Lips possessed mine! A soft but insistent tongue found its way into my mouth! It was a new experience, startling me into immobility. Moments passed before I found the wit to realize that the mouth sucking at mine and the hand that even now had found its way under my skirt were those of a woman!

My resistance was tentative at best, for with my lips possessed by those of Madame Kooshay, others had taken control of my body. In seconds I was being lowered, gently but firmly, onto the floor.

The compartment was silent exept for the sounds of our breaths, rapidly rising in an ever-faster cadence. I was only dimly aware that the train had come to a halt inside the tunnel.

There were many hands now. They unfastened my bodice and raised my skirt. Two of them grasped my ankles, spreading wide my legs.

Lips brushed my bare breast, then returned, opening wide to hold captive the pneumatic flesh while a soft female tongue swirled round and round the aureole. Even the thought of resistance was wrenched from my mind as that same tongue, with sudden purpose, flicked my now turgid nipple. I felt, rather than heard, my own involuntary gasp of rapture as suddenly my senses were bathed in sensations to which I had hitherto been a stranger.

Fingers caressed my naked thighs. As I had that day, as on most others in the summertime, refrained from wearing drawers, there was no encumbrances to the hands that even then were nearing their virginal target. How many hands? Two? Three? Fifteen delicate ladyfingers! But one seemed bolder than the others. The bravest of all probed forward, finding its way, an exquisite explorer searching for treasure in a silken forest. My body tensed with expectation and this time it was I who thrust my tongue forward into a soft mouth that sucked on it as if it were a sweetmeat. I was learning my lessons quickly, when suddenly the lips on mine were replaced with others. An instant later, not just one, but both my breasts were being suckled.

The intrepid finger was finally home. With featherlight footing, it crawled the length of my mossy glen.

In seconds the single digit was joined by another that lost itself in the dewy folds. I felt myself trembling with expectation – though for what, I knew not. But despite my ignorance and lack of experience, instinct informed me that what I assumed to be a pinnacle of pleasure was as nothing compared to the heights that lay ahead. I was spread-eagled in pitch darkness, deliciously vulnerable to the lustful machinations of three heated females!

The intrepid finger, with great delicacy, inserted itself into a tight-fitting, secret passage that had known none before it. My hips, on a volition of their own, thrust upward, demanding more. But the proprietor of the enchanted finger denied it, drawing back so as to preserve intact the natural (or unnatural?) barrier that blocked full, lascivious entrance.

For a moment my nether regions were free of caresses. Before I could react to the sudden emptiness, the delightful digits had been replaced with lips and tongue! I had never dreamed such things were done!

Somehow I knew that the joyful, fluttering tongue was that of Madame Kooshay! Curled into a more tensile tool, an oral cock, it fucked me slowly . . . then more and more rapidly – penetrating – opening and softening me with each heavenly thrust! My bum was a pneumatic machine, oscillating in some predetermined, sensuous rhythm. Rivulets of female nectar ran down my thighs.

Once again, the lips I was kissing so passionately were

replaced by others. Ah . . . these were different! They were softer, damp with a savoury moisture, delicately pliant, fringed with a cushion of silken strands. My tongue penetrated to find itself in a much different kind of cavern. With a groan of ecstasy, I lost myself in the young woman's quim, sucking, licking, laving its pulpy mass with the flat of my tongue. The juices were sweet, with a tangy taste – ambrosial!

She sighed, uttering the first words since we had entered the tunnel: 'Ah . . . *gamahuche, chérie*!' The words impressed themselves on my passion-fevered brain. They were the first of that lovely language I was to memorize.

Meanwhile, Madame Kooshay's tongue had found the small pink cuntal button that is the seat of heavenly pleasure – the zenith of exquisite sensation – the special joy of womankind! And until her sensual probing, I had not even known of its existence.

I pressed upward, forcing my honey pot into Madame Kooshay's mouth. My hips rotated madly. Simultaneously, I was receiving instructions at one end while demonstrating my new-found knowledge at the other. I searched out the succulent oyster of my other lover, sucking her erect nub between my lips, titillating it with my rapidly gyrating but gently applied tongue. Her reaction was gloriously akin to mine. Our moans and cries were a sensuous duet climbing the scale to climactic crescendo. I grasped her buttocks, pulling her lovely, squatting body downward till she was actually sitting on my face! At my other end, Madame Kooshay was licking furiously. All about me were the deliciously liquid sounds of female lust, the cries and moans and whimpers of joyful women!

My face was buried – lost – in my lover's lush garden as both of us spent in explosive synchronization! I was certain I was dying a most beautiful death.

My resurrection came slowly. Drenched in perspiration, I realized that the train was moving once again. I sighed with fond satisfaction and leaned back against the soft leather.

Then, quite suddenly, we were in the open once more. Green hills stretched gently to the horizon. Beside me, Madame Kooshay, her beauteous head tilted becomingly, was exhaling gentle, ladylike snores. With befuddled eyes, I glanced round the compartment. Yvette, her blonde tresses flowing in the breeze, was staring out the open window. Yvonne sat demurely reading a small, elegantly bound book.

But surely this was impossible! Only minutes ago, perhaps just seconds, one of these ladies had been squatting over my face! The two others had been devouring my breasts! Madame Kooshay herself had been cupping my plump arse cheeks in her long-fingered, elegant hands, her face buried between my twitching thighs! My heart, even then, was still racing from recent exertions! Yet there they were, each involved in a private pursuit as if nothing of the kind had occurred!

Had I suffered a strange, momentary brain fever? Or perhaps I had dreamed it all in feverish sleep brought on by the unaccustomed speed of the railway – the rhythmic swaying of the coach? But then why was my bodice unfastened? And why was there still on my tongue a savoury, unmistakably feminine essence?

TWO

I was to realize in later years that bondage was not my favourite dish, though it did have a certain piquancy. [J.E., 1899]

The train sped through the countryside on its way to London and my future. In a little while my three strange companions were sleeping. They remained so as we slowed, then stopped at a place labelled Cardiff. Looking out on the platform, I could see that some passengers had disembarked and were having tea at a small shop in the station lounge. Perhaps, thought I, it was just what I needed to dispel the cobwebs clouding my brain. I was still shaken from my recent experience with the equestrians and perhaps, too, still just a wee bit inebriated. A nice cuppa would surely revive me.

Gingerly, so as not to awaken the ladies, I opened the compartment door, stepped onto the platform and, with legs of India rubber, made my way. I ordered tea and a bun to go with it. It seemed an invigorating combination. But lost in my pleasure at the end of the counter, I was unaware that I had become the sole patron. My fellow passengers had returned to the train. Through the open door I could see that it was moving!

I shot out of the lounge and raced frantically down the platform. But even as I reached my carriage, it outpaced me. In seconds, the train, with ever increasing speed, was passing me by! Soon it would be a swift juggernaut disappearing in the distance.

Despite the fact that my efforts had become a losing game, I continued to run beside it. My feet, encased in inadequate shoes, pounded awkwardly on the wooden platform.

Suddenly, a man of imposing proportions materialized on the narrow runningboard. With one hand grasping the doorjamb, he reached out with the other. It quickly encircled my waist and I was borne into the air! An instant later I found myself on the runningboard, secure in his protective embrace.

Inside was another gentleman. They seated me and placed in my hand a glass of Scotch whisky they insisted I should down for its calming effct. As the first whisky to pass my virginal lips, it caused me to sputter and almost choke, but it accomplished its purpose.

Their names were Mr Thisby and Mr Woodcock. The compartment was of the first class. Instead of cheap leather the seats were upholstered in real purple velvet. The wood was even more highly polished, and a collapsible table was laden with fruit, cheese, wine and something called *pâté de foie gras*. Mr Thisby and Mr Woodcock were quite concerned for my welfare and insisted I imbibe still another glassful of comfort. I appreciated their thoughtfulness.

With a feeling of panic, I realized that my luggage was still in the compartment ahead. My rescuers advised me not to fear, for when the train arrived in London I would be able to return, via the station platform, to my own carriage in order to retrieve my goods. (British railway coaches of that period consisted of compartments comprising the entire width of the carriage. There was neither passageway nor aisle to enable passengers to move from car to car or even to make their way through an individual car without braving the narrow, exterior catwalk that ran along each side.)

Relieved and feeling safe and secure in the presence of two gallant gentlemen, I fell into a deep, inebriated sleep, to dream in full, vivid detail of my recent erotic adventure with the foreign horsewomen.

Having no idea how long I lay in the arms of Morpheus, I awakened into a state I assumed must be yet another randy dream. A lascivious titillation centered on my breasts, spreading in waves throughout my body. With my eyes still closed, I squirmed about, though for some reason the slightest movement seemed difficult. But the soft velvet was luxuriant against my naked skin. Naked? Surely this was a most realistic dream! Then, too, I was aware of a difficulty of movement. It was as if I were in some strange, dreamlike state of paralysis. . . .

With a sudden jolt of awareness, I opened my eyes. The sight that greeted them was not the stuff of dreams, but rather a reality that shocked me to the core. I was indeed naked! Mr Thisby had the nipple of my left breast between thumb and forefinger! Mr Woodcock's face was buried in the pillow of my right breast, his mouth sucking the soft flesh! And worse; in attempting to move out from under my erotic tormentors, I found I was bound and gagged, hand and foot! Surely, I thought in horrified astonishment, the ways of the British railway system were most peculiar!

Terrified, I struggled with my bonds, as the train hurtled through the English countryside. It was to no avail. Mr Thisby placed a calming hand on my head. In a civil voice he said, 'Ah, Jenny, you are with us again. Now we can begin your education. You are fortunate to have two sophisticated men of the world to instruct you. Think of it; had you not come into our clutches, you might have fallen prey instead to some ignorant clod. First experiences create lasting impressions, and so we intend to launch you on a career of lust second to no woman in the empire. You will surely thank us.'

'Enough talk,' said Mr Woodcock, pinching my nipple painfully.

Terrified, I stared up at him. My own fear had me paralysed. Even unbound, I doubt I could have moved.

'A moment,' said Mr Thisby. Then, turning to me once again, he said, 'Whilst you slept we investigated and found you to be a virgin, just as we suspected you'd be. But we are gentlemen and will leave you intact.' Much like a headmaster instructing a recalcitrant student, his smiling face transformed itself into a stern visage. 'If you are a good child and pay attention, no permanent harm will come to you. If not, you might, after all, be fucked. In any case, you are sure to be whipped, and that, young lady, will pain me as much as it does you. Mr Woodcock, however, will be pleased to do the honours as he gets a good deal of pleasure from that sort of thing.'

Realizing my predicament, I fought desperately against panic. These were surely madmen!

Mr Woodcock leered down at me. I moaned my discomfort through the gag, causing his expression to grow pained. He glared as if at an incorrigible daughter who had misbehaved. He was joined in this by Mr Thisby. The two stood just inches away, both formidable, naked men, all bulges and angles, muscles and hair. It was a double shock as I had never previously seen even one naked man. In fear I glanced away from them – downward – to be greeted with incongruous shards of formless flesh hanging from their hairy groins.

It was, of course, my first view of the masculine member. A most dismal view. My father was a blacksmith, therefore I had some familiarity with physiognomy, and fearfully had assumed the device of the human male to be of a similar scale to the horse. But the horse in this respect was the far nobler beast. The pair of sad protuberances facing me seemed hardly useful except, possibly, to piddle from.

Was this indeed the deep and fearsome secret kept from young girls in order to protect them from a fate worse than death? What was there to fear? It all seemed much ado about very little. Despite my situation, I felt a poignant stab of disappointment. One of girlhood's darkest, most profound mysteries fizzled like a defective bomb.

Fortunately, I was shortly to be disabused of this depressing notion. Nature, as someone has said, will out. In a manner of speaking, it did exactly that. Just inches from my face, Mr Thisby grasped his organ and proceeded to pump it gently to and fro. Before my very eyes it grew – expanded – as if the result of some music hall conjurer's trick. Magically, a bulbous head, wearing a soft, purplish hat, emerged. Before my astonished eyes, the small sausage grew into more and more of a massive organ, beveined and seemingly rock hard. Ah then, I thought, this is a horse of another colour!

Glancing to my left, I perceived that Mr Woodcock, too, had undergone a transition. From between his legs a weapon of dramatic dimension pointed skyward. A flagpole, I conjectured, worthy of the Union Jack!

In my growing fascination with the performance before me, I almost forgot that I was bound. No longer the least bit fearful of my fate, but rather with increasing randiness, I watched, bug-eyed, as the men frigged themselves – Mr Woodcock, now with both hands, as if he were wielding a club. I squirmed about in my bonds as a shiver descended my spine to find a home in my twitching buttocks. Mr Thisby, as if aware of my awakened interest, smiled at me, and bobbed a performer's bow of appreciation to a captivated (and captive!) audience. For surely that was what I had become.

Mr Woodcock's breathing was increasing in intensity, his face flushed, his groans of pleasure extended into a sustained, reverberating rumble. He frigged at an ever increasing pace, the monstrous, steel-hard piston grasped tightly in his huge, white-knuckled fist – on and on!

I had never even imagined such things, nor dreamed them. Through widened eyes I stared at the swollen head that was beaded now with glistening, miniature pearls of male essence.

With his eyes burning into mine, Mr Woodcock manhandled the object of his affection till it came into contact with my right breast! A hot poker of pleasure seared my skin! The gesture came as a surprise so intense I thought surely my heart would stop beating! Breathlessly, I looked downward as Mr Woodcock, using both his thumbs, applied gentle pressure to spread open the small slit at the tip. Then, with one hand holding my breast steady, he applied the opening. I watched spellbound as my engorged nipple was literally swallowed whole by the hungry prick!

Cupping my breast in one hand, Mr Woodcock, slowly at first but then with increasing fervour, pumped his rod against its plump, fleshy cushion. My distended nipple, inserted, transmitted the throbbing pressure throughout my body as if I and his cock were one!

Mr Woodcock's eyes were shut. His voice was a husky whisper. 'I'm spending. . . .'

'Yes! Now!' Mr Thisby called out, 'Shoot it on her tit, you randy bastard!' His hand clutched even tighter, frigging faster in tempo with his friend.

Mr Woodcock's battering ram throbbed. I could feel it, and thus share in the intense pleasure it was affording him. I tried to imagine what was about to happen. Being new to the phenomenon of the orgasm, I had till now no inkling that the male of the species possessed a capacity for this ultimate joy. But in what form? I twitched with lustful curiosity.

Mr Woodcock's pego was alive. I could feel each spasm more intensely than the last. Then, before my very eyes, a puddle of thick white ooze formed explosively on my breast around the swollen cock head! A most curious . . . yet marvellous phenomenon!

I squirmed, pressing my bottom against the floor. The insides of my thighs were dripping with cuntal essence, echoing the spunky wetness smeared on my breast.

As Mr Woodcock's prick even now pulled away from my breast, its hungry little mouth grasped, fighting valiantly to retain its grip – pulling on my nipple as if reluctant to part from its lover.

Mr Woodcock, in a lewd gesture that sent my head spinning, reached out with the palm of his hand to massage his claggy ooze into the virginal skin of my breast.

'It is,' said Mr Thisby, 'a most satisfactory elixir for the complexion.' He looked deeply into my eyes, then turned to his mate who lay recovering on the velvet-covered rear-facing seat. 'Perhaps we might remove the cloth from her mouth now.'

Both Mr Woodcock and I nodded affirmatively, though my nod was somewhat the more emphatic of the two. It took but a moment to untie it. I flexed my jaw and then in a quiet, most ladylike voice said, 'And the ropes . . . I promise I won't try to get away. . . .'

'Where would you go, if you could?' asked Mr Thisby.

'She's to stay bound,' said Mr Woodcock in reproving tones. 'And if she utters another word, the gag will be replaced!'

Mr Thisby took a step forward. His weapon, just inches from my face, was still at attention. He grasped it with both hands, a determined fireman directing a hose.

'It's for the best,' said the kindly Mr Thisby, smiling down at me. 'We will all probably enjoy it the more if you remain tied up.'

I was about to speak further on the subject but caught myself in time.

'And now, young Jenny,' said he, 'you are going to suck your first prick.'

I nodded fearfully, one part of me recoiling in horror and trepidation, the other thrilled by the prospect. The conflict brought tears to my eyes; I turned my head to hide them. The internal war raged back and forth on the littered battlefield of my mind.

The brutal words had elicited an immediate and voluptuous stirring in my soupy quim. I licked my lips, feeling a sudden, almost overpowering longing to have Mr Thisby's fat pego between them! The war was over.

The aggressive forces of lust had won the day over the defensive garrison of fear.

A firm hand was on my head, turning it. The giant organ presented itself. Tentatively, I licked out at it, my tongue flicking its tip. Then, more boldly, I leaned forward, swirling it around the velvet-skinned head.

'Ah, you like it then, you little devil!' said Mr Thisby.

Now lapping the underside, I glanced up at him. My lewd demeanor answered his question.

'Then take it in your mouth . . . suck on it, my dear, like it were a nice fat bit of sweet treacle.'

'Mmmmm . . .'

'And if you're a good girl and do it properly, I'll reward you with some marvellous custard. . . .'

I opened my mouth to accept its gift. Gently I ran my tongue around the tip, then under the little hat. My action brought a spasmodic response and a moan of pleasure from Mr Thisby. I experienced a momentary satisfaction – nay, pride – with the realization that I had sought out and located a secret, highly sensitive spot. I was immediately aware that this new and exotic endeavour called for the same degree of skilful dedication as was required for performance in most other sporting activities. I suspected I possessed a native talent and vowed, then and there, to be a superlative student.

Curling my tongue so that it remained in place, I took more of Mr Thisby into the lustful cavern of my mouth. I fluttered rapidly but softly against the secret underside. It was as if his prick were a piccolo and I the musician.

In turn, I sucked and slobbered, diddled and fluttered. Then, with my lips ovaled, I presented my lover with a cuntlike sheath to fuck. Soon I was taking it all, each thrust penetrating to the portals of my throat. I quickly learned to relax the muscles there and control my breathing so as not to gag. With lustful longing, I hoped for a mouthful of 'custard'.

'Suck me, Jenny!' Mr Thisby's voice was hoarse, raspy and breathless from erotic exertion.

'Fuck the bitch's mouth. Shoot your spunk into it!' echoed Mr Woodcock, stepping to my rear. Roughly he raised my rump, then proceeded to paddle my plump buttocks with the flat of his hand. At first I sensed the action as a purely painful experience, but as the flesh warmed, the lustful heat was transmitted to my excited puss and then throughout my body. Soon I was heaving and twitching in cadence with the stinging slaps on my backside and the counter rhythms of the gallant cock thrusting in and out of my eager mouth.

Then suddenly, with no warning, Mr Thisby's fat organ withdrew, trailing spittle. In sad farewell I thrust out my tongue for a final lick at its gorged head.

Before I had the chance to close my mouth, Mr Woodcock's soft peg had gained entry. It was as nothing compared to the giant that had just vacated, but I was thrilled by my power to transform this diminutive object into a similar monster.

In strict, authoritarian voice, Mr Woodcock warned me of my teeth, threatening to pummel my bum till it was a bloody pulp if I bit him. He went on to say that no *true lady* ever bared her teeth. He needn't have feared. In that respect, at least, I vowed to be a *true lady*.

I placed my lips gently around the succulent tip, thrilling to the sense of his soft, bulbous knob emerging from the fleshy folds of its secret holster. Then, making a perfect oval of my lips, I flattened my tongue into a soft cushion and sucked him in.

Mr Woodcock bent forward, his body arching over mine, his hands now cupping my buttocks as I sucked on his prong. He groaned, shoving his still somewhat flaccid prick into my mouth till his large, hairy bollocks pressed against my lips. 'Fuck! Spunk!' he called in a shrill voice.

'Suck him well, Jenny,' said Mr Thisby, stepping behind me.

'Fuck her arse!' cried Mr Woodcock, his now hardened machine pistoning into my mouth with increasing fury. 'Up her bum!'

I could hardly believe what I was hearing! Was it possible? Were women's nether openings sufficiently accommodating? Surely, such an act must be painful!

I had no time to dwell on these scientific considerations, for at my rear, Mr Thisby was fondling my cheeks, kissing them, running the wet appendage of his tongue into the deep crevice between them. Slowly, his hand reached beneath me and curled upward until his skilful fingers brushed my dripping cunny. An educated digit found the virgin clitoris, causing my entire body to respond with a series of excruciating thrills that had me close to fainting.

Then, suddenly, the hand was withdrawn. I felt a thick sausage between the plump flesh of my nether cheeks. Was he to do that awful thing now? I tensed myself expectantly as Mr Woodcock's cock shuddered in my mouth. But no . . . it was not Mr Thisby's intention to bugger me. His monstrous engine passed downward between my slippery thighs. Was he to be first to enter? To break his word and rid me of my rosy virginity? I hoped so. But . . . no again. Instead he seemed content to thrust his cock back and forth in the open folds of my sopping cunt. My bum, as if controlled by a mind of its own, rotated in lewd circles, enhancing our pleasure.

With Mr Thisby taking his pleasure at my rear and Mr Woodcock at my front, our moans, groans and whimpers were a joyful chorus. I felt I might spend from just the sense of it!

One of them – I knew not which – called, 'I'm going to cum!'

Another cried out, 'Spunk fuck! I'm spending!'

With that, Mr Thisby transferred his thrusting prong once again to the soft, hospitable crack of my arse. With one hand he frigged himself furiously at the very portals of my twitching, nether opening! No longer fearful of the possible pain, I thrust back at him, longing for the rude, mysterious penetration . . . anything! But again, Mr Thisby, every bit the true gentleman, refrained from such violation. Instead I felt his diddling digits playing in the moist garden once more. My gooey little cunny welcomed him. Two of his lovely fingers pranced amongst the folds while a third found its way, once more, to my clitoris. I had become so randy that the instant it was touched, my lust-wracked body erupted into an orgasm of an intensity greater even than my first, less than two hours earlier. With a sustained roar of exultation, Mr Thisby exploded between my palpitating cheeks. His slimy spunk filled my bottom crevice to overflowing!

In the midst of my own spending, Mr Woodcock withdrew his bursting affair from my mouth, rubbed it up against my left breast and – not to be outdone by his friend – ejaculated glob after glob of thick, creamy jism. Both my breasts had now been anointed. I thrilled to the lewdness of it all and to a dawning concept of female sexual power.

Soon afterwards I was unbound. Now that they had finished with their lewd festivities, Mr Woodcock and Mr Thisby seemed concerned for my welfare. We dressed and they insisted I eat something in order to regain my strength. They prohibited any further whisky but instead served me a cup of hot tea poured from a cunning thermal bottle.

When I had composed myself and was seated, demurely now – fully clothed as if nothing had occurred – Mr Woodcock asked, 'Do you travel the railways often, Jenny?'

'No,' said I. ''Tis my first journey.'

'And how do you like it?'

'Well,' I said, blushing, 'is it always so . . . educational?'

'Yes, of course.'

'Then I must travel the rails more often.'

'But only British rail,' said Mr Thisby seriously.

We sipped our tea and continued our pleasant small talk. I told them of my aunt in London. Mr – or rather – Colonel Thisby was by way of the army; Mr Woodcock, a government minister, was his brother-in-law. I felt flattered to have made friends with two real gentlemen so far above my station.

As we neared London, each of them, despite my protestations, stuffed fivers into my bodice. The instant the train came to a stop, I accepted hasty kisses on the cheek and leapt from the carriage whilst they were still fussing with their baggage. I hastened up the platform to my original coach just behind the still steaming engine. Clambering aboard, I found the equestrian ladies gone. My luggage, both bags containing all my wordly goods, was also gone. I raced into the station proper, frantically searching for them but to no avail. Finally, fighting back the tears, I stood in the midst of the evening crowd. I owned naught now, except the clothes on my back and a ten-pound gift presented by two kindly gentlemen. It was thus I arrived in London to begin my new life.

THREE

The term 'cunt', and most other lewd words at that time, were foreign to me as a young girl new to London. I use them here, however, in proper context for the sake of those historians, both amateur and professional, of a dim and distant future, who may be reading this in order to gain knowledge of how we spoke the Queen's English in Her day. [J.E., 1920]

It was late afternoon. Flagging a hansom, I arrived in front of my Aunt Portia's house in Bayswater just in time to observe the movers loading the last of her personal possessions onto their van. She was surprised to see me and, in her preoccupation, seemed to have forgotten completely about the arrangement made with my father. In fashionably cut widow's weeds, with her face reflecting the ravages of recent tears, she told me of her misfortune. Mr Pflumshawe's tragic death at sea had left in its wake an ocean of debts. Everything had been taken for their payment: the tea warehouses, the bank account, the railway and shipping shares, the house and all its furnishings. Poor Aunt Portia was left with nothing but her wardrobe, her marriage bed (the creditors had been kind enough to permit her to retain it) and a few 'jewelled baubles' she had managed to squirrel away. These she had sold, on the quiet, in order to raise enough money with which to purchase a cottage in Brighton.

'But,' she said, her voice pitched in the dulcet tones of

the newly bereaved, 'it is a very small cottage with room only for myself.' She sniffled, searching in vain for a handkerchief. 'It's as much as I could afford.'

'I'm sorry.' I handed my aunt a handkerchief, wondering what else I could say.

'Thank you, dear Jenny. What a pretty little thing you are.' She snorted into the handkerchief. 'And no servants. I can't even manage a maid on what I've got. What is to become of me?' (Aunt Portia was only a year in Brighton when she wed an elderly American dentist. She lived the rest of her life in the American state of Texas.)

With that, my Aunt Portia – the paupered Widow Pflumshawe – pecked me on the cheek, then stepped into a hansom cab, which, following the van, turned the corner and disappeared. Once again I was alone.

Where to go? I knew no one in London . . . ah, but I did! Madame Kooshay! Even now, my bags rested in her possession. I rummaged in my purse for her calling card.

Twenty-two Highcastle Road was a big Georgian house in Mayfair. The brass shone, the windows gleamed, the few stone steps were as spotless as bone china. I stood on the narrow portico and pulled the bell wire.

It was answered by a butler, the first I'd ever seen close up and in the flesh. I gave him my name. His was Samuel and he was all I imagined a proper butler would be. His bearing was erect; his livery in perfect taste and well fitted; his attitude and tone properly respectful with just a hint of cordiality. I was ushered through a heavily brocaded portiere into a small reception hall furnished in, I was later to learn, the French style.

Taking my coat, he said, 'I'll announce you to the madame.'

I sat, staring at a picture on the wall. It was of a naked young woman with a big purple orchid sprouting from her vagina – a genuine oil painting. Shocking! The eyes looked right out of the picture into mine. It was as if she were alive and about to leave the frame to sit beside me. I hoped she wouldn't.

'Ah, Jenny. I see you like the painting.'

I turned to see Madame Kooshay standing between the large double doors. 'Yes, I think I do,' said I.

She was beautiful, dressed in some sort of black silk dressing gown that was more revealing than any I'd ever seen even in pictures. She said, 'It was painted by a young devil named Whistler – an American. An exchange of professional services, so to speak.' She smiled at me. 'Your bags are safe. I felt they would have been stolen had we left them on the train. When you didn't return we were quite concerned.'

'I almost missed it,' said I. 'Some gentlemen pulled me into their compartment in the nick of time.'

'Well then, all's well that ends well.' She took my hand and patted it. Hers was very warm. I found it difficult to take my eyes off her. The black silk did little to hide her charms. It clung as if it were wet, delineating her legs from hip to floor.

She noticed my interest. 'It's French,' she said, wetting her lips with a sinuous tongue. 'They call it *lingerie*. Very new.' She brought my hand to her breast. 'Feel how lovely.'

I could sense the heat of her body through the thin fabric. Her breast was full, its nipple titillated the palm of my hand through soft silk that seemed but another layer of skin.

'Yes,' I said, blushing to the roots of my hair. 'Lovely.'

'Would you care for a nice cuppa?'

'Don't mind if I do, thank you.'

Tea was served by Samuel in what Madame Kooshay called her 'sanctum sanctorum'. Before leaving, he lit the gas, enhancing the beautiful room in a rosy glow. It was a large room, an indoor garden of potted palms and rubber plants. A row of French doors lined one wall, while ornately framed paintings punctuated the others. A half-dozen Oriental rugs were scattered about. At the far end, surrounded by a veritable jungle of greenery, was a large Oriental booth covered with what seemed a hundred pillows of varying colours, shapes and patterns. It was a room of clutter and warmth – comfortable and overstuffed.

I sat in an elegantly carved armchair upholstered in heavy brocade. Madame Kooshay lay, stretched out near me on a wide chaise longue, her black lingerie contrasting gorgeously against bright red velvet.

She spoke small talk – the weather, the discomforts of train travel. (I disagreed silently, thinking rather of both the *joys* and the educational value of modern British rail transportation.) As she was speaking it occurred to me that I hadn't noticed till now her lack of a foreign accent. She spoke like a well-born Londoner; A's broad, H's audible, all filtered through a mouthful of mashed potatoes. Perfect English. A miraculous change.

I told her of my Aunt Portia's bad fortune and of my dilemma. Madame Kooshay listened, a most sympathetic expression lighting her beautiful face.

'You are welcome to stay here,' said she, 'until you get situated.'

'How kind of you . . . but I wouldn't want to presume . . .' I feigned pleasant surprise at her offer, but her words, I must admit, were exactly what I hoped they'd be. I simply had nowhere else to go.

'It presents no problem, dear Jenny. For the moment I have more rooms than I need. It will be lovely to have you with us.' Once again, Madame Kooshay reached out to take my hand.

'Perhaps,' said I, 'there is something I might do to earn my keep?'

'Perhaps. But first you must make yourself at home here for a few days, meet the ladies. You might find you don't like it here.'

'Oh, no. I'm certain I'll like it . . . it's beautiful. . . .'

'Well, we'll see.' She squeezed my hand. 'In the meantime I'm sure you'll want to freshen up after your journey.'

'Yes, ma'am.'

'But first . . .' She pulled me to her, onto the red chaise longue, '. . . a kiss.'

Recalling the strange interlude with Madame Kooshay and her friends on the train earlier that day, I was only too willing to be kissed – or more, if it came to that.

Her parted lips touched mine gently. She spoke softly into my mouth, 'You are a pretty little thing, Jenny . . . so very delicate, so sweet . . . a virgin rosebud awaiting its opening.'

A velvet tongue slithered between my lips to make sinuous contact with my own. She placed my hand on her breast. I thrilled to its rotund fullness through the gossamer silk.

'A sweet virgin,' she whispered.

I spoke into the soft flesh of her neck. 'How could you know?'

'Tight . . . on the train . . . my finger . . .'

The memory of that particular caress sent a hot chill coursing through my body. We kissed again. I rolled her nipple gently between thumb and forefinger, in the manner I had learned earlier that day.

Madame Kooshay took me in her arms, hugged me affectionately, and then she was standing, her svelte curves towering above me. She smiled, saying, 'It would be quite easy to get carried away, dear Jenny, but the witching hour approaches. I must rally my ladies. And you must be fatigued after such a day.' She pulled a bell cord hanging to the right of the fireplace. 'Mrs Rose will show you to your room and draw your bath. I'm sure the two of you will get along.'

FOUR

Hats off to Thomas Crapper, the inventor of the first practical flushing device! Surely he should have been knighted by a grateful queen. [Buckingham Palace was amongst the first to be so equipped.] In terms of his contribution to humankind, he deserved at least as much credit and notoriety as was awarded the American Wright brothers or Thomas Edison for their lesser inventions. Of what use was flying about, if after one landed at one's destination, one was still forced to brave the elements, the stench and the general discomfort of that awful outdoor facility? The mere addition of Edison's electrical light would not have improved matters. Of course, in her day, Madame Kooshay was by way of a pioneer, well ahead of most. Her two gas-lit bathrooms were amongst the earliest in London to sport indoor plumbing and flush toilets. [J.E., 1920]

Mrs Rose was a portly woman in her fifties or perhaps her sixties. She wore a severe black dress and bore a striking resemblance to the queen – bless her – except that Mrs Rose seemed a happy person, quite jolly.

My room was lovely. The bed was huge, overflowing with a feather mattress. The wallpaper was purple. There was a large chest, a wardrobe, a chenille mirror, a chaise longue and a beautiful Oriental rug on the floor. Two windows were heavily draped in maroon. My bags stood at the foot of the bed, across which was draped a pure white lingerie similar to Madame Kooshay's black one. I was delighted by it all and deeply grateful to Madame Kooshay for her kindness.

Next, Mrs Rose showed me the *bathroom*. 'A room just for washing?' asked I.

'Oh yes,' said Mrs Rose. 'Isn't it lovely?'

I had never seen a room anything like it. I pointed at a strange, ugly-looking device squatting in the corner. 'And that?'

'That's a water closet, dear. It's where you go . . . a toilet.'

'Indoors?'

'Just like a real throne.' She lowered an open, wooden seat. 'The seat goes up for men. When you are finished, there is paper and then you pull this.' As she spoke she reached up and grasped a wooden handle attached to a metal chain.

There was an immediate gurgle that quickly developed into an almost deafening cataract. The water, I could see, was flowing down through a pipe from an ingenious wooden box suspended above the throne. In the bowl it formed a violent whirlpool – a most astonishing sight!

Mrs Rose lit the gas in an ornate, cast-iron boiler sitting at one end of the large wooden bathtub. I was to wait a half hour, then turn off the gas and open the large water cock. A hot bath would be the miraculous result.

I returned to my room, opened my bags and hung my clothes in the wardrobe. I disrobed with some excitement, donning the beautiful white gown that Madame Kooshay had supplied. I had never worn silk before. As I moved about, it made a swishing sound, caressing my naked skin in a cool, sensuous embrace.

Aroused, I viewed myself in the chenille mirror. The gaslight behind me revealed the full curves of my body beneath the thin silk. My hands thrilled to the feel of my own supple female flesh. My nipples, engorged now, stood out, denting the fabric like two tiny fingers. I tweaked them, first the right, then the left, sending shivers of delight down the length of my body to centre in the moist haven between my thighs. But enough. Surely the half hour was up. It was time for my bath.

With soap and towel, I entered the bathroom only to find the tub full and someone sitting in it. We introduced ourselves. Her name was Elvira. She smiled shyly at me with a face dominated by arched, almost Oriental eyes. 'Oh, the bath must have been yours. I'm truly sorry. But,' said she in a lyrical voice, 'there is more than enough room for two. Why not join me? That way neither of us will be forced to wait another half hour.' She smiled an invitation, moving to the head of the tub.

I felt her eyes on me as I stepped out of my gown. Gingerly I inserted a toe. The water was delightfully hot. It was all far different than the weekly tepid baths to which I was accustomed in the tiny, hand-filled zinc tub in the kitchen at home. Sighing, my eyes closed contentedly, I lowered myself slowly into its embrace. I had always thought of bathing as being a necessary chore rather than a luxuriously pleasant experience. One could do this every day, even if it was, as some said, unhealthy when done to such excess. I slumped down, allowing the water to rise all the way to my neck.

Elvira smiled at me. 'Isn't it lovely?' she asked. 'Ah. . . . Look how your breasts float – like two pretty islands.'

I glanced down at them. Lovely, indeed. 'And yours too.'

'Yes, but yours are nicer than mine . . . fuller.' She was silent for a moment, then. 'May I touch them?'

'Yes,' I said without thinking further.

She ran a tentative finger across my left breast. I closed my eyes once again, savouring the sensuous warmth. I heard my own sigh of pleasure, the rippling of water, as, encouraged, she leaned forward to cup my breast in her hand.

In husky tones, she said, 'If you'll stand, I'd be happy to soap you.'

I opened my eyes and rose with some difficulty out of

the water. She stood in front of me, brazenly surveying my body. Taking her cue, I did likewise.

Elvira was shorter than I, more sparsely fleshed. Her perfectly formed breasts were teacups to my melons; her curves, though sinuous, less pronounced. Her belly was flat, lacking the slight curvature of my own. I glanced downward at her motte. It was profuse, a blond nest of fine silk that matched her crowning glory. Staring into my eyes, she lathered the white soap cake in her small, delicate hands. Then, taking my arms, she turned me about till my back was to her. The cool air raised small goose bumps on my dampened skin.

We spent the next fifteen minutes rubbing, caressing, lathering and rinsing each other. But soon, the water cooled. A knock on the door indicated that there were others equally interested in bathing.

Back in my room, after the lovely bath with Elvira, I was pleased to find, laid out on a small table, a fine supper of roasted lamb and sprouts. I ate slowly, ruminating on the strange events of the day and my good fortune in having made the aquaintance of the gracious Madame Kooshay. Where would I have been without her kindness?

I found myself wondering about my attraction to those of my own sex. Before the dawn of this very day, I had no idea that such things went on. Were these sisterly activities indeed common practice amongst all women? It was all quite confusing. I felt vaguely anxious.

On the edge of sleep, I lay in darkness between the crisp sheets of my new bed, attempting to relive the events of the day. Outside, there was the sound of carriages on the cobblestones.

Suddenly, despite my fatigue, I was wide awake. I crawled from the bed to open the heavy drapes on one of the windows. In deep shadow on the road below, a passenger was debarking from a hansom. As he did so, the front door to the house opened, bathing the scene in a pool of yellow light. The passenger was wearing a tall black hat and carrying a walking stick; obviously, a gentleman. He entered. Then once again Highcastle Road reverted to a darkness relieved only by the dim glow of the gaslight at the corner.

I stood at the window, my mind churning with excitement. This wondrous place – this greatest of all the world's cities – was to be my home; the place where my future would unfold! Day by day, year by year . . . what marvellous things awaited me? What trials and tribulations? Pleasures? Triumphs? Would I marry? Would I grow old and die here?

*

During the next few minutes, there were three more cabs, each carrying a single gentleman. I found such activity strange at this late hour. But, of course, London itself was strange to me. I was a bumpkin of but one day's residence.

Feeling the need to piddle, I ventured into the hall. As I neared the grand staircase I became aware of the sound of laughter – of music and festivity. Curious, I descended to the second landing to peer over the rail. A party was taking place in the main parlour.

The music was from a string quartet tucked away behind a forest of potted palms. There were about a dozen ladies who were outnumbered by half again as many gentlemen. Except for a few couples waltzing graceful circles around one another, everyone was sipping champagne, engaging in what I assumed was witty conversation, laughing and flirting. From my secret perch above them I observed the festivities, and breathed the air of excitement and expectation generated by the roomful of happy participants.

The ladies were gorgeously dressed. A few were gowned and jewelled like royalty, others were half naked, their breasts discernible beneath gossamer wisps of chiffon.

Some were slim, curvaceous, like elegant, long-legged gazelles. A few others were plump, pinkish nymphs, nude except for daring, tight-waisted corsets that emphasized fat tits and good-natured, jiggling rumps.

The gentlemen, all formally clothed, varied in age from those barely out of their teen years to those barely into their seventies. Despite this disparity of years, they shared an ease of manner of men of the world. The scent of floral perfume mingled with a smoldering aroma of Cuban leaf wafted up the great staircase. I inhaled it with pleasure and a growing envy. Perhaps someday . . .

I searched the room for my new friend Elvira to find her dancing with an extremely tall young gentleman who seemed no older than herself. She wore a gown of beautiful brocade and a glittering tiara, like a princess from some fairy kingdom. Nearby stood Yvette, dressed as a jockey, snapping a riding crop against her leg as if making an adamant point to an elderly, mutton-chopped gentleman in full, formal military array. With her trousered legs spread in confident stance, her jockey's cap tilted at a roguish angle, she seemed incongruously boyish. I wondered vaguely of what they were speaking.

As I watched, two formally dressed arrivals, escorted by Samuel, were met by Madame Kooshay. I thought it peculiar that her words of greeting, rising above the general hubbub, were phrased in a magically restored French accent.

I stared down onto the gay tableau, longing to be part of it. Perhaps someday I, too, would be lovely, sophisticated, capable of wearing beautiful clothing and sipping champagne while engaged in witty small talk with elegant gentlemen.

Yvette, on the arm of her whiskered, military companion, had started up the staircase. Wary of embarrassment, I made haste to ascend before I could be discovered.

In the bathroom, I piddled, flushing three times for the

experience. Then, returning to my giant bed, I sought, once again, the arms of Morpheus.

I doubt if I had been asleep for more than half an hour when I was awakened by strange sounds coming from what seemed to be the adjoining room. In the dim window light, I bestirred myself, this time to make my way to a door that I assumed connected my room to the other.

Peering through the keyhole, I was greeted with a sight far stranger than any I had yet observed. Yvette, the jockey, was riding! The role of horse was filled by Mr Mutton Chop, the elderly gentleman with whom she had ascended the stairs. Fully clothed, she sat astride, flicking her crop against his flabby, naked flank. Somewhat awkwardly, they cantered about the room. As mount and rider turned broadside I could see, hanging from between his legs, a monstrously erect horsecock. It was of greater dimension than either Mr Thisby's or Mr Woodcock's – so much so that had it extended another two or three inches it would be dragging on the floor! As I watched, she manipulated the crop to his underside and with some vigor flicked the heavy organ. Their voices, though muffled, were understandable.

Mr Mutton Chop groaned. 'Please . . .'

'That is not the sound of a horse!' Yvette's French-accented voice was shrill, commanding. She grasped a handful of his remaining hair and pulled his head back till his eyes bugged. 'Horses do not talk!'

Mutton Chop whinnied!

It was an equine impression far from perfect but it nevertheless seemed to mollify Yvette. 'Ah, that's better,' she said, releasing his hair. 'Giddap! Take me to the bloody bed!' The sound of her crop on his bare arse was resounding.

Though the scene before me was bizarre beyond anything I could even imagine at the time, I was nevertheless quite affected by it. I felt a tingling sensation at the base of my spine and through the use of an inquiring finger was made aware that, once again, my sap was running.

Through my keyhole I observed the wilful victim stretch

out on his back. Yvette disappeared from my view momentarily, then returned with a length of rope. I observed breathlessly as, with what seemed to be practised skill, she bound her guest into supine immobility. It took her less than three minutes to pass the rope twice beneath the mattress, locking both his arms and legs akimbo.

Because of the height of the bed, I could see little of him except for the massive priapus, which stood like a monument to their childish game.

Yvette was soon as naked as he. Her body was similar to my own; big-breasted, liberally but not overly fleshed. She crawled onto the bed, grasped Mr Mutton Chop's weapon in both hands and began frigging him slowly.

Said she, 'You're not to cum until I order it.'

Said he, 'Yes . . .'

'Yes what?'

'Yes, mistress.'

'If you spend, I shall piddle on your face and whip you to within an inch of your life!'

'Oh yes, mistress, beat me, piss on me!' He spoke breathlessly, his voice sounding husky and trembling with expectation.

'Not if you spend,' she said, unaware of her contradiction.

With that, Yvette straddled him. He struggled for a moment to place a pillow under his head, raising it so that it was now in my field of view. She was squatting over his face. His tongue, stretched to its fullest, was just able to make a feathery contact with her quim. She allowed only that access to her pleasure garden which his tongue tip could reach, staying just barely in range, teasing him thusly while pumping his cock in ever increasing tempo.

Overwhelmed by what lay before me, I touched my own cunny with a tentative hand. It was spongy and hot through the soft silk of my new gown. I pressed tighter, moving my hand in slow circles as the heat spread through my body.

Suddenly, with no warning, Yvette lowered herself abruptly so that she was actually sitting on her victim's face. She released his prick, braced her arms on his chest and bore down.

'Suck my cunt.' Her voice climbed the scale of passion. 'Fuck me with your face . . . drink my juice!'

Her body moved back and forth with increasing violence, grinding her pussy into his face, almost smothering him in oozing female flesh!

With my eye pressed to the keyhole, I raised my gown, brought my hand into closer contact with my own gushing cunny. Attempting to gain some of the rapture Yvette was experiencing, I pressed tightly, my thumb in delicious contact with the base of my clitoris.

'I'm spending,' cried Yvette. 'Suck it out of me!' I watched as her bottom rotated in quick jerks, pressing downward on his face, her arse cheeks trembling in repeated spasms.

The lewd tableau transported me into a fit of complete abandonment. I pinched my engorged clitoris between two fingers. In a passionate whisper, I mouthed some of the new words I'd so recently learned. 'Fuck . . . cock . . . cunt . . . quim . . . tits . . ' Yvette was spending, as was I! 'Spunk . . . bollocks!. . . . cum . . . cum!'

I reached upward and grasped the doorknob to balance myself as Yvette's squeals of rapture sang lascivious harmony with my own. Then, suddenly, as I leaned forward for support, the door gave way. It swung open fully, depositing my still twitching body onto the thickly carpeted floor of my neighbour's room. In a twinkling I had passed from delicious fantasy to startling, embarrassed reality!

A heavy masculine voice boomed, 'Egad! What have we here!'

FIVE

The oft repeated statement referring to women is a rude falsehood: 'Turn them upside down and they are all the same.' It has, however, a certain validity when applied to the male of the species. To wit: 'The male sexual paraphernalia, whatever its state at the given moment, presents no indication as to the station of its master, be he emperor or beggar.' A handsome prince may possess a diminutive staff of little functional value while the ugliest, most ignorant of Croatian fishermen might be the proud proprietor of a magnificent and highly talented rod. [J.E., 1913]

Mortified, I lay sprawled on the floor. I looked up to see Mr Mutton Chop straining at his bonds, peering at me. Yvette had risen from her squat over his face and was standing on the bed straddling him. The insides of her thighs glistened from spittle and female love juices. She looked down at me, her startled expression giving way to a most diabolic smile.

'Not to fear,' said she to the supine figure on the bed, her French accent momentarily forgotten. 'Just a little busybody named Jenny who's had her eye to the bloody keyhole.'

'I'm sorry. . . .' said I, unable to think of anything else to say. I noted that Mutton Chop's iron pole had collapsed into fleshy innocence.

'She has come to join us in our little games,' said Yvette.

Then she lowered her voice. 'You like to play the games, *chérie*?' Once again, as with Madame Kooshay, her words had taken on their earlier Gallic inflection. I wondered if I, too, could learn the charming technique.

I managed a wary smile. My randiness of just a few moments ago was gone, replaced by an unsettling nervousness. I said, 'I'm sorry, but it is well past my bedtime.' I got to my feet.

'Ah,' said the gentleman on the bed, 'what a pretty little thing.'

'Jenny,' said Yvette, 'this is my friend Sir Randolph Tatter, Earl of Bainbridge.'

'How d'ya do,' said Sir Randolph, straining at his bonds.

'Pleased to meet you, sir,' said I, curtsying awkwardly. I'd never seen an earl before.

'Charming,' said Sir Randolph. 'She's bloody charming!'

'I must go now. . . .'

'Yvette, get her to remove her shift so I might see her motte – see her tits and all that sort of thing.' His prick had regained half its previous size and was growing before my eyes.

'Good night,' said I, turning to go back into my rom.

'Wait,' said Yvette. She moved quickly behind me and placed a hand on my shoulder. 'It will do you no harm, *chérie*, to honour Sir Randy's little innocent request . . . yes?'

'I don't know,' said I, feeling suddenly confused by it all. What was expected of me in this strange place?

Before I could think more about it, Yvette had turned me around into the room again. Without another word, she reached down and hoisted the new gown to my hips, exposing for her gentleman's gratification my nether parts. She fluffed the silken pubic hair with her fingers as if preparing a coiffeur.

'Charming,' said the earl. I stared, fascinated by his

pego, which had regained all of its heroic stature. Were such heroic proportions common to the peerage? Despite my embarrassment, I reaped a pang of gratification from the knowledge that I had been somehow responsible for an awesome transformation.

Yvette pivoted me slowly till my bare botom was exposed to him. I could hear his heavy breathing behind me.

'Charming.'

Then the gown was over my head, blocking my sight. Once again, Yvette turned me. Blindly I felt her fingers pinching my nipples.

'See how they grow,' said Yvette, her voice slightly muffled through the fabric gathered around my ears. 'You're a lewd little devil, aren't you, chérie?'

I moaned an affirmation. My head swirled in erotic confusion.

'Charming!'

Yvette cupped my breasts. 'These are perfect, are they not?'

'I want to stick my tongue up her arse and fuck her cunt!' The earl's voice boomed as if he were issuing orders on a field of battle.

'Perhaps one, but not the other,' said Yvette. 'She is a virgin and Madame intends she should remain so for a while.'

I wondered at this but was distracted as she led me, head still encased in its silken tent, towards the bed. I felt, in the back of my neck, in my buttocks and nipples, the beginnings of a lustful expectation quietly displacing my earlier, nervous embarrassment.

'Leave her head covered,' said the bound Earl of Bainbridge. 'It's her bottom parts I'm interested in!'

I felt a sudden, unaccustomed flash of irritation at his words. Angrily I tore the gown from my head. Then, looking down at him as he lay immobile on his back, I felt the irritation melt away. *When all was said and done, it was he who was the victim, not I*!

'Sit on his face, Jenny,' said Yvette.

Without further ado, I carried out the lascivious suggestion. I squatted above him and lowered my arse until it was firmly seated. No sooner had I done so than I felt his wet tongue invading my crevice.

With her laughing eyes on mine, Yvette said, 'And now that you're comfortable, Jenny, you can act as pin setter.'

'Pin setter?' asked I, taking pleasure from Sir Randolph Tatter's luscious laving.

With that, she straddled the gentleman's hips. His iron prong pointed straight up between her thighs, its straining attention centred on the mossy quim just an inch above it.

Yvette reached out with both arms to balance herself on my shoulders. 'You are,' she said, wetting her lips in what I took to be nervous expectation, 'to guide his prick into my pussy.' She glanced down at the impatient battering ram, her eyes wide, unblinking. 'Hold it with one hand and spread me with the other, dear Jenny. . . .'

I leaned forward, grasping the awful thing as directed. My fingers were barely long enough to encircle it. With my right hand, using thumb and forefinger, I spread her cuntal portal. The mons veneris was pink, plump, luscious. The pads of sweet, moist female flesh were firm and elastic. Her clitoris, emerged from its cocoon, was like a tiny, perfectly proportioned, erect penis. I leaned even closer, managing to keep my bottom firmly seated on the face beneath it. This was to be my first view of fucking. I felt a thrill of voyeuristic expectation.

Yvette began to lower hrself. 'Mind your aim, Jenny.'

My eyes were riveted on the point of impending contact. The final secret was about to be revealed to me. But how was it possible? In awe of Yvette's courage, I tightened my guiding grip on Sir Randolph's thick, oversized sausage, convinced it would never fit into the small, mysterious, feminine tunnel that I held open with my fingers.

'Oh, Jenny . . . I'm about to be fucked by the biggest prick in the British empire!'

I directed it carefully as contact was made. With baited breath I observed the tip of the giant pass through the portals. Then, as Yvette lowered herself a bit further, the purple hat was all but submerged.

'Ah,' said she, wriggling her bum in slow circles. 'Bloody heaven it is!'

She took a little more, while at the earl's other end, his tongue circled my nether rosebud, causing my body to twitch uncontrollably. Yvette's delicate cunny seemed stretched to its maximum. I looked up to find her unblinking eyes staring into mine.

'Oh, it's so good . . . kiss me, Jenny!'

I released the gentleman's partially implanted prong to put my arms around her. Her open lips were delightfully soft and receptive. We leaned into one another, sucking each other's tongues, our bottoms revolving, each in its own rapturous orbit.

Then suddenly, as I held her, she dropped a full six inches, her overstuffed orifice swallowing the remaining two-thirds of Sir Randolph's gigantic tool. At the same moment his tongue, a stiff probe, deftly wriggled its way into my nether opening.

My squeal of delighted surprise blended with Yvette's deep-throated groan. 'I've got him all, Jenny . . . his whole cock is in me!' she moaned into my open mouth as we held each other. 'Oh heaven! I'm being fucked by a monster from hell!'

She proceeded to bounce up and down wildly, cunting and uncunting, her long ebony tresses flying, her eyes wide but unseeing, her mouth gaping as if fighting for air. I watched, fascinated, as each upward thrust emptied her of at least half of Sir Randolph's fat bludgeon. Then the downward plunge would swallow it again till, with a liquid sound, it disappeared inside her, leaving only his giant bollocks exposed. Cunt and cock were one, a well-lubricated, perfectly coordinated engine of lust.

'Cock! Spunk!' she cried.

'Cunt! Fuck!' I replied.

She reached out with both hands to pinch my nipples. I reciprocated while pressing my bum even tighter against Sir Randolph's face, thrilling to his long, diddling tongue. Hearing myself squeal yet again, I wriggled with increasing rapidity.

'Yes, Jenny . . . what's he doing to you?'

'He's buggering me with his tongue!'

'Oh, we're so bloody lewd!' Yvette began a mad gyration, her bottom swinging in a dozen different directions simultaneously.

'Fuck him, Yvette!' I cried.

'Yes . . . fuck . . . fuck . . . up her arse!'

Her nipples, between my fingers, had grown fat and hard like tiny pricks. I twisted them, crying, 'Cummmm!'

'Yes . . . I'm going to spend!'

Suddenly, Sir Randolph dispensed with his anal preoccupation to transfer his oral affections to my pussy. The flat of his tongue licked its full length – back and forth. I bore down, almost smothering him in oozing female flesh.

Yvette cried, 'I'm cumming!. . . . Ohhh!'

'And me!' I, too, felt the pressure of an impending release. I raised up slightly, allowing the earl's now stiffened tongue access to my twitching clitoris. It vibrated against the supersensitive female flesh like a tuning fork! He applied more and more pressure. He was a genius at the game, fetching me till, once more, I settled on his face, exploding . . . my pussy . . . my breasts . . . my legs . . . my belly . . . everything, flying off in all directions in rapturous detonation!

Afterwards, we released Sir Randy from his bonds and bent him over the brass footboard with his white arse in the air. Yvette, using a long black leather whip, laid on while I knelt at his feet and, using both my hands, masturbated him. He spurted on the fifth strike. The earl's emission was copious. Yvette and I rubbed the sticky cream into the skin of our faces, to enhance our already rosy complexions.

Finally in my own bed, I watched the London sky grow pink through my open window and mused on the fact that my working-class arsehole had played host to the imperial tongue of British aristocracy. Just yesterday, as but the common daughter of a Welsh blacksmith, I wouldn't have even dreamed of such a possibility! I was exhausted but happy. I'd come a far distance in a short time and it had been a long day.

SIX

At a time when the human population of London was well over 3 million, the equine population was estimated to be almost 500,000 . . . A half million horses deposited their by-products a few times daily onto the cobbled thoroughfares! By day's end, Piccadilly, Regent Street, Pall Mall, were each paved with a fragrant carpet of manure through which ran meandering streams of acidic urine. The general ambiance was gloriously pungent! As is the case with all disagreeable facts of life, however, one adapts and accepts and soon becomes inured.

Just a final thought on the subject and I will leave the reader to his supper: London was as a flower garden compared to more tropical metropolises such as Rome and New York. [J.E., 1919]

For five days I roamed the streets of London's West End, attempting to familiarize myself with at least a part of that marvellous city. Its complexity, its variety of shops and restaurants, its fashionably clothed pedestrians and its hustle and bustle left me breathless.

I took most of my meals in pubs and tea shops, foregoing, except on one occasion, the communal dining arrangements at Madame Kooshay's. I felt intense gratitude for her gift of domicile and refrained as best I could from taking undue advantage. I did little more than sleep there. Even my sexual education seemed to have come to a halt following that first night with Yvette and the earl.

I soon realized that parties, similar to the one I had observed, were a nightly affair. So, too, were Yvette's squeals of delight, which along with heaving groans of masculine pleasure continued to penetrate our connecting door and thus disturb my sleep. It was, however, a welcome disturbance, providing a stimulant to my newly developed erotic imagination – meat for my masturbatory fantasies.

Early one morning, while everyone was still asleep (they were all late-rising), I explored the premises. It was luxurious beyond the dreams of such as myself, a bumpkin born and bred in a shabby blacksmith's cottage.

The first floor consisted of a large parlour, a cosy billiard room, a dining room and Madame Kooshay's 'sanctum'. On the second and third floor were ten bedrooms and two bathrooms. The attic had four bedrooms and maids' quarters. The basement contained an extensive kitchen, larder, laundry room and additional servants' quarters.

It was a strange and beautiful house, as were its congenial inhabitants. A dozen young women and their hostess appeared to live for nothing but parties, rich foods and drink and the ecstatic pleasures provided them by an endless stream of gentlemen who, as far as I could tell, asked nothing in exchange for their manly services.

Madame Kooshay was indeed a gracious and generous soul. Where would I have been without her? It occurred to me, however, that sooner or later I would have to give up this friendly sanctuary. But where to go? What to do? I had vowed not to return to Liverpool; I was determined to become a Londoner. Perhaps when I had learned more of the ways of the city, something by way of employment would present itself. For the moment I put the problem out of my mind.

Late on the fifth morning of my stay, as I was preparing to leave the premises for yet another day of exploring, Elvira asked me to join her at breakfast. It was to be my first communal meal with the ladies.

As the hour – though nearing noon – was considered

somewhat early for the denizens of Madame Kooshay's, we were the first four at the breakfast table. In addition to myself and Elvira, there were my noisy neighbour, Yvette, and a blond girl, Magnolia – of delicate features and physiognomy – whose robust attitude towards life, I was to find, gave the lie to her frail appearance.

The table was resplendent with platters of fried codfish, kidneys, grilled tomatoes, bacon, toast, kippers, eggs, a pitcher of hot milk, a large jar of marmalade, three teapots, and two crocks of butter of a consistency only slightly firmer than that of whipped cream.

After being introduced, I noted that the girl, Magnolia, had her left wrist done up in a bandage. I inquired politely as to the cause of her infirmity.

'The right honourable, bloody Sir Bertram Whitehead of the bloody home office is who did it to me!' She crunched down on a kipper and chewed furiously. 'You ask Elvira, she was there, naked just like me.'

'He imbibed a bit too much bubbly,' said Elvira.

'I'll say he did . . . bloody drunken acrobat he was!'

'He was funny,' said Elvira. 'Diverting . . .'

'Like a bleeding music hall turn!'

'He stood on his head and had us do likewise. And that was just the start. Poor Magnolia is not very athletic.'

'I'm a nice girl, I am,' said Magnolia, her mouth full now of bacon and toast. 'I don't hold with nasty things like athletics and the likes. The dirty old bastard had me twisted like a pretzel! Try to tell me what that's got to do with anything? Broke me bleeding wrist, he did!'

'It's not broken,' said Elvira, 'it's merely turned. T'will be good as new in a day or so, mark my words.' She placed her hand on Magnolia's arm in sympathy.

'You must have fared well with such goings on,' said Yvette.

'Sir Bertie is always generous,' said Elvira. 'There was an extra fiver to share last night.'

'We didn't share the broken bones!' said Magnolia. 'Why should we share the bloody fiver?'

With a forkful of kidneys poised at my lips, I said, 'You mean – he paid you money?'

Yvette said, 'When gentlemen request something out of the ordinary, they usually add a little on for the girl. It's a sort of understanding, if you know what I mean.'

'Add a little?' It was all somewhat confusing. 'To what?'

'Diabolical,' said Magnolia, her mouth open. I glanced around the table. They were all staring at me in frozen silence as if I were some alien creature from the mysterious purple grottoes of the moon.

Finally, Yvette, speaking in a low-pitched voice, said, 'We're harlots, Jenny.'

'Whores,' said Elvira.

'You mean,' I said, 'you take money from men for . . .'

'Yes. It's a profession like being a doctor or a barrister.'

'We sell our bodies,' said Elvira.

'Rent them, actually,' said Yvette.

'We usually get them back filled with spunk but none the worse for wear, as they say.' Magnolia giggled at her own words, almost choking on a kipper. 'Except this time he broke me bloody wrist.'

'Whores?' asked I, flabbergasted.

'Whores,' they chorused.

'But I thought that whores were terrible, dirty women who walked the streets – hellish, diseased creatures. . . .'

'Fire and brimstone,' said Elvira. 'That's what all the goody-goodies would have you think with their bible-thumping. But there's a lot worse than whoring for such as us.'

'Starving's one,' said Magnolia.

'You mean,' said I, 'that men pay you money in order to give you pleasure?'

'They usually take more than they give. The money is to make up the difference.'

Elvira reached out and took my hand in hers. 'You really don't know about fancy houses?'

'No,' said I, looking about me in confusion.

'You're sitting in one now, dear Jenny.'

'And eating good food,' said Yvette. 'And sleeping in a big soft bed and taking hot baths whenever you choose and being waited on hand and foot by real servants and hobnobbing with real gentlemen – even sirs and lords – just as if you were a high-born lady or a princess of the realm.'

'If you were one of us, you might even be putting a little away to open a flower shop or comfort your old age.'

Said Elvira, 'This is a good house, Jenny. Madame lets us keep the extras and never steals from us. She listens to our troubles and takes good care of us and even puts out our money at interest. And our gentlemen are the *crème de la crème*. I don't know where I'd be if I weren't here.'

'I bloody well know where I'd be,' said Magnolia. 'I'd be on the street with all the others or slaving in a scullery somewhere or married to some brute who beat me and kept me having babies one after the other while he spent his bloody money on whisky and me and the wee brats freezing near to death with nothing to eat but gruel. If you're not high born, the best thing you can be in London is a whore in a good house.'

I was quiet after that. Later that day, when I had returned from my walkabout, I sought out Elvira and asked her how she had acquired such a fine accent, seeing that she was working class.

'Mr Reginald Nottingham,' said she. 'He's a gentleman who comes here quite often – friend of madame's. When he takes a fancy to one of the girls he teaches her.'

'To be a lady?'

'Yes. Proper English. That makes one a lady, doesn't it?'

I nodded, saying, 'And Yvette, too?'

'Reggie taught her to be a French lady.'

That night I paid no heed to the usual sounds of rapture from Yvette's room, but rather lay awake staring at the ceiling, trying to think of myself as a whore. Despite the obvious advantages of such an avocation, and the good, secure life it offered one, I had vaguely uncomfortable doubts as to its suitability for myself. Little did I realize that tomorrow was to put those doubts to the test.

SEVEN

Things have changed over the years. Virginity nowadays is valued mainly by the Irish and by certain primitive tribes. Probably, before the end of this century [the twentieth], the hymen will be relegated to a status equal to that of the tonsils. [J.E., 1920]

'Jenny', said Madame Kooshay, her French accent once again dominant. 'It is time, *chérie*, we spoke of your future.'

We were sitting, enjoying tea and scones in her sanctum. We were both comfortably clothed in our lingerie. It was late afternoon. Rain was streaking the windows. The atmosphere was cosy. A small fire burned in the grate. I sunk deeper into the multi-coloured pillows of the Oriental booth, losing myself in the warm ambiance of a friendly forest of potted plants and the muted hues of paintings and books lining the walls.

'As you do not possess the good fortune nor the means to be a lady of leisure,' said she, 'have you considered finding a situation?'

'Yes,' said I, responding brightly. 'I would like to work in a hat shop. I've visited a few and I believe I have a calling for millinery.'

'Ah yes, millinery. All women must be hatted.' Her lips, above the rim of the teacup, formed a pleasant smile. 'A most laudable ambition.'

'I thought I might go about to some shops and make inquiries. . . .'

'Perhaps you might. But it would, I am sorry to tell you, to be no avail. Unfortunately, dear Jenny, many apply but few are chosen, and at this moment, you have neither the experience nor the presence for such employment.'

'Presence?'

'Accent, *chérie*. Just a single word from your lips and your roots become obvious. And surely you have, despite an admirable predilection for *les chapeaux*, no experience at all in that or any other endeavour. Certainly you must know that in Britain, station is everything and labouring-class girls, especially those with no experience, be they English or Welsh, are never engaged in trade except on the street as flower girls or match girls or whores. Only in America is it otherwise. I'm sorry to inform you of this ugly fact but s'truth and for your own good.' Despite her words, her tone was kind. 'You are a naive, provincial slip of a girl, who, it seems has been sheltered from everything.'

Suddenly downcast, I stared into my cup. What was I to do? I was indeed ignorant. Was I about to be ejected from my comfortable sanctuary? Had Madame Kooshay arranged this meeting, after six days, merely to inform me that I was now an unwelcome guest? It seemed so. I sipped my tea nervously, feeling a rising panic. 'I appreciate your thoughtfulness on my behalf,' said I, 'and am grateful for the succour you have provided me.' To my own ears, the words sounded stiff and insincere. I shuddered, feeling as if I were about to weep. My voice grew suddenly breathless as I fought the tears. 'Please . . . what can I do, where can I go?' I looked up at her.

'Back to your cosy smithy in Liverpool, my dear. I will shortly have a need for your room and prefer not to abandon you to the streets. They are not for the likes of you. If you have no money, I'll provide you with the fare.'

I slumped into the pillows; the tears, now released, trickled down my cheek. 'Thank you. . . .'

Madame Kooshay took the teacup from my hand. Then, gently, she embraced me. I melted into the comfort of her arms, sobbing. 'I so wanted to stay in London . . . to make my own way. . . .' Her breast was a soft cushion beneath my cheek. I felt a momentary desire to turn my head and bury it in the deep cleft between the twin beauties.

'You're an ambitious little thing,' she said, patting my head. 'So perhaps there's hope.' She pulled away from me, retaining a tight grip on my arms. 'Do you realize you possess something quite saleable?'

'No,' said I, wondering what she could be referring to.

'Something that many men value highly?'

'What could that be, Madame?' I sat erect, my interest aroused.

Madame Kooshay's French accent was gone again. She spoke in cool, businesslike tones. 'A rare and valuable jewel between your thighs – a gorgeous ruby waiting to be mined.' She held up the extended index finger of her left hand. 'You possess an unviolated quim. In other words, Jenny, you're a tight litle virgin. I determined that on the train.' She lay the finger on her lower lip, licked at it slowly with a long pink tongue as if it were a bit of sweet treacle. 'Mmm, delicious . . . and worth a fortune.'

A shiver ran down my spine. 'My virginity is worth money?' It seemed so unlikely. Yet, so much in the past few days was new and strange.

'Precisely, my dear. Virginity is a prerequisite for female respectability, honour and Christian morality, and therefore its selling price is high. The male of our species values it more highly than he does any other female virtue. It is the currency of holy wedlock; men consider it unthinkable to marry a woman who cannot bestow its gift on the wedding night. Yet many of these same men have lied, even raped and plundered, for the privilege of bursting this barrier of innocence while simultaneously standing ready to defend with their lives the virginity of their sisters. And women themselves, dear Jenny, place an equal value on it. They consider its out-of-wedlock violation a fate worse than death itself.'

Madame Kooshay stood, her long, lithe body looming over me. In a voice now soothingly affectionate, she said, 'A spot of sherry would be nice now, don't you agree?'

'Yes . . . please.'

At the sideboard, she poured two portions of amber wine into graceful crystal glasses. 'There are men,' said she, 'who value that silly little pink nubbin – that shard – of female flesh so highly that they are willing to pay or promise almost anything for the honour of destroying it.'

I was amazed by her words. Haltingly, I said, 'But surely a man would prefer a woman of experience over an ignorant virgin.'

'Men prefer what is forbidden, Jenny.'

'Are all men this way?' asked I, accepting the sherry glass.

'Hardly, my dear. There are some who appreciate the educated talents of experienced women. These are men more interested in experiencing pleasure, and even sometimes of sharing it with their partners, rather than merely verifying their virility. I have no doubt that you'll be bedded often by both types during your lifetime. And when you fall in love, as I'm sure you will do many times, I hope it will be with a gentleman who respects your passion as much as he respects his own. In my eyes, a true gentleman will always do so . . . as will, conversely, a true lady, whatever be her station.'

She was quiet for a moment – introspective – as we sipped our wine. Finally, she said, 'But to the matter at hand, my dear; you have an innocent beauty that will stand us in good stead.' She looked me in the eye as if to judge my reaction. 'If you are agreeable, I will pay you thirty-five pounds. That's over six times what your little cherry would bring you on the street. I will put you up for auction. The highest bidder will win a night in which to have his way with you – to deflower you as he sees fit.'

'Will it hurt?' I could think of naught else to say.

'The merest pop, and it will be all over. Your innocence

will be gone with the wind and you will be a full-fledged woman. Of course, if the man is a bull and at the same time inconsiderate, there will be a certain discomfort. But you are a passionate little thing and I'm sure you will find yourself accommodating in a short time.' She sat close to me on the pillows and placed a gentle hand, once again, on my shoulder. Then softly she said, 'It is a rare opportunity, Jenny; the beginning of a career that might very well carry you far. You have little else now but your body with which to create a future. It is a lovely body, and if you permit me to exploit it wisely, it can be your fortune.'

Her hand left my shoulder, trailing downward to caress my breast. Then her lips were on mine and she was whispering into my mouth. 'If you decide against my suggestion, then perhaps I can offer you employment as a maid at eighteen shillings the week. But soon the golden opportunity will be gone. You will squander your virginity on some clod or other who will leave you weeping and with nothing to show for it but a damnably big stomach.'

'Yes,' said I, my voice a hoarse whisper as she lowered me onto the pillows, lifted my gown to press her lips fondly against my naked belly. With my hands buried in her golden hair, her fluttering tongue left a trail of spittle as it made its way to my pussy. She spread her lips and sucked the soft flesh into her mouth.

'Yes,' I repeated. Then I melted.

EIGHT

It has been my experience over the years to note that men, in terms of their sexual preference, are categorized into two types: tit men *and* arse men. *Tit men are notorious for their violent nature, their unpredictability, their self-delusion, their coarse humour. Arse men, on the other hand, are strong-willed – true gentlemen of even temperament, high intellect, noble motivation. It is a well-known, historic fact that Jack the Ripper, Kaiser Wilhelm, and Black Bart were tit men. It has also been established that Benjamin Franklin, Sir Richard Burton, H. G. Wells, and Ludwig van Beethoven were arse men. Of course, a 'pure' example of either type is rare. Most men are hybrids with one side or the other somewhat dominant. [J.E., 1915]*

Finally, I was to attend an evening's festivities downstairs. I was not, however, to be a guest but rather a display, who, we hoped, would elicit at least a pound sterling for each pound of my flesh. Or as Madame Kooshay explained it, I was to be a silent princess who would bring out the 'best' in a congregation of gentlemen competing for my maidenhead. And the winner, she assured me, would indeed be the most gallant of them all.

At precisely ten o'clock, wearing a 'diamond' tiara and a gown beaded with pearls, I was escorted by Madame Kooshay and two of the girls to a temporary platform at one end of the large room. There I stood while my two attendants undressed me to murmurs of appreciation from twenty attentive gentlemen (nine of whom were there for the occasion by special invitation).

Atop the small stage was an ornate, thronelike chair. Naked but for the tiara, I sat in regal splendour – perfumed and powdered, my cheeks and nipples rouged, my pubic tresses shaped and coiffed into a beguiling heart shape. The men stared up at me with eager eyes, causing me to tremble self-consciously. But as I grew accustomed to their admiration, that negative feeling melted slowly into a positive one. *They were there for me! Me, little Jenny Everleigh! I was the centrepiece, the sole object of their yearning. Above all the others, I was the female for whom they lusted*!

Madame Kooshay stood to my right. She spoke in a clear voice, tinged with French, 'I will accept an opening bid of thirty-five pounds.'

'Done!' said a tall young officer clothed in the formal regalia of the Coldstream Guards. With a proprietary grin, he surveyed me head to foot as if he were already the high bidder making his rightful claim.

'Forty!' shouted an elderly, portly gentleman on the edge of the group.

'Fifty,' responded a vigorous-looking man in his thirties, sporting a full black beard. One of his arms was around Yvette's waist, the other he raised, champagne glass in hand, to make his bid. With his eyes on mine, he toasted me and in one gulp drained the ration of bubbly. Yvette, her full body pressed against his side, smiled at me encouragingly. She was dressed in gartered black silk hose and a black corset that squeezed her breasts into fat globes, forcing them upward till they seemed just under her chin. I could not help but note that together they formed a kind of fleshy table onto which one might place a tablecloth and serve luncheon.

No sooner had Yvette's bearded friend announced his bid than the portly old gentleman's arms were raised again. He shouted, unnecessarily, 'Fifty-five!'

From that point on, the bidding was brisk. Most of the gentlemen participated, raising each other in five- and ten-pound increments. I felt the rising tension of competition, indeed shared in it, my heart beating wildly. Which of them would win the right to initiate me into the lascivious art of fuckery?

I began to favour Yvette's handsome, bearded chap. He seemed the coolest of all, bidding only when the calls lagged. I caught his eye, nodded imperceptibly. He returned my encouragement with a wry smile. I closed my eyes momentarily, attempting to visualize his naked body covering my own. I opened them to see his brazen hand on Yvette's breast. I squirmed in my seat as my nipples tingled from his lustful gaze. His eyes were fondling my breasts just as his hand was fondling Yvette's! He was an erotic magician making love to me across a crowded room! The heat rose in my loins as his gaze trailed downward. Was such a man destined to be my champion? I prayed it were so.

In my preoccupation, I became deaf to the bidding, blind to the attentions of all the others. The feelings so miraculously wrought by the erotic power of my distant lover's eyes grew more and more intense. A chill passed through my body; my nether regions twitched with delicious cravings! Could I actually be fetched by this alone? If the game continued, would I spend in full view of the congregation? I shuddered with the knowledge that it was quite possible – nay – probable! His passionate gaze was as a soft tongue laving the folds of my secret nest. The cushion beneath me grew sodden.

Dimly I was aware of madame's voice. 'Jenny, dear . . .' The two words, stated gently, returned me to sobriety. It became suddenly clear that I must put an end to the sensuous game we were playing. In her subtle way, Madame Kooshay had pointed out that there was serious business afoot and it was incumbent upon me to be fair and impartial to all. Favouritism was certain to be noticed and might preclude some from bidding. With great effort, I tore myself away and stared out impassively at the congregation.

As the bids grew higher and higher, the participants, one by one, dropped out. Finally, when the bidding reached two hundred and ten pounds, only a pair remained in the game: the portly gentleman and my bearded champion.

It was an enormous amount of money! Surely, thought I, this could not be serious. It must be a game – a lighthearted charade they played from time to time. There were those in Britain who would consider such a figure a lifetime's income.

'Two hundred and twenty,' said the portly gentleman.

'Two fifty!' said my knight.

Was there to be no end? I gasped in disbelief! Next to me, I noted that madame did the same. It seemed that she, too, was surprised by the heights achieved. Then, for the first time since it had begun, the bidding ceased. The older gentleman displayed a dejected frown, the younger a triumphant smile. Yvette, her painted mouth to his ear, was whispering something. He laughed outright then smacked her affectionately on her plump, lace-covered rump.

Madame, ignoring the impropriety, said, 'Is that the final bid?'

There was silence. All eyes turned to the portly gentleman. His saddened attention seemed centred on the now quiescent, mossy garden squeezed between my thighs. Despite my intense attraction toward his younger competitor, I experienced a rush of sympathy for him. I was being unfair – selfish. Christian charity dictated that I help the poor man. Perhaps with a bit of encouragement he might still have a chance. I commanded my legs to relax their modest stance, allowing them to assume a more naturally spread posture so that he might see what he was bidding on.

'Gentlemen,' said Madame Kooshay, 'surely there must

be one among you who has the taste to appreciate the extremely rare, virgin beauty you see before you. Two hundred and fifty pounds is an insult to her innocence!'

There was a cough, a momentary rustle of silk, a throat clearing, a feminine titter. Silence.

'Mr Mulberry?' asked madame. The old gentleman's eyes dropped from my quim to his own feet. He spread his hands in resignation.

'Jenny, dear,' said madame, 'please stand.'

I stood, my hands crossed demurely over naked loins.

'Jenny . . . your hands, my dear.'

I placed them at my sides.

'Now turn, slowly.'

Once more I complied with my mistress's command. As I revolved in place my weight shifted from one leg to the other, causing my hips to swing provocatively from side to side. I took pleasure in this new-found adroitness of hip. It had come to me naturally.

'The bid is two hundred and fifty pounds. Will I hear, gentlemen, two hundred and sixty?'

Silence reigned. Madame Kooshay's voice shattered it. 'A certified virgin, dear friends. There is none more charming, more eager in these islands . . . nor even in *la belle France* itself! . . . Going for two hundred and fifty pounds . . . Mr Mulberry, Lord Bainbridge, Mr Farsley, Mr McMuggle . . . this is your last chance. Going . . .'

'May I touch?' asked the old gentleman.

'Briefly, Mr Mulberry.'

I froze in place, my back turned to my audience, my right hip extended. I felt his warm hands on my buttocks. They squeezed gently, then were gone.

'Two hundred and fifty-five,' said Mr Mulberry, his voice cracking on the fifth syllable.

'Madame,' said another voice that I recognized as belonging to my champion, 'may I also sample the goods?'

'Briefly, Mr Nottingham.'

I shifted my weight to the other leg, rotating my hips to

the left in order to present a somewhat different aspect to the prospective buyer.

The 'sample' came as a sudden shock – a resounding slap to my right buttock! It stung the plump flesh, sending tremors through my body. Fighting the shock, I remained perfectly still, knowing somehow that submission would win the day for Madame. Slowly – provocatively – I rotated my hips to the right again, bent forward slightly in order to present my buttocks as an even better target. I was aware of a murmur of appreciation from my audience. This time it was my left cheek that experienced the impact. The slap was sharper than the one previous, palm and arse flesh meeting in perfect, total and resounding contact. I felt the heat course through my body.

I gave no hint of painful reaction but rather, once more rotating my hips, I turned to face my energetic assailant. With eyes half closed I stared into his, freezing the grin from his face. I was onstage, the audience was mine. My hands went to my breasts, cupped them, allowing the elongated nipples to peek through my fingers.

'Magnificent,' said Mr Nottingham, his voice husky, barely audible.

A voice from the audience called out, 'Two hundred sixty!'

Another shouted, 'Two sixty-five!'

Still another, 'Two hundred seventy!'

'Three hundred pounds,' said my bearded assailant, his eyes still on mine.

Then a new voice, one that had remained silent till now, thundered from across the room. 'Three hundred and fifty pounds! And let there be no further nonsense about it!'

He was totally bald. A hulk of a man in black, he was off by himself, reclining on one of the chaises, his polished dome reflecting the warm gaslight. His eyes, however, reflected nothing but rather, seemed to burn with a crystalline light of their own. His face was heavy, with a coal-black beard and large eyebrows – an evil visage that sent chills of trepidation up my spine.

Stunned silence reigned. *Three hundred and fifty pounds!*

Finally, Madame Kooshay called in a voice strained with incredulity, 'Three hundred fifty pounds has been bid. Do I hear three hundred and sixty?'

Silence.

There was no further bids.

'Sold to Major Horace Piltdown, O.B.E.!'

I was to be fucked by the Devil.

NINE

Fashions of that day were designed to preclude hurried or impetuous disrobing. This had little effect on the birthrate but was a great disadvantage to the illicit pursuit of passion. Beneath a dress or gown replete with hooks, eyelets, buttons and ties lived an assortment of perhaps a half-dozen petticoats, a chemise, a pair of long-legged drawers, a chemisette and possibly a set of hoops. If by some chance, amorous intentions survived the fevered machinations of female disrobing to that point, one was then confronted by the most formidable barrier of all: the corset. It was a diabolical device of torture and constriction; the iron maiden of its time; a suit of armour, constructed to be impervious to the impetuous arrows of cupid. The corset's stated purpose was to mold its stylish wearer into an idealized hourglass. Its actual function was to make the weaker sex even weaker, subjecting her to shortness of breath, fainting and unspecified internal problems. To divest oneself of it in a reasonable amount of time required the aid of another woman; for no man, unless he be long married or practised in military engineering or in bridge construction, would dare such an intricate undertaking.

All in all, the nineteenth century and its industrial revolution put an end to romantic or sensuous undressing for all but the most dedicated women. The gracious folk art of disrobing was not to be fully revived till the twentieth century and the invention of the French panty and the blessed American zipper.[J.E.,1921]

My deflowering was to be consummated two nights after the auction, between supper and breakfast. It was to take place in the 'bridal suite', a pink and white room designated for 'special celebrations'. A massive canopied bed fitted out with silk sheets floated like an island in a sea of lilacs and gladiolus. The effect was breathtaking. Could any girl ask for a more perfect setting in which to consummate one of the most important events in her life? As for myself, I was fussed over, pampered and fitted with a white brocade bridal gown done up specially for me by a local seamstress.

'And,' said Madame Kooshay, 'since the enormous fee you commanded was the direct result of your own superb talents, I am doubling the amount I promised you. Seventy pounds. You should be proud, my dear.'

'Thank you, Madame.'

'And afterward, if you wish, you may stay on here and be one of our girls.'

'Oh, thank you, Madame.' I was flattered by the attention being displayed toward me, almost overwhelmed by my new status.

'Your fortune is made, dearest Jenny.'

'Yes, Madame.'

'Though I must say, I thought for a moment that you were about to do yourself in.' She laughed, kissed me on the cheek.

I had no idea what she was speaking of. 'How is that, Madame?'

'Reginnald Nottingham – it appeared as if he were about to be the high bidder.'

'The bearded gentleman with Yvette?'

'The same, dear Jenny. It was obvious to one and all that you were taken with him. You caused him to forget himself and stake far more than he should have. He might have ended up high bidder – t'would have been a disaster.' Madame Kooshay smiled, ran her hand affectionately through my hair. 'But fortunately, my sweet, you seemed to have realized it in the nick of time and saved the day.'

'I felt I was being unfair to the others – and to you, Madame, by making my preference obvious.'

'Unfair?' She held me at arm's length. 'You mean you didn't know?'

'Know what . . .?'

'Reginald Nottingham was what gamblers call a shill. I should have told you.' She smiled sweetly. 'A shill, Jenny, is someone who bids falsely in order to heighten the bidding of others. Reggie Nottingham himself couldn't even have afforded the opening bid! He is practically a pauper, recently disinherited. He was carried away with you – lost his power of judgement and for that, I must say, I hardly blame him.' Madame kissed me affectionately on the lips. 'Reggie is an amusing fellow, a good friend. All of our ladies like him and from time to time he helps us with one thing or another. He is handy to have about – sort of a friend of the family. This time we made use of one of his many talents in exchange for a few of Yvette's. She was more than willing and so all's well that ends well.'

I felt a sting of jealousy. 'You mean that Mr Nottingham had been bidding for me so that he might poke Yvette?'

'Ah, that troubles you.' Madame Kooshay put her arms around me. 'Well then, you'll be pleased to know that Mr Nottingham is also interested in you. He asked if there was anything more he could do in the future – some service or other in lieu of payment, as with Yvette and a few others. As I mentioned, we often arrange such things, Reginald and I.'

I was annoyed and wondered why. 'What did you tell him?'

'I said it was up to you.'

'No,' said I. 'I hate him.'

The following evening, dressed as a bride, with my train carried by four of the ladies, I ascended the main staircase to the 'bridal suite'. A dour Major Horace Piltdown, standing in the doorway, greeted my ceremonial entrance with little more than a grunt, then turned his back to stare out the window. He remained thus till the bridesmaids left.

I swallowed my disappointment at his gruff reaction. It is not every day that a girl gets to make such a flamboyant entrance. A single complimentary word would have sufficed, even a warm kiss on the cheek or an extended hand. Perhaps, I allowed, he was merely exhibiting a rather shy nature – poor fellow.

A marvelous supper of oysters, roasted pheasant and champagne had been laid out in the room. But Major Piltdown's seemingly ill-tempered silence destroyed my appetite. Neither of us ate much, but rather toyed with the food, stared at our plates. The champagne went unopened. By the time we got to the trifle, I was fighting panic. Surely one of us should speak.

'It's a lovely evening,' said I, aware of the tremor in my voice.

'It is far from a lovely evening, Miss Everleigh. It is raining.'

I pushed my plate away. He was a surly man, probably violent. I eyed the door, then taking the bull by the horns, I turned to him. 'If you don't want me, Major Piltdown, then why did you buy me?'

He seemed not to hear me. He said, 'I hate virgins!'

In a state of anxious confusion, I stood, almost upsetting the table. 'But you paid three hundred and fifty pounds for me!'

'Yes.'

'Perhaps,' said I, 'Madame Kooshay will return it.'

'No. I couldn't ask her to do that.'

He looked up at me and I felt that what I had taken for surliness was actual fear – a fear even greater than mine. He was totally unlike the men described by madame. In contrast to my initial feelings of fear and repulsion, I now found myself feeling sorry for the poor devil.

'I have a phobia about virgins. I'm repelled by the very

idea,' said the major, gritting his teeth. 'And blood – I never could stand the sight of it. Furthermore, what pleasure can be had by poking a completely ignorant, immature, disgustingly innocent young girl, who at best would be fearful and uncooperative? What need could any man have for such bother when the world is filled with charming, experienced women who are eager to be bedded by such as I?'

'Then why . . .?'

'I admit it is a contradiction, but I purchased you simply because you are the most beautiful young woman I've ever set eyes on. My bid was an irresistible impulse.' He spoke rapidly, in an undertone, his eyes on mine. 'I fell in love with you the moment I saw you.'

Touched by this unexpected admission, I stepped closer to him and took his hand in mine. I said, 'But I am not inexperienced.'

He brightened. 'You mean, you're not a virgin?'

'No, Major Piltdown, I'm surely a virgin – certified – but I am not what you term ignorant – nor am I innocent or uncooperative.' Taking charge of the situation, I lowered myself into his lap and reached to loosen his cravat.

'Certain pleasurable activities are not unknown to me.'

'Good Lord, I . . .'

Before he could finish what he was about to say, I pressed my lips to his. In shock at my unexpected action, he recoiled, almost tipping the chair. But I persisted. My insistent tongue forced its way past his stiffened lips. His arms, finding themselves around my waist, seemed unsure, tentative.

I pressed my body against his, whispering into his gaping mouth. 'Major Piltdown, we have the entire night in which to rid you of your foolish phobia.'

'Please, Jenny . . .' He pulled back, releasing my waist. 'It would not be advantageous to either of us for me to try.'

With cool deliberation, I stood up, pulling the pins from my hair. I was determined to provide the poor man with three hundred and fifty pounds worth of pleasure. I was an honest girl who believed in *value given for value received*; a credo I would honour for a lifetime.

'Please, lend a hand, Major,' said I, turning my back to him, flipping my hair out of the way. In silence he complied. I could feel his warm breath on the back of my neck as he struggled with the hooks and buttons. It took him some minutes to complete the task, thereby affording me time to plan a strategy.

If, as he stated, he preferred experienced women to all others, then, despite the fact that I was new at the game, I would do my best to assume that role. Since leaving home only two weeks earlier I had learned much and I was confident that my imagination was capable of filling whatever gaps remained in my education.

Finally unfastened, I stepped back. As Major Piltdown watched with wary, but nevertheless appreciative eyes, I allowed the white gown to slip from my shoulders. There was nothing else to remove. In a trice, I stood naked before him. I turned a sensuous half circle in order to afford him a complete view of what was to be his. With my back to him, I felt a sense of gratification at his gasp of pleasured surprise.

I turned to find my reluctant paramour gaping at me out of widened eyes. For moments he seemed paralysed, his mouth open but unable to speak. Was I indeed that beautiful?

Finally, in a hoarse whisper, he said, 'I've never seen such an instantaneous transformation from clothed to unclothed.'

'Prepared in advance for your pleasure, Major.'

'Ah, Jenny . . . for a second time my eyes feast on perfection!'

'But you, Major Piltdown . . .'

'*Horace*,' said he in a gentle voice.

'Horace,' said I, standing now with my legs slightly parted, my hands clasped demurely, yet at the same time provocatively, over my naked pubic coif. 'But you are still clothed. It's unfair that only I am naked.'

He removed his waistcoat and proceeded to unbutton his shirt. Feeling a delicious sense of power, I stepped closer to him.

'Let me help you,' said I, descending to my knees.

He sighed, his body rigid, much like a soldier's at parade rest. As I unbuckled his shoes, he stepped out of them. I unfastened his trousers and pulled them down past his knees. Beneath them his bottom parts were clothed in white linen drawers extending from waist to knee. Slowly, I lowered them to join the trousers around his feet. His pego, a jolly but still diminutive playmate, sprung happily to view.

I glanced up to observe a barrel chest sporting a dense blanket of ebony hair that more than made up for the total lack of it on his massive, square head. Then, returning my attention to other matters, I cupped his gonads in the palm of one hand whilst with the fingers of the other I made gentle traceries about the base of his boodle. From what I had observed of the two gentlemen on the train and of Sir Randolph, such machinations on my part should result, quickly, in a stiffening and lengthening of the flaccid tool. Sadly, such was not to be the case with Horace. Though I had no inkling of such things at the time, the poor fellow was to require a much different and more rigorous stimulation.

TEN

Treachery! I speak not of male treachery towards the female but rather the ofttimes treasonous behaviour of the penis towards its proprietor. Wilful and quite often disobedient, the disloyal male organ, taking no cognizance of desire, passion or the object thereof, is capable of countermanding the orders of its master and remaining comatose.

As if with a mind of its own, this most prefidious of organs is also capable of low comedy of a contrary sort. For how many respectable gentlemen of good intentions have been blessed with unnecessary and, certainly embarrassingly unwelcomed erections in shops, public corridors, omnibuses[forcing them to ride past their stop], and on tailor's or speaker's platforms? To add injury to insult, how many of these same well-meaning gentlemen have found, just hours later, when they have finally bedded the object of their affections, that their contrary weapons on the very eve of battle have now taken it upon themselves to remain flaccidly uncocked?

Such is the male affliction that deserves, from all the women of Britain – of the civilized world – a deep sympathy and understanding.[J.E.,1903]

Kneeling at Major Piltdown's feet as he sprawled in the chair, I licked and sucked his soft prick in an effort to transform it into the state of rigidity necessary to pierce the ripened fruit of my maidenhood. Though the act was a pleasantly sensuous experience, it created, neither for myself, nor seemingly for the major, the driving passion of my few earlier adventures. There must be, I mused, while tonguing in gentle circles, a great deal of variation in the responses of men. Perhaps each was different from the other. If so, then what a wondrous variety must exist in the machinations of giving and receiving pleasure!

But if that were the case, would it be considered proper etiquette for one to ask her partner to describe those special desires that set him apart? I felt a sudden dejection. I might very well go on sucking through the night with no more response than I was now receiving: Major Piltdown's hands playing laconically in my hair. I had thought it all quite simple, but now I began to realize there was probably much in this line of which I was unaware. I was but a suckling babe playing at a very complex, grown-up game.

I allowed the soft member to flop from my mouth. I looked up at him. 'Major Piltdown?'

'Horace, my dear . . .'

'Horace,' said I, aware of the plaintive quality of my voice. 'What should I do?'

'You said, dear child, that you were experienced.'

'Perhaps not quite as much as I thought.'

The major pulled me to my feet. 'There is, dear Jenny, something we might do to improve matters if you are willing.'

'Anything, Horace,' said I, pressing my naked body against his.

Silently, he bent to retrieve his trousers from the floor. As I watched with growing curiosity, he removed the belt, a thick, wide leather affair sporting a large brass buckle. I felt a momentary stab of fear. Was it to be his pleasure to beat me with it? Before I could react further to that idea, he took me by the hand to the bed. There, with his deep eyes staring intensely into mine, he placed the belt in my hand. Then he lay face down on the bed, his legs spread.

'Whip me, Jenny . . .'

Ah, thought I, shades of Sir Randolph. I grasped the strap by its buckle, wondering whether pain and pleasure were universal or merely a diversion shared just by a few.

'Do it,' said he.

'Where?'

'On the arse,' said Horace, his voice muffled in a pillow.

'But surely it will smart . . . sir.'

'Lay to, Jenny!'

With a delicate reluctance, I brought the strap around in an awkward movement, allowing only its inertial weight to propel it. Despite the lack of force, the impact was like a pistol shot. In seconds, an ugly red welt appeared on the victim's milk white flesh.

I hesitated. Was that to be all? Were we now to get on to the matter at hand? The silent question was answered as the major arched his back, raising his naked rump a foot off the mattress.

He called out in hoarse tones, 'What are you waiting for, you little bitch? Strike . . . strike!'

Once again, I brought the thick strap across Major Piltdown's bepimpled buttocks. Then again, this time with increased force. He groaned, wriggled his arse in what I assumed was further invitation. Becoming more practised now, I laid the strap across both cheeks. His body twitched, silently. I felt an awakening interest creep into my loins.

CRRRAAACK!

'Whip away, me little darling!'

In rising heat, I responded with a vicious snap to the deep crease of his arse.

'Oh, lovely!'

CRRRAAACK!

'Marvellous!'

CRRRAAACK!

My heart was beating wildly. For the first time that evening, I felt now a familiar warmth radiating deliciously out from my groin to my breasts, my belly, the back of my neck – to the very arm wielding the vicious strap . . .

CRRRAAACK!

'Rapid fire, me lads!'

CRRRAAACK!

'Wrap the Moslem bastard in a pigskin!'

CRRRAAACK!

With his waffled bum elevated to receive its due, Major Piltdown was writhing uncontrollably on the bed.

CRRRAAACK!

'Oh . . . Cunt! Fuck! Prick! Spunk!'

A strange, wild exhilaration suffused my body. Quite suddenly, I was carried away – maddened – seething with perverse power! Blindly, I struck again and again! The sound of leather on bare arse flesh set a lewd rhythm in counterpoint to our heavy breathing and to Horace's manly grunts and groans. Now he was struggling to his knees, calling out I knew not what. Fevered with lustful power, I lashed out, this time catching him across the small of his back! He was down again.

CRRRAAACK!

'Let up, Jenny . . .'

CRRRAAACK!

'Enough!'

CRRRAAACK!

'No more, mistress!'

Finally, aware of his words, I stopped. He was face down; his arse a patchwork of hideous welts; his body bathed in sweat, twitching uncontrollably.

'Delightful,' he said in a quiet, gasping tone.

Breathless with exertion, my mind a seething blank, I could think of nothing to say. I dropped the strap, ready for come what may.

Painfully, Horace rolled over. With gaping mouth and wide eyes, he seemed a heaving fish out of water. His cock was rampant, its bulbous, purple head capping a thick shaft at full staff.

'Glorious,' he said, his eyes on mine. 'You are an angel!'

'Thank you,' said I, recovering my senses, I lowered my

gaze once more to his stiffened pego. Surely it was ready now to do its duty.

I was mistaken . . .

Major Piltdown, his gigantic prong grasped firmly in hand, spoke in firm, authoritarian tones. 'And now, little Jenny, you are to perform yet another service.'

'Yes, sir,' I said.

'Yes, Horace . . .'

'Yes, Horace . . .'

'First, you are to blow out one of the candles on the table.'

'Yes?'

'Do it, girl.'

Wordlessly, I obeyed, wondering what was afoot.

'Now, sweet Jenny, remove it from its holder and roll the tip around in the butter.'

Once again, I complied.

'Be sure to get it nice and greasy.' He grinned up at me like a mischievous little boy. 'The tables are to be reversed, dear little girl. It is *I*, not you, who will receive the first fucking of the evening.'

Dimly perceiving his meaning, I stared in awe at the candle. The ways of men were seeming curiouser and curiouser.

'Come here, Jenny.' He reached out for me and ran his hands down my flanks, between my legs. He cupped my dampened quim in a congenial palm. 'Soft like a nightingale's belly,' said he, diddling lightly with his fingertips. He removed his hand and licked his fingers as if he'd just eaten a succulent sweetmeat. 'Delicious . . . a rare cuntal vintage, somewhat young but nevertheless, properly aged.' With three fingers in his mouth, his grin seemed grotesque.

Still on his back, he raised his knees and grasped them, pulling them back till they touched his chest. His nether region was completely exposed to me, topped by a proud staff that towered majestically from a tangled forest of black hair. Beneath his massive sack of balls a wrinkled arsehole stared up at me, unblinking. In a voice trembling with lewd expectation, he said, 'The candle, Jenny.'

'Yes, Horace.' I held it up. A full ten inches remained unconsumed.

'Gently, dear girl . . .'

I placed the tip against the puckered portal, pressing lightly.

'Ah . . .'

The slippery wax phallus slipped into its tight sheath. I found the sight of it, at first, somewhat unnerving.

'Ah . . .'

A full inch disappeared before I met resistance. I glanced upward for further instructions to find my view of the major's face blocked by his rampant priapus.

'Push it in, Jenny,' said Major Piltdown hoarsely. 'Up me arse!'

I pressed harder . . . another inch. He groaned and quite suddenly the orifice relaxed. The way was clear – open to his chosen tool of perversity.

'Lovely!'

Fully half the candle was implanted; the remainder protruded grotesquely from his arsehole. He groaned.

I pulled the waxy instrument partway out, watching wideyed as his elastic anal rim clung to it as if reluctant to give up its rude intruder.

'Ah . . .'

I pushed it in again. The major's breath hissed through his teeth.

'Fuck!' He grasped his cock just under the head and proceeded to frig it.

I drove the candle in and out with increasing tempo.

'Bugger me, dear girl!'

I plunged – withdrew – plunged – rotating the waxy phallus in small, tight circles, spreading his arsehole, feeling once again a voluptuous heat course though my body to settle in my neglected pussy.

'Fuck my arse!'

With the candle clasped in both hands, I fucked him with wild abandon. Once more I was being carried away on the wings of Major Piltdown's lust!

Then the sight of a tiny, glistening pearl on the tip of his prick created in me a sudden, uncontrollable desire. Without thinking, I lowered my head to take the bulbous cock head between my lips!

'Suck it, Jenny!'

I took his fat sausage into the rapturous sanctuary of my mouth – sucking – licking – savouring the mouthful of lewd male flesh! Then, suddenly, his thighs were clasping my head. He rolled – and I with him – till my back was on the bed and he squatted above me, his cock still in my mouth. The candle, temporarily free of my guiding hand, protruded from his clutching anus. I reached up, grasped it once more, held it steady whilst he fucked it with rotating, thrusting hip movements.

'Fuck! Suck!'

The major was fucking and being fucked simultaneously – fucked in the arse with a candle whilst he fucked my mouth! I made a tight ring of my lips, a cushion of my tongue. The mere thought of what was going on was almost enough to fetch me – almost – but not quite. With my free hand I reached down to my soggy quim. Lightly, I touched my clitoris. It was free of its sheath and painfully sensitive. I placed a finger on either side of it, straddling, then slowly, in half time to Major Piltdown's thrusting hips, I frigged.

'Suck, fuck!' he cried. 'Suck it out of me, bitch goddess!'

My body was twitching, the tension building unbearably. I slowed my cuntal manipulations, feeling a strong desire to spend at the same time as my paramour.

'For queen and country!' cried Major Piltdown.

His cock, violating my mouth as I had hoped it would violate my still virgin pussy, was fucking into the portals of my throat. For a moment I was certain I was about to choke, but in the nick of time, I discovered a way to relax my throat muscles. Soon I was taking all of him, his heavy bollocks bouncing against my chin!

'Hold your fire, men!'

I twisted the candle as it drove in and out. Everything was happening at once . . . Sucking! Fucking! Frigging!

'Steady lads . . .'

Major Piltdown withdrew his swollen organ till only the bloated head rested on my tongue. It spasmed and twitched as if it were alive, independent of its master. I, too, was twitching, writhing on the sheets now damp from gushing quim. Both the major and I were about to explode!

'Ready . . .!'

Suddenly, all motion ceased. My back arched in orgasmic tension as we hung on the brink. Major Piltdown groaned a deep, drawn-out, surging rumble that seemed to emanate not from his vocal chords, but from his entire body. Then, in a commanding voice pitched a full octave above normal, he called, 'FIRE AT WILL!'

His weapon exploded in my mouth!

My body sung out in glorious release as waves of rapture found their way to my breasts, my fingertips, my belly, my neck! In my mouth, his twitching pego spurted acrid spunk onto my waiting tongue. I swallowed quickly, only to be rewarded with yet another spasm.

Minutes passed before I was once again aware of my surroundings. My eyes opened, not on the major's hairy belly, but rather on the dimly lit ceiling. His spunk, so recently hot and creamy, was clotting on my lips, my cheeks, my chin.

The major himself, I discovered, was sitting on the edge of the bed, staring down at his feet. As I stared, dumbly, he muttered something. I know not what, then he stood and proceeded to dress.

Within minutes he was standing in the doorway, fully clothed, his polished head gleaming in the candlelight. 'You are,' said he in kindly tones, 'a fine and talented whore . . . dear Jenny.'

'Thank you,' I said, hardly cheered by the gracious compliment, my voice pitched just above a sorrowful whisper.

'Cheerio . . .'

With that, Major Horace Piltdown opened the door and exited the 'bridal suite.'

Madame Kooshay found me a half hour later seated at the small table, dressed once again in my now wilted bridal gown. In a fit of sobs, I blurted out the disgraceful news. She held me as I wept on her shoulder.

'I am a disgrace to this establishment,' said I. 'I have shamed its good name!'

'No, Jenny, dear. Quite the contrary . . .'

'And I have not the slightest notion of what I did wrong – '

'You did nothing wrong,' said Madame Kooshay, taking my hand. 'You are quite the most beautiful girl here and, from what I have heard, probably the most talented. You lack only experience, dear Jenny, but that is, of course, the natural state of a true virgin.'

'But he paid so much for me and then left me as he found me! Surely I'm a failure.'

'Hardly. Major Piltdown, before he left, spoke of you in the most glowing of terms.'

My sobs were cut short. 'He did?'

'Yes, my child – glowing.'

'He didn't complain?'

'Why should he?'

'I thought I had been, in some manner, distasteful to him.'

'No, my dear, he only praised you. You provided him with what he said was the most exciting and fulfilling evening of his life.'

'I don't understand . . .'

'The major,' said Madame Kooshay, 'got what he paid for – more, in fact – he got his virgin, the most charming and beautiful in all of Britain. But unlike most men who value female carnal innocence, his desire was not to deflower his prize, but rather to use her in lewd ways more congenial to his particular predilection.' She smiled at me, ran her graceful fingers lightly across my cheek to brush away an errant tear.

'Men are most peculiar,' said I, sniffling.

Madame Kooshay produced a handkerchief from her bodice. I dried my eyes, blew my nose and returned her smile.

'Yes,' said she, 'most peculiar. But as women we can profit from their peculiarity. In this case we have gained from Major Piltdown's perversity. You are, Jenny, still a virgin and therefore a good deal of money is still to be made. Surely that will cheer you up.'

'Another auction?'

'No, I'm afraid we couldn't do that as it might create malicious gossip. There are those – hardly gentlemen – who would leap at the chance to malign the poor major as having been unable to rally the tool of his manhood at the moment of truth. Some might go even further.' She stood and picked at the untouched roasted pheasant on the table. 'I will find the right client. Of course, we can't expect the enormous fee you've so recently commanded, but it will be substantial nevertheless. As a matter of fact, I do have someone in mind.'

'That would be lovely,' said I.

'And your share, dear Jenny, added to the seventy pounds you've already earned, will certainly leave you with over one hundred pounds sterling – surely a fortune for any young girl!'

'Oh thank you, Madame!' I was overjoyed. I was not a failure after all! In addition, according to Madame Kooshay, I was soon to be rich beyond my dreams.

She was silent for a moment. Then she said, 'Of course, there is the possibility of another course we could take . . .'

'What is that, Madame Kooshay?'

'Reginald Nottingham . . .'

'Yvette's young gentleman?'

'None other.'

'But you said that he is almost penniless.'

'Ah, true, young Jenny, he is that, indeed. But Mr Nottingham can bestow on you something far more valuable than mere money.'

'Yes?' I was alive with curiosity.

'He can make you into a proper lady. He can teach you to speak the English language as if you'd been born to the peerage and all that – like a duchess, my dear. He does that sort of thing rather well.' She pulled me to her, pressed her body against mine and kissed me lightly on the lips. 'And in this country, one's accent is a key to one's future. If you speak like one of the upper class, they will accept you as one of their own. If not, then you will never rise above the level on which you were born. 'Tis your body and therefore your choice.'

I was astounded at my potential good fortune. 'Oh please, Madame,' said I in little more than a whisper, my mouth less than an inch from hers. 'It is what I want more than anything – more than money.'

'An admirable choice. I'll speak to Reggie this very evening,' said she. 'It would be advantageous to me also. On these premises a beautiful lady will be far more popular and command higher fees than the daughter of any Liverpudlian blacksmith, no matter how charming.' She ran her tongue across my lips, slipped its tip into my mouth then crushed her lips against mine.

'Oh, Madame . . .'

'And now,' said she, 'a treat, something you deserve as a reward for your excellent behaviour with the difficult Major Piltdown and for upholding the good name of this establishment.' With her graceful hands on my hips, she held me at arm's length. 'But first we must get you out of this gown.'

She had me naked in a trice. Then, with my pulse beating rapidly, I sat on the edge of the bed and watched as she disrobed. Despite our earlier adventures, 'twas the first time I had seen madame without her clothing. She was much slimmer than I, unstylishly so. Instead of the full-blown, plump pneumatic curves so highly valued in fashion, her body was gently curved, her stomach flat. Madame Kooshay possessed the body of a ballet dancer, a sleek body adapted to action and speed, like that of a lynx.

She threw herself onto the bed. Lying on her back, she surveyed me with moist eyes while speaking in a hoarse whisper from moist lips. 'Sweet Jenny,' she said, 'come here for your reward . . .' She reached up to pull me to her. 'We are going to involve ourselves in what knowledgeable, sophisticated women call *soixante-neuf,* sixty-nine to the less initiated. You will soon understand why it is called that. Just lay atop me thusly, my sweet, and we will seek to advance your education.'

Madame Kooshay manipulated my eager body so that my thighs straddled her face, thus bringing my oozing quim into contact with her lips. At the same time, I had only to lower my head in order to bring my lips to her own garden of delight. Sixty-nine, indeed! It was the most ingenious and voluptuous of all the sexual configurations of which I had hitherto been a part.

A century later we raised our dripping faces to smile at each other.

'Lovely,' said she.

'Lovely, indeed,' said I, wondering if my education was now complete.

'You should be hungry,' said she. 'Young girls are always hungry afterwards.'

Still damp with passion's juices, I joined my benefactress at the table. In minutes, between us, we consumed the pheasant, the oysters and all of the sweetmeats.

ELEVEN

There were, in my earlier days, sporting gentlemen whose pursuit of the forbidden included a perverted desire for child virgins as young as the age of nine. A profitable industry was founded to service this horrid taste. It included, in addition to kidnapping, the purchase, by unspeakably evil procurers, of children from their poverty-stricken parents. It pleases me to state that Madame Kooshay was one who had never degraded herself nor her profession thusly.[J.E.,1907]

The following evening, dressed this time in a fawn negligee, I was once more sharing my room with a gentleman. Again, things were to work out differently than I had been led to expect.

Reginald Nottingham spoke in heavy, resonant tones. 'You are a most beautiful young woman.'

'Thank you, Mr Nottingham.' I felt the compliment was a satisfactory beginning, but more than that, the tone of his voice sent a thrill coursing through my body.

'You're welcome, and you will call me Reginald except when we're working.'

'Working?'

'Yes, precisely,' said Reginald. 'And I can assure you it will be hard work. I have a plan so magnificent, so astonishing that it will make my reputation wherever English is spoken. A miracle! I will be known worldwide as Reginald Nottingham, the world's greatest dialectician.

Although that is not quite the term I would apply to myself, no other describing what I do has yet been coined. Perhaps in the future those who take up the gauntlet will be called Notterists or Nottomotrists or somesuch. But at the moment it is a new scientific pursuit that, as far as I know, is practised only by myself.' He paused, as if awaiting my reaction. I smiled at him sweetly, wondering if and when he was going to make love to me.

As if satisfied that I found his every word fascinating, he continued. 'Up till now I have created, just for a few females, merely an exterior façade, a rough familiarity with proper English and deportment – nothing more. But all the while I've been loooking for the perfect subject. I have spent nearly two years frequenting this brothel and two others, awaiting the ideal subject. And now, just when I was about to give up, I found you!'

'The perfect subject?' I was growing nervous under his intense gaze.

'You, my dear.'

'Me?' I closed my eyes to avert his diabolical stare.

'Yes, you are perfect. You possess intelligence, sensitivity, natural beauty. But your accent is an abomination. You sit when you should stand and stand when you should sit. You possess the figure of a lynx, yet you have the posture of a hippopotamus and, I might add, comparable table manners also. You are incapable of pursuing a conversation on any subject but yourself. In short, I repeat – the ideal subject. He turned away and threw his arms up as if taking applause from an unseen audience. 'She's perfectly marvellous!'

I felt a sudden, almost overpowering anger. 'You're bloodly mistaken if you think you have the right to talk to me this way!' With enraged abandon, I directed a kick at his arse. He turned quickly, caught my ankle and brought me down.

'You damned fool! I'm going to make a lady out of you!'

He held me down with muscular arms. At the top of my

voice, I said, 'You have a call on my virginity, not a licence to insult me!' I struggled to free myself from his iron grasp. Then, an instant later, his words flashed to life in my brain. Wondering if I'd heard correctly, I said, 'A lady?'

'Exactly.' He released my arms and glared down at me. 'The qualifications I mentioned are shared by two-thirds of the women in London. But you, dear Jenny, have others that I have found are rare indeed. I believe you to possess the three essential ingredients lacking in all I have interviewed – intellect, a certain pliancy that will permit real change and lastly, an ability to commit yourself, courageously, to new experiences without either precondition or prejudice.' He stood. 'Actually, I am not entirely certain of any of this and so I might be making a mistake. But I doubt it. I have been asking about you, observing you; it's the little things. All my instincts tell me that you are the one, the ideal subject. For that reason, you excite me beyond measure! I felt this when I first set eyes on you at the auction. Like shiny gold from dull, common ore, like a lovely butterfly from an ungainly caterpillar. I can help you transform yourself into a thing of beauteous perfection. And more, I can open you to the world!'

Reginald paced to the end of the room, then returned to stand, once again, looking down on me. Stunned by his words, I reclined awkwardly on the floor where he had left me. I had difficulty discriminating between insults and what I perceived to be compliments. Surely he was mad.

'It is not my intention,' he said in the spirited cadence of a candidate for Commons, 'to create yet another façade, to teach yet another young harlot, as I have those few others, how to emulate her betters; to parrot them – monkey see, monkey do. No, dear girl, I'm going to work with you from the inside out. When we're finished, you will not merely look, speak and act the part, you will actually *be* a high-born lady! It will be as if you were born to that station! Think of the triumph . . . you, an insignificant whore from Liverpool, will, when I'm done with you, be accepted by the upper class, by the peerage, perhaps even by the nobility, as if to the manor born . . . one of their own!'

I was dazzled by his proposal – confused, angered and at the same time, impressed by this man as I had never been by another. I stared at him, unable to conjure words with which to construct a coherent sentence. He grinned and extended a hand to help me to my feet. He held me close for a moment, then in soft, seductive tones, said, 'As for that other thing – my reward – it will await your emergence as my social equal . . . nay, possibly my better. I do this because I much prefer to deflower a virgin lady than to diddle away an evening with an ignorant, Liverpudlian harlot. There are plenty of those – but that is not your true calling. How say you?'

My heart was beating madly. If for no other reason than that promised union, I would agree. But was his promise sincere – or was I destined to remain, for the rest of my life, the most sexually experienced virgin in London? A lady! Could he really accomplish such a feat? I stared up at him, feeling a desire so intense that I felt my insides were on the boil.

'Well?'

I nodded dumbly.

'Agreed then,' said Reginald. 'And in the meantime, Jenny, dear, you are to refrain from indulgence in any other carnal pursuits. Like the caterpillar you currently resemble, such activity will have to await your metamorphosis into a butterfly.'

Dumbly I asked, 'Everything?'

'Yes.'

'But I will be a lady?'

'Yes.'

'A real lady?'

'Yes! With God's will, my genius, your capability and much hard work, Jenny Everleigh, my love, we will surely do it!'

It seemed, at the time, more than worth the price of waiting.

TWELVE

A word about regular bathing. At this time, the daily bath was coming into fashion. There were still those, however, both in and out of the medical profession, who insisted it was destructive to one's health. Less than a decade previously, the full bath was for many, a monthly affair [if that].

Previously, there had been strong odours that differentiated the sexes. Gentlewomen smelled highly of a variety of floral colognes they used in order to camouflage an accumulation of stink. [This was before ingenious French perfumers – the alchemists of love – conjured up those exotic, artificial scents that had naught to do with flowers and were, in fact, completely unknown to nature.] Their gentlemen, more often than not, stank from, amongst many other things, a deep brown smell of stale cigar smoke. Thanks to the advent of indoor plumbing, by the second half of Victoria's reign the atmosphere in the vicinity of ladies and gentlemen was somewhat fresher than it had been during the first half. [J.E., 1919]

Famous Danes play dangerous games in sewer mains. It was a sentence I would grow to hate! *He who makes hurried haste is hired.* Loathsome! There were others, but these two stand out. They became a catechism repeated ad nauseam for weeks till I had them right, the 'aitches' and the 'ayes'. In so doing, much else seemed to fall into place (or 'plyce', as I used to pronounce it). But it was all just the very tip of the iceberg.

There were considerations almost equally important as

accent, such as deportment, grace, manners and poise under pressure. (*One must bathe every day whether one needs it or not. No true gentleman will take your hand, unless it is offered.*)

As for daily baths, I was long since committed to them, ever since I had been introduced to the wonderful tub in the *bathroom*; not as a discipline but rather as a joyful activity. My only quarrel with such ablutions had to do with their now solitary nature. I longed for Reginald to join me in the big tub. It was, of course, a forlorn yearning softened only by masturbation in the hot, relaxing water. Did that, too, fall under his category of *all other carnal pursuits*? Fearing a negative reply, I refrained from asking. I had fallen in love with him – damn his pledge!

As for two entire days devoted to 'offering one's hand', I was to learn that such was not, as might seem at first glance, merely a *passive* feminine activity. Rather it was both a science and an art. There seemed an infinite number of variations: the firm grip; the soft, demure grip; the limp, disinterested grip; the subtly squeezing, invitational grip; the gracious curtsey; the eye contact; the looking away (*where* one directed her eyes could be significant); and the cold and haughty or the casually insulting refusal. Offering one's hand was a means for communicating complex messages of acceptance, rejection, friendship, disdain, love (at first sight?), disgust, submission, dominance, trust, suspicion.

There was more, months of it: how to stand, how to walk (with a book atop one's head), how to sit, how to hold a teacup. *Heavy hangs his human heart when Helen hastens away.* How to eat with a knife and fork, how to address servants, how to serve tea, how to use one's handkerchief. *Saintly ladies refrain from laying about on painfully rainy days. ENOUGH*!

We laboured, often ten hours a day for days on end; the mornings in Madame Kooshay's parlour; the afternoons and evenings, in my room. For the first few months I would fall exhausted into bed, feeling, each night, as if an alien presence had occupied my brain. In the mornings I would awaken, not quite sure who I was.

Endless reading filled all the blank spaces in my day and, to a decided extent, my nights. The first, Milton's *Paradise Lost*, was as Greek to me, but then I had not as yet developed a habit of reading books. I improved. I even began to look forward to those reading sessions as a respite from almost constant drill. I became avid, accepting each volume from Reggie as if it were a gift. There was Henry Fielding, Lord Byron, Shelley, Keats, Jane Austen, Boswell, Sir Walter Scott, Wordsworth, Thackeray, Dickens, and my favourite, Emily Brontë, and her masterpiece, *Wuthering Heights*. There were also journals to be read: the *Tatler*, *Blackwoods*, the *Spectator*, the London *Times*. On a number of occasions we ventured forth on what Reggie characterized as 'field-trips'. At the National Gallery I became conversant on the Dutch and Flemish masters and to a somewhat lesser degree the sixteenth-century Italian painters. We attended the British Museum where I was awed by the Rosetta stone.

The change was gradual. There came a time when the old Jenny Everleigh seemed dimly foreign to me, like a frock I had outgrown. But the entity replacing her seemed equally foreign: cold, unnatural, only partially formed. I was a shell inflated with an amorphous, gaslike personality. I walked, talked, sat, stood and recited as if directed from outside myself. My only true feelings involved my mad schoolmaster, my dedicated mentor, my nemesis, Mr Reginald Nottingham. Poor old Jenny Everleigh had fallen in love with him, while I (whomever she might be) found my affection weighted heavily with petulance, frustration and pride.

Then one day, seven long months after we had begun, Mr Reginald Nottingham, in the middle of a drill on 'small talk', abruptly broke off his discourse in mid-sentence. He lurched to his feet, assuming the stiff, artificial posture of a guardsman standing to attention. He said in a strong, definitive voice, 'Enough, Jenny. We are through – finished. I have done everything I can.'

Stunned, I fell back into my chair. 'You mean I have failed?' I fought valiantly against tears.

'Sit up, you ninny! Arched backbone! Extend your neck! Hands in your lap! Knees together! One toe out, one toe in!'

Instinctively, I obeyed him, my heart sinking. 'Perhaps a little more time – another month,' I said forlornly. 'I'm sure I can get it right . . . we can go over the . . .'

He laughed, his head thrown back, his arms spread wide. I watched him, feeling I would dissolve in the acid of shameful ignorance. I had failed and the insensitive beast was laughing at me! Nevertheless I sat upright in the stiff French chair, a living waxwork, staring fixedly at his rude display. Then, as if the rigid posture was imparting courage, I heard myself say, 'It is unfair for you to laugh at me, Reginald, ungentlemanly. As did you, I also did my best.' He continued laughing as a rapidly rising gorge of temper displaced my despondency and self-pity. Louder now, but still in measured cadence, I said, 'Perhaps it is you who has failed.'

His laughter faded. He stood looking down at me, unblinking, his expression suddenly masked.

'You little fool,' he said flatly. 'Surely you must know.'

'I know nothing,' said I. 'Only what you tell me. Perhaps it was all too great a task . . . but if you laugh at me again, I will forget what you have taught me and strike you with this bloody candlestick!'

'Bloody?' Once again he laughed.

I stood, and foregoing the candlestick, slapped him across the face with all my strength. Then in as dignified a voice as I could muster, I said, 'Since I have failed at becoming a lady, I neither have to speak nor act like one!'

He grasped my arms in fingers of iron, his face reddened from the blow. 'Ah, but you are mistaken, you foolish girl.

No one has failed and I was not laughing at you. I was laughing out of sheer joy and you should have been laughing with me!'

'You mean. . . ?'

'We have succeeded beyond all my hopes!' He held me at arm's length. 'Between us, dearest Jenny, we have created a masterpiece!'

It was then I permitted my tears to flow.

THIRTEEN

What man would not take pride in being told by a satiated woman in breathless convincing voice that he is a superlative lover? Sisters, take heed: Flattery will get you everywhere. [J.E., 1921]

Reggie, in a show of tenderness that was his first since I had known him, kissed my joyful tears away. Then, suddenly, his arms were about me, his lips on mine.

He whispered into my mouth, 'Now, Jenny . . . finally.'

'Yes, Reggie . . .' My heart stopped beating. I felt his tongue searching for mine. It was a kiss that lasted a century. I was breathless with passion when our mouths finally separated.

He held me at arm's length, his hooded eyes surveying me hungrily. 'You were a guttersnipe when I first set eyes on you, and now . . .'.

'And now,' said I, grinning mischievously. 'The guttersnipe has vanished and quite miraculously you are about to make love to a lady who speaks the queen's own English and is capable of holding a teacup properly.'

He undressed me slowly, kissing each part of my body as it was exposed to him. 'Lovely . . . delightful . . . charming . . . beautiful . . . gorgeous . . . astonishing . . .'

'Oh, Reggie,' I panted. 'Touch me, kiss me, devour me.' The kind of pleasure I was experiencing was new to me – not the convulsive, one-dimensional passion of previous encounters, but rather a more subtle and complex emotion, tender and far more intimate.

Finally I stood naked. He pulled back, taking in every inch of me adoringly. His eyes seemed to have a miraculous, tactile quality; I could actually feel them on my skin – thrill to them – as his gaze traced its way slowly downward . . . my neck . . . my shoulders . . . my armpits . . . my breasts . . . my belly . . . my silken nest and quivering thighs. He looked up again, locking his eyes with mine. We smiled knowingly at each other. We would soon be sharing the body he seemed to be admiring so intensely. (Ah, yes, gentle reader, and we would also be sharing his.) But there seemed little hurry. 'And you, my darling,' said I, reaching out to unbutton his shirt. 'I long to see you as you see me.'

He lifted me off my feet, then cradling me in his arms as if I were weightless, carried me to the bed. There, propped up on silken pillows, I watched my lover disrobe.

Reggie, his eyes never leaving mine, took his time, carefully folding each piece of his clothing as he removed it, then letting it fall incongruously to the floor. It was a silly, yet charming love ritual. Time was of no importance. Between us there seemed a tacit agreement to stretch each second into a minute, each minute into an hour. With great expectations I watched him undress as one watches the raising of a theatrical, first-night curtain.

For the first time in my young life I was in love! A delicious emotion! I gazed at the object of my affection, thrilling to the sight of a strong, healthy male body, wide shoulders and hairy chest. His arms seemed capable of great deeds. His belly, delineated by gently swelling muscles, was flat, without a trace of paunch (the first male I had seen, thus). And this beautiful man was to be my first true lover!

Then his prick was free from its confinement. Semi-erect, it was a handsome sight, nestling in a forest of shaggy red hair. It was fat and had a massive, purplish helmet and at its base, a pair of symmetrical, perfectly matched bollocks. *My lover's cock*! The voluptuous device that would soon rid me of my troublesome virginity at last! Daily, I had stretched out in my warm bath, masturbating, conjuring visions of holding him in my arms as he pistoned in and out of me. How fortunate that it was to be wondrous Reggie rather than Major Piltdown or some other, lesser man for whom my only feelings would have been those of lust.

Then he was in my arms. The full length of our bodies pressed, one to the other. We lay on our sides, our lips joined, my breasts crushed against his chest. I cupped his face in my hands, caressing his tongue with my own while gentle fingers strolled the length of my back. Like titillating feathers, they descended slowly to my buttocks, then up again to the sensitive skin of my neck.

My legs parted to make room for his insinuating thigh. Soon it was pressing gently against my virginal nest. I moaned into Reggie's mouth as my hips, of their own volition, began to rotate in a slow, barely perceptible dance of passion.

'Darling,' he whispered, 'I want to kiss you there . . . suck you, eat you up. . . .'

'Lovely,' said I, grasping his hips to bring him even tighter against me. 'But to do that, you would have to go away and I want you to hold me like this forever . . . closer . . . closer. . . .'

'Oh yes, Jenny, me darling.' One hand cupped my buttock. The other reached between our bodies to caress my breast. A gentle forefinger traced the sensitive aureole. It was joined by an insistent thumb. Between them the amorous digits grasped my nipple and rolled it back and forth in tempo to match the slow-humping motion of my hips.

His hardened shaft rubbed against my leg. I reached down. It was a fat sausage in the palm of my hand. I ran my fingers to its underside, just beneath the glans, where I stroked lightly, titillating the exquisite flesh. Reggie groaned under his breath and suctioned my tongue into his mouth to suck it just as I would have sucked his cock had I been willing to break our embrace.

He withdrew his leg from between mine, manipulating our limbs until I was able to place the now massive member between my thighs. I released a sigh of built-up tension as it pressed up against my moistened quim. Heaven! Soon I'd have it all inside me.

Clasping each other's buttocks, we began a slow, lascivious dance, he thrusting his arse in short little jabs while I rotated mine in small circles. The bulbous head of his cock travelled back and forth in its juicy furrow. The hardened shaft pressed tightly against my naked clitoris. A rapturous tremor radiated from its focal point between my legs, to my breasts, the back of my neck.

'Dearest,' said I. 'Tell me what you're going to do.'

'I'm going to fuck you, Jenny.'

'Oh, Reggie. You'll be the first.'

'I'm going to fill your pussy with cock.'

'Oh yes.'

'Where no man has ever been before . . . deep inside you.'

'Oh yes!'

'I'm going to pump my spunk into you.'

'Yes, my darling. . . .'

'Tell me, Jenny. Let me hear you say it.'

'You're going to fuck me.'

'Soon, my dear.'

'You're going to push your big, fat beautiful cock into me, pierce me with it, fuck me . . . fuck me . .. fuck me! I'll open for you, Reggie. My cunt will suck your cock into my body, swallow it!'

'Oh, darling Jenny . . . your cunt. . . .'

'My sweet, open cunt – my beautiful, luscious cunt. Promise me you'll shoot your delicious, slimy spunk into it. Promise that you'll fill me up!'

'I will . . . I will!'

'Then it's yours, Reggie. All yours! Do it to me, darling!

I've waited so long. Fuck me now, my hero, my champion, my love!'

He rolled me over on my back. I lay legs akimbo, looking up into his eyes.

'Yes, now, my sweet,' he said.

'Now, my darling,' said I glancing downward for a last look at the battering ram that would soon deflower me. Then, inexplicably, despite my passion, a sudden fear took hold of me. Would it fit? How could the tiny, untried sheath between my thighs possibly accommodate such a huge mass of rock-hard cock flesh? Surely it would split me in two!

As quickly as it had appeared, the momentary panic dissipated. It was as if I'd passed through a darkened railroad tunnel but was now once again speeding through a bright sunlit world. My passing fear mattered not. If indeed there were pain, I would accept it gladly. I had no doubt that inevitable joy would far outweigh any initial pain, no matter the intensity. How could it be otherwise? I was soon to be a woman and this would be the first of many. How many? Hundreds? Thousands? There was a lifetime of ecstasy ahead of me. I spread my legs even further in open invitation. Let the brute do its worst; I would accommodate it or die trying!

My darling Reginald placed one of the silk pillows beneath my eager arse, propping it up, in order to make his target even more accessible.

Then, grasping his hardened prick, he brought it to the entrance to a glistening shrine of lust through which no man had ever passed. We both watched with baited breath as the helmeted warrior pressed forward. Suddenly, overwhelmed by the sight before me, I reached down and, using my forefinger, proceeded to diddle my clit in gentle circles. The lewd gesture seemed to meet with my partner's approval. He looked up at me momentarily, an excited smile lighting his face. I shivered with passion.

His cock head, aided in its efforts by an outpouring of

oily cunt sap, was slowly gaining entrance. I heard myself speak in a husky whisper. 'Ah, Reggie, such a lovely sight.'

'Lovely, my dearest.' He pressed downward, firmly, yet gently insinuating the lustful weapon into its tight-fitting sheath.

Finally, the head was fully inserted. At last my puss was receiving its due! A cock was inside me! A man was fucking me! A wondrous cock! A glorious man! Reggie and I – little Jenny Everleigh – were connected, one to the other with an iron column of flesh.

'I'm in you,' he said. 'Inside you.'

'It's a marvel, my love, a miracle.' I removed the finger from my clitoris so as not to confuse the sensation.

'What does it feel like?'

'A glorious fullness.'

'It's just the head, Jenny, the tip. There's a great deal still to come.'

'Then thrust home, my love!'

'There will be pain. . . .'

'Damn the pain! Kiss me and thrust home. . . .'

He lay atop me, supported on his elbows. I grasped his head with both hands and fucked his mouth with my tongue as he would soon be fucking my cunt with his prick. His hips pressed downward, slowly but steadily burying his fuck machine inside me. Then, suddenly – an explosion of pain as if a bomb had detonated inside me! I stifled a scream, but even as I did so the sudden pain was but a memory . . . in moments, just the memory of a memory as it faded to dullness. Our groins touched, pressed together, entangling the silken strands of red and blond pubic tresses.

'I'm in you,' he whispered. 'Every inch of me – all the way.'

'Yes . . . yes!' I clung to his lips; my eyes clamped shut.

'Does it hurt, my darling?'

Touched by his concern, I gazed up into his eyes, just inches away. 'Only a little now,' I said, smiling. 'Oh, Reggie, you've made me a woman!'

'How does it feel?'

'Glorious! I'm filled with you. I could burst with joy!'

I raised my legs and wrapped them around his waist in a lover's embrace. His cock stuffed my tight little cunt to the very portal of its womb, and still I pressed his body to mine in the hopes of swallowing more.

We fucked. With Reggie's cock fully buried, we ground our bodies together in slow, loving circles. His balls caressed the cheeks of my arse. The pressure on my clitoris varied with each orbit as, little by little, my poor distended pussy accommodated him. Pleasure merged with pain as I thrilled to an excruciating fullness. I was a woman! All that mattered was to *feel!*

FOURTEEN

A major revolt was taking place in the dark cellar beneath the sturdy edifice of Victorian morality. Whilst the wives, mothers and matrons of the great middle class were covering their bodies in layer upon layer of protective sheathing and dressing their naked piano legs to the tune of fire and brimstone mouthed by the ministers and guardians of public morals and propriety, a naked, sexual revolution was being fought just under their feet. [J.E., 1920]

'We are going to test our handiwork,' said Reggie. 'The judges are to be the most critical in England. But I have no doubt you'll pass muster with flying colours.'

I had not seen him since he had made love to me three days previously, and I had thought of nothing else since. My muscles still ached and my constant reliving of all those heavenly hours had kept me in a perpetually randy state. Now the mere sight of him set my battered quim to salivating.

'There is a ball,' he continued, 'Friday night, in honour of Tewfik Pasha, the son of the Egyptian khedive. Everyone of note will be there, including, dear Jenny, Edward himself.'

'The Prince of Wales?'

'The same, my sweet.'

I was struck dumb. 'I'm certain you will be presented,' said Reggie.

'No, it's too soon – I'm not ready. . . .'

'You are as ready as you will ever be.'

The mere idea sent me into a fit of nervousness. 'But surely, dearest Reggie, that can wait until I'm a little more confident. I mean, why do I have to be tested?' I placed my hand tenderly on his cheek.

His voice grew cold. 'Because I want you to be.'

'But you said you were pleased, happy, overjoyed with our accomplishment. Surely that's enough. Why do we need the approval of outsiders?'

He stared at me silently. I glanced down at the floor, and in a quiet, nervous, little voice said, 'I haven't seen you in three days. Ain't you going to make love to me again?'

'Ain't?'

'I mean: *aren't* you going to make . . .'

'I taught you to look at the person to whom you are speaking!' His words were packed tightly together, like a military command. 'Straighten up!'

I complied, staring at a point on his forehead. 'Please don't force me to go. . . .'

'Stop snivelling and listen to me! Four months ago I took as raw material a lowly child and not only created a well-bred English lady, but in the bargain made her into a *woman*. I expect you to act the part, to *be* what you've become!' He grasped my forearm in a grip of iron, squeezing it to punctuate each word. 'I expect you to take pride in our accomplishment, to look forward to bearding them – those pompous asses – in their own den, just as I look forward to it!'

'But suppose I fail, suppose they see through me. . . ?'

'Then you will make an ass of yourself; you will be mortified and I will step away from you as if I had never known you. I've no time for students who don't measure up.'

'You'll desert me?'

'Yes.'

'You beast!'

'It's up to you to stand on your own two feet. And if you

haven't the confidence now, you certainly will, after the ball – unless, of course, you fail miserably. And Jenny, dear, the only thing that can cause you to fail is a lack of courage.'

I felt tears welling up, self-pity and anger duelling for ascendancy. 'You would leave me standing there, mortified?'

'Yes.' Reggie released my arm, paced the room. He turned and faced me. 'I will be here on Friday evening to escort you to the ball. It is into the valley of death for you. You can do what you will till then – cry your little eyes out if you desire – but from Friday night on you will be poised and beautiful.'

'You bloody beast!'

'*Bloody*, dear Jenny?' He looked at me as one might look at a peculiar breed of insect. 'I taught you better than that.'

By Friday afternoon I was beside myself with trepidation and anguish and had decided not to subject myself to what I was certain would be a shattering humiliation. I would not go to the ball. Once again, Madame Kooshay consoled me.

She held my hands in hers. 'I have faith in you,' she said. 'If I were seeing you for the first time in four months, I would not recognize you. Perfection – a miracle. Reginald is a genius, and you, Jenny, are equally a genius. You are, in every way, a lady of style and culture.'

'He's a beast,' said I, hardly hearing her. 'He possesses not an iota of human compassion . . . inhuman.'

'You are mistaken, my dear.' She poured the tea. Then peering at me over the top of her cup, she said, 'there is something you don't know about Reggie, a secret he's kept from almost everyone, even some of those closest to him.' She was silent for a long moment. Then quietly, she continued. 'I believe it would be best for all concerned if you knew.'

My curiosity was piqued. I stared at her questioningly.

'Reginald Nottingham,' she continued in lilting voice, 'is not what he seems, just as you are not what you seem.' She hesitated, her usually beautiful and benign face breaking into a frown. 'No, perhaps I am not expressing it properly. What I meant to say was that you're not what you once were, not what you were born to. To put it bluntly, Reggie was born in a work house in the East End. His mother was one of us, but of a much lower status – a miserable creature of the streets. She died of the consumption when he was only six. He remained an orphan till age twelve when he escaped. Reggie has lived by his wits since then.'

I was astounded. 'But his accent, his behaviour. . . ?

'He taught himself, just as he taught you and, I might add, just as he intends to teach others.'

In sheer astonishment I collapsed into the chair. 'Then he is, Madame Kooshay, indeed, a genius!'

'Indeed.'

'I would never have known!'

'Yes, just as no one will ever know with regard to you.'

'Good Lord . . .'

'And that's not all,' Madame Kooshay said. 'Reginald can place anyone in Britain within a mile of his birthplace simply by listening to a few of his or her words. He has written two books on modern English linguistics and has been asked, innumerable times, to lecture as a guest at Cambridge.'

'And he, a poor orphan,' said I incredulously.

'Born in a work house,' said she, 'he has hoisted himself by his own boot straps to the highest status one can attain – a true scholar of the human condition and of the fairest language of them all!'

'How courageous!' said I. 'I feel ashamed.'

'And well you should, dearest Jenny.' She looked directly into my eyes, placing equal emphasis on each word. 'He has a right to expect the same courage from you, his first protégée.'

'I see.'

'It is what he means when he speaks of a test.'

'Of course. . . .' My mind was a cauldron of conflicting thoughts and emotions.

Madame ran a tender, reassuring hand through my hair. 'At the ball, tonight, Jenny, you'll meet not your betters, but rather your peers. What say you, dear girl?'

'I will attend the ball,' said I. 'I will go there on my champion's arm and I will make him proud of me.'

'Ah, that is noble indeed,' said Madame Kooshay. 'And afterwards, when you return, you shall be the second lady of this establishment. You will demand a fee higher than any of our girls, higher than any *fille de joie* in the empire. And I, too, will be proud of you!'

FIFTEEN

Little did any of us dream that 350,000 handsome, virile young Britons, of all classes and stations, were soon to perish, to drown in the mud of Passchendaele. The remainder of that entire generation was also to die in the horrors that followed. It was the end of the world as we knew it. The new world has yet to announce itself and I shudder in expectation. [J.E., 1919]

I was the belle of the ball! My debut at the Egyptian embassy affair honouring Tewfik Pasha was a success beyond my most fervent imaginings! Within minutes of my arrival, my card was filled, except for five dances I kept open for contingencies.

From the top of a wide marble staircase I gazed down into an ornate ballroom populated with the glamourous and influential upper crust of international society. The sound of the Majordomo's voice was electrifying, causing my spine to tingle from an incongruous mating of pleasure and trepidation. '*Mr Reginald Nottingham and niece: Miss Jenny Everleigh. . . .*' Reggie had arranged for us to arrive a half hour late, knowing that I would be the focus of one hundred pairs of socially prominent eyes. It was to be thus for the duration of the ball.

On the receiving line, Tewfik Pasha, dressed in a robe embroidered with gold, took my hand. 'You are, dear woman, the most desirable female I have yet seen on this peculiar island.' As I came erect from my curtsey, his deep black eyes glared into mine. My training dictated I should look away demurely. I did not do so but rather accepted his stare for what it was: a challenge.

'Perhaps, sir,' said I, 'you should seek further.' Our eyes were locked in sensuous combat.

'There is no need to.' He broke the contact, glancing downward but not in defeat. As if surveying a potential battlefield, he took me in from head to toe, resting for a full ten seconds in the vicinity of my bust. I was aware of embarrassed coughs behind me. Finally, with his satiated eyes on mine once more, he said, 'Would you be so kind as to reserve the first dance for me? I believe your custom dictates this as my prerogative, but I refrain from exercising it and simply ask.' He spoke with a curious lisping sound heavily flavoured with French.

'I should be honoured, sir.' Now it was my turn to view him from head to toe. Beneath the exotic robe I suspected a roly-poly body, the result of soft living and rapacious appetite. (As the reader will also discover in due time, it turned out that I was mistaken in this.) I did not, however, find him unattractive. There was a quality to his voice and his commanding attitude that set my blood racing. It was as if he possessed understanding of all my intimate desires and detailed knowledge of each of my bizarre fantasies. There were no secrets to be withheld from this strange, young, bearded, Oriental potentate. I felt suddenly faint under his intense gaze.

When the time came, Tewfik Pasha chose to sit out his dance. We conversed in a relative privacy monitored by two of his colourfully clad retainers who stood a few feet from us, massive arms crossed over their chests as if guarding the royal treasury.

In a voice flavoured with the accent of the East, he said, 'I would be honoured, dear lady, if you would accept an invitation to be my guest aboard the *Maratini* – my yacht – on its return voyage to my ancient homeland. Think not ill of me for asking; there will be other guests – compatriots of yours. You will be well chaperoned. Before we dock in Cairo we will attend the ceremonies honouring the opening of the Suez Canal. They will be most exciting, I assure you.'

I was thrilled by his offer. In demure tones, I said, 'I should be delighted, sir, but such an undertaking on my part would require permission from my guardian.'

'Mr Nottingham?'

'Yes.'

'Then we shall see,' said the son of the Khedive.

It was left at that. There followed a whirlwind of waltzes and polkas with a varied assortment of partners: young swains and older gentlemen, diplomats, officers, titles – some of them outright bores, others adroit conversationalists but each, in his own way, intent on finding out more about me, possessing me. It was all quite exhausting but at the same time, invigorating. Soon I had no trouble accepting my new identity. I was comfortable in the role as if I had been born to it.

I wore a white silk ball gown provided by my gracious madame. It was amusing to see the gentlemen's eyes drop momentarily into its daring décolletage as they took my hand during introductions. Reggie introduced me as his niece and ward. Most of the gentlemen asked if they might call on me but, of course, under the circumstances, I was forced to put them off. Consider for a moment, dear reader, the French ambassador come to call, inadvertently pulling the bell cord at Madame Kooshay's exotic establishment!

There were many stunning beauties present, but my dance partners, to a man, told me that I was by far the most beautiful of all. At first I thought it just vain flattery but as the evening wore on, the compliments seemed unending, finally causing me to accept totally their evaluations.

The most satisfactory of all was from my own, dear Reggie. 'You are an unqualified triumph,' he whispered. 'So much so, that I'll wager they wouldn't believe the truth even if it were told to them!'

'But surely you wouldn't tell. . . .'

'Have no fear, Jenny. The secret pleasure I feel is more than sufficient reward.' He smiled at me. 'You have been fully accepted and can do no wrong now, even if you tried. You are the subject, this very moment, of a hundred wagging tongues all about the room. You are, dear heart, a woman of mystery! Just minutes ago, I overheard the Transylvanian ambassador describe you as being the illegitimate daughter of the prince of Bavaria. You have been, according to that particular pundit, attending school in England for the past ten years! Delicious, when you consider the idiot is unaware that the prince of Bavaria is himself in attendance!'

'Yes,' said I, laughing briefly into the back of my lace-gloved hand. 'I danced with the crown prince earlier and *he* was trying to get me to admit that I was Lord Churchill's mistress!'

'How they buzz with false conjecture! The women are envious and the gentlemen are intrigued. . . . Ah, but once more the music starts.'

Again, I was surrounded by men competing for my attention. Glancing at my card, I saw it was an open dance. The choice, however, was not mine to make. The Prince of Wales extended his hand and the others withdrew. He swung me out onto the floor.

'Miss Everleigh,' he said, smiling down at me, 'may I call you Jenny?'

'I would be flattered, Your Royal Highness.'

'Ah, then you may call me Edward – in private, of course.'

'Edward,' said I, my heart fluttering. I had come far in but a short time. Little Jenny Everleigh addressing the future king of England by his first name!

'Jenny,' said he, 'your guardian is a brilliant man. I read his book on London regional dialects and found it fascinating. But he is brilliant in other matters also.'

His words startled me. Surely he hadn't found us out. . . .

'I mean,' said the Prince of Wales, 'that his staging of your debut could not have been better planned. Keeping you hidden away all this time to unleash you all of a piece at the start of the season and in this company – a shrewd tactic – delightful. You have burst like a star shell on this company! The most beautiful, most charming lady in all our realm has appeared amongst us, unheralded, her very existence unsuspected . . . 'tis indeed a surprise treat to us all.'

'Thank you, Your Royal Highness. . . .'

'*Edward*, my dear. Despite the crowd, we are essentially alone.'

'Then Edward t'will be.' I looked up at him, hoping my eyes were innocent even as I was not. 'When we're alone.'

'And will that be soon?'

'Will what be, Edward?'

'When we're alone – I mean to say, really alone.'

'You flatter me, Sire.'

'I don't mean to.'

'It's surely a game you are playing.'

'No, dear Jenny, I am quite serious.'

Glancing down, I found he was indeed serious. There was a sausagelike extrusion distorting the thigh of his left trouser leg.

He caught my glance. As we whirled to the music, he said, 'You don't blush at the evidence of my desire?'

'No, Edward,' said I. 'It is, as you pointed out, quite serious and I would add, impressive.'

'Gad! There is more to you than I reckoned.'

'Quite a bit more, Your Royal Highness . . . Edward.'

'Then may I call on you? Discreetly, of course.'

There was little doubt that the future king desired me! It required but seconds to plan the necessary tactics. In a soft, seductive voice, I said, 'Mr Nottingham – my guardian – would be shocked by such a proposal. If he knew of it, he would whisk me from London in a trice.'

'Is he by your side constantly?'

'Oh no,' said I, 'he leaves London from time to time.'

'Then perhaps in the near future. . . ?'

'I am unaware of any such plans at the moment.'

'Pity.'

As if in deep thought, I was silent for a moment. Then, as we twirled to the centre of the floor, I said, 'But I'm sure something might be possible.'

'Yes. . . ?'

'If he had to attend a series of interviews at Cambridge that would keep him overnight.'

'Is such in the offing?'

'No,' said I, 'but surely it might be arranged.'

We stopped dancing. The Prince of Wales guided me to the edge of the floor. 'Just what are you getting at, Jenny?'

'He would certainly be absent from London if they wanted to speak to him regarding a permanent chair in linguistics.'

'At Cambridge?'

'Yes, but Oxford would do as well.'

'You are a sly puss, Jenny Everleigh.' He laughed, then grew serious, as if lost in thought.

Taking the opportunity to move close, I allowed a surreptitious hand to brush across the bulge in his trousers created by the royal pego.

His eyes shut momentarily. 'You make a strong case,' he said.

'As do you, Edward,' said I, an innocent tone and demeanour contradicting my words.

He was silent for a moment, then said, 'I do have a certain influence, rarely used. . . .'

'Well,' said I, 'perhaps we will meet again at another ball.' I turned away, speaking over my bare shoulder. 'But now I must leave. There are those on my dance card I am honour bound to attend.'

'Wait . . .'

I turned to him, my eyes wide with innocent conjecture. 'Sire?'

'You say a chair in linguistics?'

'Yes, I believe Mr Reginald Nottingham to be more qualified for such a position than any man in England.'

'So he may be.' He laughed briefly, allowing his eyes to stray to my bosom. 'You drive a hard bargain, young lady.'

'I do so, Your Royal Highness, in order to benefit future undergraduates and thus the intellectual glory of this kingdom.'

'Where may I call on you?'

'I think it best,' said I, 'if I call on you.'

'So be it! On Wednesday next, at eight, I will be at the home of my friend, James Whistler.'

'Ah . . . how I look forward to seeing you there, dear Edward! I shall arrive promptly, with eager heart.' I offered him my hand, which he kissed, his eyes on mine. 'But, of course,' I continued, 'all depends on the whereabouts of my guardian. If he is present on that evening, I will be unable to embark on such a romantic voyage.'

'I assure you, madam, he will be in Cambridge discussing with the authorities there what you so aptly described as the intellectual glory of this kingdom.'

I handed him my dance card, watched breathlessly as in silence he wrote down the address. Then, clutching it to my bosom, I said, 'Till Wednesday, then, Your Royal Highness.'

'Till then, Miss Everleigh.'

The rest of the evening was a blur of faces and Strauss waltzes. But I had done it! I had passed the test!

SIXTEEN

Over the years I have found that, of all nationalities, the English have the greatest natural propensity for sexual madness of a certain sort. As for myself, the reader of these journals will discover that I, too, have taken pleasure from an occasional paddling of my rump. I have found, however, that it is somewhat more comforting to give than to receive. [J.E., 1911]

'I knew you would do it!' Madame Kooshay poured the champagne, gesturing gaily with her other hand.

Reggie grasped me around the waist, twirled me about till I was dizzy. 'She more than did it!'

'Let's hear it for our Jenny!'

'Hip, hip, hooray!' The ladies joined in. 'Hip, hip, hooray!'

I stood, blushing, Reggie's arm around my waist. It was a surprise party that had greeted Reggie and me when we returned from the ball. All the ladies were present. The premises were closed for the night.

'You should have seen her with Edward,' said Reggie.

'Edward who?' asked Magnolia.

'The Prince of Wales, you ninny! She had him in the palm of her hand . . . and the French ambassador and the prince of Bavaria and the first lord. Every man there was falling over himself to gain our Jenny's favour! And the women – green with envy! She was the belle of the ball, the mystery woman. You should have heard the theories – she was a foreign princess educated in England; she was the mistress of lord so-and-so; she was the illegitimate daughter of the king of Freedonia, or some such place! Jenny was the focus of all eyes, the subject of a hundred wagging tongues. Even Tewfik Pasha, that sly wog, was captivated. He has invited our heroine to sail to Egypt on his yacht!'

'Will you accept?' they chorused.

'I don't know,' said I.

'He is royalty in a way, isn't he?' asked Mrs Rose.

'It will be the making of you,' said Yvonne.

'Jenny and I will discuss that later,' said Madame Kooshay. 'In the meanwhile, since Mr Nottingham is our only male guest, it is proper that he dance, at least once, with each of us.'

Madame had retained the musicians for the night. The girls danced with each other while Reggie went from couple to couple, breaking in. More champagne was fetched up from the cellar. We were indeed a gay crowd. Finally, Yvette, a glass of bubbly held aloft, called out, 'A game. Let us play a game!'

'Which one?'

'Blind man's bluff,' said someone.

'With Reggie as the blind man!'

'We will each remove our clothing,' said Elvira. 'When he catches one of us he has fifteen seconds to guess who.'

'Capital!' said Yvette. 'And the forfeit?'

'If he guesses incorrectly, he must do the lady's bidding.'

'And if I guess correctly?' asked Reggie.

'Then you are free to go to the next.'

'Unfair,' said Reggie. 'If I'm right, then the lady should do *my* bidding.'

'Agreed!'

The musicians were dismissed, then Reggie was blindfolded. In a trice we were all naked, including Mrs Rose, the tipsy housekeeper. We made a circle about him.

The first tagged was Lesley, a new girl from the great

metropolis of New York, in the New World. He ran his hands quickly over her smooth flanks, cupped her teacup breasts, thought for a while, then said, ''Tis surely Maria!'

'Wrong!'

Reggie whipped off his blindfold, staring dumbly at Lesley. 'You have exact facsimiles of Maria's breasts, which I know as well as I know the West End.'

'The forfeit!' we chorused.

The American girl considered for a moment. Brightly, in that peculiar accent they all have, she said, 'I will have my way with you for exactly ten minutes. If during that time you spend, you will be required to gamahuche all fifteen of us until we do likewise.'

Reggie groaned. In mock seriousness he said, 'That is a most damnable and undeserved punishment! Surely my tongue will sprain before I can conclude such a task!'

We all cried, 'Forfeit! Forfeit!'

'And,' said Lesley, 'since you mistook me for Maria, she will act as my aide-de-camp.'

Reggie was laid out on a convenient couch. Madame, silently counting the seconds, acted as official timekeeper. Reggie's pego was flaccid, the first time I had ever seen it in such a restive state. We all watched as Lesley ran delicate fingers over his balls, then underneath to that secret male place between the base of the gonads and the anal orifice. (It is there, I have been told, where men sport a kind of primordial clitoris.) With her other hand, she reached up to pinch his tiny nipples.

'And I,' said Maria who stood by. 'What would you have me do?'

'Titillate him,' said our American girl. 'The mental is just as important as the physical with this sort of thing.' She cupped the head of Reggie's prick in a graceful hand.

Maria, with one foot on the floor, raised the other to straddle Reggie's head. His eyes stared straight up into her lovely quim, observing her as she played with it, spread it, stroked it.

As Madame Kooshay called out the first minute, I was surprised to observe his tool still uncocked – a relaxed state I had never before seen it assume. I felt admiration for a heroic effort. This courageous obstinacy lasted for another minute and a half. By then, Lesley, making admirable use of a long and graceful tongue, was stroking him from bollocks to cock tip. Suddenly, his tool shot erect. He groaned as Lesley, making a wide oval of her lips, took him to the balls. In a slow, steady rhythm, she fucked the poor man with her mouth.

Maria was now attempting to feed him a perfectly formed breast. At first he disdained it. She played it across his face, teasing him, muttering small sounds of encouragement and little squeals of pleasure. Suddenly, as if engaged in a losing battle, Reggie surrendered. He opened his mouth to the plump offering and was soon licking circles around the puckered pink aureole, alternately sucking then nibbling on the fat, distended nipple. The ladies applauded as Madame Kooshay called out the passing of the third minute.

Reggie's strategy was clear to me. He was using Maria's breast to distract him from Lesley's expert cock-sucking.

As the minute passed, Maria unbeknowingly provided my hero with an even greater distraction. Swinging her body around, she straddled his head with her plump thighs, enveloping his face in her spongy quim. Then, with her hips rotating rhythmically, she joined Lesley at the other end in a dedicated pursuit of Reggie's elusive orgasm.

As the fourth minute came and went, Lesley, grasping the iron-hard staff, passed it to Maria's open, welcoming lips. With the head implanted in her partner's suctioning mouth, she proceeded to frig it. She pumped slowly at first, then with ever increasing tempo.

From where I sat on the floor, just a few feet from the engrossed trio, I could see Reggie's nose implanted firmly in Maria's arse furrow. Her hips gyrated furiously as he lapped her swollen quim.

'Suck him, Maria,' said Lesley in breathless tones as she

pumped Reggie's cock into her friend's mouth. 'Take his spunk,' she cried. 'Drink his jism!' Faster and faster. . . .

Maria was trembling, her rotund arse cheeks rotating in voluptuous circles about the fulcrum of Reggie's face. Then, suddenly, she lifted her mouth from his cock and drew in a lungful of air only to expel it in a rapturous moan. I watched, a lustful fever growing in my body, as Maria's buttocks clenched and unclenched, echoing her delicious clitoral spasms.

'I'm spending,' she cried. 'Suck me! Spunk! Fuck! Ohhhh. . . !'

Lesley bent to take every inch of Reggie's naked cock into her mouth. Her head bobbed up and down, fucking him with her lips.

Madame Kooshay called out, 'Time's up!'

The contest was ended. Reggie stood, unspent, victorious, an arm around each of his exhausted antagonists. In a show of British sportsmanship, he kissed each of them soundly. The audience of women cheered him, a hero returned from the wars.

'Hooray!' My champion had not only won the day, but he had also bestowed a gratuitous orgasm on one of the aggressors! 'Hooray for Reggie!' I cried. The others echoed my applause but the game had just begun.

The next to be tagged was Yvonne. After cupping her buttocks (the largest in the house), Reggie guessed correctly. For the forfeit, he demanded that she place herself supine across my lap and allow herself to be spanked for five minutes. Both Yvonne and I protested, but Madame Kooshay, acting as referee, judged it a fair forfeit. I must admit to a degree of titillation as the fair and somewhat fleshy Yvonne arranged herself across my lap. Before proceeding, I ran my hands down her back and stroked her full but firm buttocks. The arse muscles were clenched in expectation of what was to come. I ran my fingers lightly across the plump flesh, halting here and there to knead it gently. Yvonne, despite her obvious anxiety, sighed in appreciation. In moments her muscles relaxed. Her hips commenced a delightful wriggle.

'Ready?' asked I in a quiet voice.

'Spare me, Jenny. . . .'

I insinuated my other hand between her thighs, bringing it into feathery contact with the luscious garden at their juncture. My other hand continued its gentle massage. Yvonne's body seemed to vibrate with a sustained, catlike purr. I stroked, patted, pinched.

'Ready?'

'Yes, anything, dear Jenny. . . .'

With one hand still locked between her thighs, I raised the other, aware that those gathered round had ceased to breathe. In order to heighten the suspense even more, I hesitated, arm raised, for a few seconds. My palm struck precisely where I intended it to – on the left cheek of Yvonne's posterior. The sharp sound of its contact was as a pistol shot, its pureness and clarity startling in the utter silence surrounding it.

'Oh.' Yvonne shifted her arse first one way, then another. Two of my fingers grasped her elongated clitoris between them while my thumb stroked its length.

I struck again, this time on the right buttock, then again on the left. Yvonne moaned, half in passion, half in pain. The resilient flesh of her ample arse gleamed red in the gaslight.

'More?' asked I.

'No. . . !'

Smartly, I slapped again. 'No what?'

'No, please . . . Mistress Jenny.'

'That's better.' I removed my fingers from her oozing pussy. 'Are you certain you want it to end, Yvonne?'

'Please, mistress.' She hesitated. Then, rotating her hips as if seeking intimate cuntal contact with my thigh, she cried, 'Oh more! More!'

I proceeded to diddle her clit while my open hand flashed again, contacting her poor, plump bottom with a resounding *thwak*!

'Do you like being spanked, Yvonne?' I asked in a gentle voice.

'Yes, mistress.'

'Should I strike harder?' I pinched her clitoris, rolling it between my fingers.

'No, mistress . . . yes . . . no . . . oh!'

Thrice more I pummelled her plump, red arse cheeks, my aim now made imprecise due to the motion of her madly rotating hips. All the while I masturbated her wildly, my index finger bent upward at the first knuckle, inserted in her seething quim in order to caress the secret spot common to all women but known to only a fortunate few.

'Oh, mistress! Give it to me! Now!'

Once again my palm descended on her ravaged bottom. Then, with my thumb stroking her clit, I stuffed three fingers into her. Her buttocks flexed, trembled, wriggling about the fulcrum of my pleasuring hand.

'Ahhhhh,' cried Yvette. 'Cumming! Cumming! Cumming. . . !'

Then all was quiet except for the deep breathing of my peers. I looked up to find them staring wide-eyed at our tableau. Two of them – Magnolia and little Clara, the tall Negro girl from Jamaica in the West Indies – were masturbating. It was an accolade equal to the applause that followed.

Once again, Reginald Nottingham was blindfolded. This time he tagged a startled Mrs Rose. He ran his hands across the slack flesh of her buttocks, palmed her flabby breasts. Then, after a moment's thought, he said, 'Elvira! I'd know her anywhere.'

We all laughed. The blindfold was removed and Reggie stood there, making a show of surprise at his 'error'. Mrs Rose stood dumbstruck.

'The forfeit is yours to choose,' said Madame Kooshay.

The older woman looked lost, her eyes appealing to us for help. I felt perhaps that Reggie's 'joke' had backfired when he said, 'Mrs Rose seems unable to make up her mind, therefore, I suggest that Elvira, since it was she I mistakenly identified, announce my forfeit.'

'Ah, then,' said Elvira, feigning angered jealousy, 'since it is up to me, I suggest you fuck the bitch to within an inch of her life!'

'Oh, goodness,' said a now self-conscious Mrs Rose. 'It has been so long. . . .' Her hands crossed in front of her in attempt to conceal her nakedness.

'Surely, you haven't forgotten how,' said one of the girls.

'If you have, our Reggie will be certain to jog your memory,' said another.

'You should demand he pay the forfeit,' said still another.

'Oh, goodness,' said Mrs Rose.

'Hardly a forfeit, madame,' said Reggie. 'Rather a great pleasure.'

'Oh do,' they chorused, gathering around the poor woman, patting her, stroking her stringy hair. 'You will love it. . . . Reggie is a champion lover. . . . We have each had him and now 'tis your turn. . . . You'll become one of the Reggie sisterhood. . . . It is always heavenly with Reginald.'

'Oh, goodness. . . .'

'Come now,' said Elvira, taking Mrs Rose's hand and leading her to a couch. 'Heaven awaits you.'

'Indeed it does,' said Magnolia.

'Indeed,' chorused the ladies.

They stretched her out on the couch, arms and legs akimbo. As Reggie bent to kiss her full on the lips, I felt a flash of pride in my friend. Surely, his was a most noble act of charity – no, not charity but rather *chivalry of the highest order*! Reggie was a man amongst men – staunch, highly principled. He was above all a gentleman of sterling character and I vowed, then and there, I would always love him.

A hush fell on the congregation as he knelt by the couch,

running his hands over Mrs Rose's slack flesh. She groaned quietly, placing both hands over her eyes as if to block out the reality of what was happening to her.

'Oh, goodness. . . .'

Then Reggie was on the couch with her, clasping her body to his. Elvira stepped forward and inserted her fingers delicately between their bodies and into Mrs Rose's hairy forest.

'Ah,' said Elvira, 'she is ready for you, Reggie. She's sopping with dew, she is, and open.' She reached upward and grasped Reggie's hardened pego to bring it into conjunction with its target. With unerring aim she set the pin. The bulbous head of Reggie's magnificent prick was poised at Mrs Rose's portal of passion.

'Thrust home!' cried Elvira.

I watched breathlessly as Reggie brought his weapon to bear. It was not a 'thrust', as Elvira had ordered, but rather a gentle insertion. Mrs Rose vented a long sigh. 'Oh, it's been so long,' said she, her eyes open now, staring rapturously into Reggie's. 'So very long since I felt the likes of this . . . 'tis heaven!'

With half his cock embedded in her, Mrs Rose was galvanized into a changed woman. She wrapped herself around him, hugging him with legs and arms, pulling him down. 'Oh, do it to me, you beautiful man!'

They were as one, a single fucking machine, perfectly synchronized – thrust and counterthrust, action and reaction! We all watched, open-mouthed, incredulous! This was not quite the tableau we expected, not merely the gallant endeavour of an active young man to pleasure a supine old woman, but rather, 'twas two sensuous individuals sharing equally in an amorous enterprise, each taking and giving joy.

We watched, incredulous, as with little apparent effort, Mrs Rose reversed the situation. Manoeuvring her bulk with ease and grace, she flipped her partner onto his back. Without breaking their lewd and intimate contact, Mrs

Rose, before our very eyes, had assumed the dominant position! A rider, sure of seat atop a bucking stallion, she rode effortlessly!

A hush descended on the audience. We were mesmerized by the sounds of fuckery: the slap of flesh on flesh, rhythmic squishings, heavy breathing, little whimpers, deep-throated groans.

Mrs Rose timed the pace. Long, deliberate strokes alternately exposed then swallowed the full length of Reggie's corpulent organ. Together, the pair of lovers seemed a powerful, well-lubricated engine of lust.

'Oh, goodness. . . !'

She's about to spend,' whispered one of our ladies. Reggie, grasping her waist in both his hands, held her suspended inches above his body. With the force of a battering ram, he thrust upward. Mrs Rose trembled convulsively and threw her head back. Her open mouth fought for air as the awesome piston plunged steadily in and out of her. Finally, her lungs filled; she released the breath in a sustained wail that, in seconds, ascended into a high-pitched caterwauling. For a moment or two we all feared for the poor woman's well-being!

Reggie's face had screwed itself into a rapturous grimace. He, too, was spending! His entire body was twitching in response to the uncontrolled spasms of his spurting pego. A low-pitched groan, counterpoint to Mrs Rose's bleating, escaped his tightly clenched lips. With a final burst of energy, he lunged upward, embedded completely in Mrs Rose's seething scabbard, then pulled her down to him. She collapsed atop his body,burying him in her ample flesh. They heaved together as a single animal and then were silent.

For a few moments there was stunned silence. Then as one we all applauded. A few more bottles of bubbly were uncorked and we toasted them as two of Britain's great athletes.

Once again, Reggie was blindfolded. Madame Kooshay

spun him three times one way, three times the other. I prayed t'would be me who was tapped. But all hope was lost as I watched him stumble away from me.

Then, miracle of miracles, Reggie seemed to gain his equilibrium. He reversed his direction, and with arms outstretched made directly for me. In an instant, before I could react to my good fortune, his fingers were on my face. I was overjoyed. It was of no concern to me whether he guessed correctly or not; the forfeit would be the same no matter which of us won.

Suddenly, Reggie had me in his arms, his lips on mine, our naked bodies pressed tightly together.

He pulled away, speaking emphatically, 'Miss Jenny Everleigh!' In a trice the blindfold was off and he was grinning broadly. 'I got this one right! At last, it is I who will choose the forfeit.'

'Anything,' said I. 'Anything at all with you, dear Reggie.'

'Ah, good. In that case you and I will retire for the night.'

There were groans of disappointment from the ladies. Someone shouted, 'Unfair!'

I took his arm and we walked slowly up the large staircase. From the first landing, he turned to the congregation. 'There is nothing unfair in love or war and tonight I believe we've experienced a bit of both.' He laughed, and we continued our ascent with his arm around my waist and his hand cupping one of my willing buttocks.

Reggie Nottingham and I made love in my big, soft bed till dawn. We slept till noon, ate breakfast and then made love again till dark.

SEVENTEEN

I have always exhibited a native talent for fellatio and a sensitive understanding concerning the hopes and fears of others. In short, I have never bared my teeth. [J.E., 1909]

Twas two days after our triumph at the ball. I was having tea with Madame Kooshay in her sanctum.

'A man called by today,' said she, 'an Arab gentleman. He announced himself as an emissary of Tewfik Pasha.'

I was astonished. 'How could he have found me out?'

'They have, my dear, mysterious ways and unlimited money. It is a combination with which some people can work miracles.'

'Tewfik Pasha must have known all along,' said I. The thought saddened me. If true, it meant that I had failed the test.

'An unlikely situation,' said Madame Kooshay. 'I believe that they simply followed Reggie until he led them here to you.'

'But why?'

'That is, my dear Jenny, a truly naive question.' She laughed. 'Do you recall telling us that Tewfik Pasha invited you to sail to Egypt on his yacht?'

'Yes, but it was so fantastic that I did not really take the proposal seriously.'

'It is quite serious.' Madame Kooshay poured the tea.

Confused and vaguely apprehensive by the turn of affairs, I sat quietly, awaiting her pleasure. Smiling pleasantly, she handed me a cup.

'These little plum cakes are marvellous,' said she. 'Mrs Rose baked them this morning – it's cook's day off and she loves having access to the kitchen.'

'Yes,' said I, taking a cake.

Madame chewed, her eyes closed in appreciation. 'Heavenly.'

'Tewfik Pasha,' said I, attempting to bring her back to the point, 'will he spread the news?'

'No. He is entirely sympathetic with your accomplishment and through his emissary, Mr Hassan, has given his word – sworn on the Koran and all of that sort of thing. Have no fear, Jenny. They will tell no one of your current situation or, for that matter, what they have surmised of your origin.'

'Thank heaven.' I bit into the cake; it was indeed delicious.

'And to make a long story short,' said Madame Kooshay, 'Tewfik Pasha has offered to pay five thousand pounds for your presence aboard his yacht.'

'Five thousand pounds!' I felt I might choke on Mrs Rose's cake.

'Exactly.'

'Good Lord! A fortune! Perhaps you mean hundreds.'

'Thousands. It was the fee we finally agreed upon, plus your return passage home.'

I was thunderstruck. It was enough money for a lifetime!

'Of course, Jenny, the decision is yours. If you agree, then I think it only fair that the money be divided into two equal parts – half for you and half for me. Your half would be deposited in the Bank of England in your name. Naturally, there will be general expenses for a wardrobe and other accoutrements. We will share those equally.'

'After all you have done for me, Madame, it is more than fair, but . . . I find it a frightening decision . . . Egypt. I haven't even been to Brighton and I've never in my life been on a boat, not even punting on the Thames!' I stared into my teacup. I was comfortable here. I had friends, a lovely home and, ahead of me, a secure and fulfilling career in my chosen profession. To risk the dangers of a sea-crossing with strangers and foreigners was an unsettling prospect. And what discomforts and dangers would await me in far-off Egypt? I knew nothing of the place other than a vague knowledge that it was mysterious and uncivilized and was occupied by a strange Oriental race called Arabs who dressed exotically and smelled differently than Englishmen. And yet. . . .

'Perhaps, my dear, you should think about it for a while,' said Madame Kooshay, interrupting my thoughts, 'though, I should mention that in order to make proper arrangements, Tewfik Pasha would like an answer by tomorrow evening.'

Distracted, I stared at her over the rim of my cup. Despite my apprehensions, I felt vaguely drawn towards the possibility of adventure, of the exotic promise of far-distant places, of experiencing the strange and forbidden. 'I'm happy here,' said I. 'Everyone has been so very nice to me. And yet . . . I don't know . . . Please, what should I do?'

'Jenny,' she said and reached across the table, took my hand. 'I'm glad that you're not being swayed by the money. I have no doubt of that. But allow me to say that you would earn an equal amount here, over a period of time. That aside, crossing the ocean on Tewfik Pasha's yacht would be more than just a voyage. If you accept his invitation, you will be embarking on, not just a sea-crossing, but a new life. To put it another way, you now stand at a crossroad. You will have many such in your lifetime, and in each case your life will be changed for better or worse, but changed it will be. Your train ride to London was just such a crossroad. Had you not been on that train, in that crriage, your world would be a vastly different place than it is now.'

'Thank heaven for that train,' said I.

'Exactly,' said Madame Kooshay. 'And now, as I said,

you face another crossroad. Will you go straight towards a destination you are reasonably sure of, or will you turn onto the new, unmapped pike?'

'And pray, where will that lead?'

'Ah, there is no telling. It may very well lead to disaster, perhaps even death or a fate worse than that. But then, too, it may well open a new world for you, a world whose satisfactions and rewards we can't begin to dream of. A gamble, Jenny – the toss of a coin. Though there is one thing of which you can be certain: it will not be uneventful and you will emerge from the experience wiser than when you embarked on it.'

Her words excited me. Impulsively, I said, 'If I refuse this opportunity, I feel I will regret it for the rest of my life!'

'You accept then?'

'Yes.'

Madame Kooshay reached over to kiss me on the cheek. 'I will send your reply to Tewfik Pasha this very evening.'

A while later, I told her of my pending assignation with the Prince of Wales. I did not, however, tell her of the bargain I had made in exchange for it. The fewer who knew of that the better. Men are peculiar and I assumed Reggie to be no exception. If all went well and he then heard that his appointment to Cambridge had been purchased with my body, he was sure to suffer a loss of pride. I had no idea what the consequence of this might be, and therefore I decided the less said the better. Discretion, in this case, was the better part of valour.

Later that evening, as I was making myself ready for bed, there was a discreet knock on my door. It was Reggie. I greeted him in my pink dressing gown. He was carrying a bottle of bubbly and two glasses. In moments we were both seated on the bed, drinking champagne. He seemed tipsy.

'I've been celebrating,' said he. 'Today I received a note inviting me to Cambridge for a discussion. They are considering me for a permanent chair in linguistics.'

'Oh, Reggie, that's marvellous!'

'Yes.' He touched his glass to mine, then drained it. 'I wouldn't have dared even to dream of such good fortune.'

'When is it to be?'

'Wednesday.'

I reached over to kiss him, saying, 'I offer my congratulations.'

'I have no idea what caused them to consider me for such an august position. I've lectured a few times as a guest, but surely that would not have been enough to . . .'

'Perhaps,' said I, growing nervous with this line of thought, 'it would be best if you just accepted your good fortune – as they say, one should not look a gift horse in the mouth.'

'Well put, my dear.' He poured more champagne into his glass and in the process splashed some onto the bed. 'Sorry . . . when I've imbibed to this extent I become clumsy, clumsy, clumsy. There was an entire bottle before this one.'

I took the glass from his hand and kissed him. Then, whispering seductively in his ear, I said, 'Make love to me, Reggie, 'tis a far better way to celebrate.'

'Ah, how I would like to, sweet Jenny, but demon rum – the spoiler of Eros – has the upper hand and the final word. I doubt if I'm capable, even with you. . . .'

'Never say die,' I whispered as I began to undress him. 'I'll slay the awful demon.'

He laughed as I pulled the trousers off him. 'Ah, my courageous champion, my heroine . . . try as you may, you're sure to fail.' He fell onto the bed, naked. 'My lance, as you see, lacks the rigidity, the strength and determination necessary to aid you in your joust. The cause is lost.'

I whispered into his open mouth, 'I shall prove otherwise.' Then, slithering down his body as if I were a snake, I took the soft mass of his penis into my mouth. I moved it about as if it were a lump of sweet treacle, bathing it, lathering it with my tongue.

Exploring between Reggie's tensed buttocks, I found the

puckered opening and diddled around it. There was method to my madness – a trick, a device of knowledgeable women, discussed by Yvette and Magnolia during breakfast just a few mornings ago. Remembering their words, I bathed an index finger in my own cunny sap. Then carefully, I insinuated the lubricated digit into Reggie's tiny nether opening. Gently, barely penetrating more than a half inch, I moved it in a slow circle while continuing to suck on his soft, cuddlesome prick. Little by little, as his anus opened to me, I pressed home. Soon I had penetrated to the first knuckle. Reggie groaned as his sphincter gave way, allowing me even greater access. I hooked my finger to massage the secret, buried gland that Yvette had insisted was common to all men.

Success! His organ was swelling in my mouth, coming alive, expanding! I thrilled to the delicious magic. The ladies had been correct. I bent to my lascivious labours with a vengeance, cued by a series of groans. Reggie had begun rotating his hips, forcing my finger even deeper.

He was hard now, hard as a rock. He fucked my mouth with deliberate strokes even as I fucked his arse. With my free hand I reached up to pinch the small nipple nestled in a lush garden of jet-black hair adorning his chest. He sucked in his breath sharply as I felt the tiny protuberance grow between my fingers. I was in control, coordinating a sensuous male triangle: cock, arsehole, nipple. Under my ministrations, Reggie heaved in rapturous agony. He breathed in short spasms. His tool, a hard muscular mass, filled my suctioning mouth. It was a handsome device, not too large, not too small, just right to slide in and out of my O-shaped lips. His hand cupped my bulging cheeks. 'Ah, Jenny,' he said, groaning. 'You are the best of all the cocksuckers in these islands. When I have my way in the government I will demand a special order to be struck. You will be knighted for your unequalled service to mankind!'

My dear Reggie showed no signs of approaching orgasm. It would require much more time. He had obviously consumed considerable alcohol. But I was a most dedicated woman. Pleasure, rather than time, was of the essence.

Grasping him tightly in order to quiet his pistoning motion, I began scrubbing with my tongue just under the plump, purple helmet. His response was immediate. His groans grew louder, his arms fluttered about my face. With his cock head in my mouth I grasped the base and proceeded to frig it.

'Oh, Jenny,' he cried, 'you've conquered the demon! Now I can fuck you!'

Gradually, I reduced the tempo, pulling my finger from his bum. He rolled me over, spread my legs wide, folding them back on to my chest. I grasped his cock to feed it to my juicy puss. Slowly, thrilling to every inch of penetration, I sucked him in. I leaned forward to take his tongue into my mouth. Then he was fucking me with long, smooth strokes as I fell back on to the bed, allowing him everything.

We grinned at each other as Reggie hovered above me, supporting himself on powerful arms. His full bollocks slapped, in slow cadence, against my buttocks and thighs.

'You make love like a lady, my Jenny,' said he, breathlessly. 'It is one thing I did not have to teach you.'

'And pray,' said I, 'how does a lady differ from others?'

'A true lady is more than just a receptacle. A true lady both gives and takes pleasure with equal gusto.'

I laughed happily. 'Then you must fuck me like a gentleman would.' With my knees pressed back against my breasts, I reached down to spread my pussy lips.

Reggie moved up slightly until his shaft was entering at a high angle, and his fat gonads pummelling the soft, delicate flesh of my wide-open quim.

'Lovely,' said I.

'Magnificent,' said he, smiling broadly. 'What we do

transcends the greatest accomplishments of mankind.'

'And womankind.'

I wriggled my hips madly as Reggie increased the pace. Supported on just fingertips and toes, he was a lewd gymnast thrusting with pile-driving intensity, his body slapping against the resilient flesh of my thighs.

As I approached the heights, he changed the tempo to one of short, quick jabs. I rotated my ecstatic buttocks on the soft, now dampened sheets as he pulsed in and out of me. My joy was complete. I spent, staring into his eyes and laughing. He laughed with me as I wrapped arms and legs around him, milking his spewing cock with my secret, inner muscles.

There were two or three small, piquant thrusts and then we lay quietly in each other's arms. I had slain the demon. I was content. Little did I know that nine years would pass before I would again bed my darling Reggie.

EIGHTEEN

During my long career as both sexual object and subject, I was to make love with many women. It should be made clear to readers of this journal, however, that men have always been my basic sustenance: the roast beef as compared to the female Yorkshire pudding. If a choice were imposed, one would live happily on the meat and easily forgo the pudding. [J.E., 1913]

'You said on Wednesday,' said Madame Kooshay. 'We must outfit you immediately. I suggest Fortnum and Mason's this morning and Staunton's this afternoon.'

'Wednesday,' said I, a feeling of dejection sweeping through me.

'Yes. But what's wrong?'

'I have an engagement with the Prince of Wales on Wednesday . . . I told you.'

'Ah yes. He may well be the future monarch, but you'll either have to change the day or cancel it entirely. One can't have everything, young lady.'

'But I must go to him on Wednesday. I promised faithfully.'

'No such thing, Jenny. A lady always has the prerogative to change her plans. You can blame it on the curse. It is a ploy that rarely fails as long as one keeps track.'

'I cannot, Madame.'

'Why?'

Quietly, I told her of my bargain with Edward. 'To

Reggie, the loss of a career would be a far greater sacrifice than either twenty-five hundred pounds or an ocean voyage would be to me. A bargain is a bargain,' said I.

'You have noble qualities,' said Madame.

'Thank you.'

'Does Reggie know of this bargain?'

'I thought it best not to tell him.'

'An admirable decision.'

'Then I can hold you to a similar promise.'

'Most certainly.' She paused, then continued, her tones now businesslike. 'I will have to inform Hassan that you cannot possibly sail till – let us say – Sunday.'

'Do you think Tewfik Pasha will agree to wait?'

'I'm sure of it. If he is willing to pay five thousand pounds for your presence, I feel he might be equally willing to put off sailing for a few days. Of course, I won't tell him the true reason for your tardiness. The less that foreigners know about the amorous activities of our future monarch the better. Such information is none of their affair.'

In gratitude, I leaned forward to place an affectionate kiss on her cheek. Madame immediately laid claim to my lips. In seconds we were on the bed. I spread her kimono in order to kiss her breasts.

'Ah, Jenny,' said she, sighing, 'I shall miss you.'

I responded by allowing my fingers to stroll down her body, across the soft expanse of her belly and downward to their final voluptuous destination.

NINETEEN

Since they invented virtually everything else, it is arguable that the art of sexual pleasure was an invention of the Hebrews. It is my notion that this momentous concept was brought to fruition during their wanderings in the Sinai in order to counteract the arid, desert boredom. All mention of this artistic innovation was probably excised from the Old Testament early in the Christian era. As evidence I can point to the unalterable fact that the world's most accomplished male lovers are not Croatian fishermen, nor are they, as some insist, Parisian artists or Japanese warriors. No, my naive sisters, the best are well-educated Englishmen of the Hebrew persuasion. [J.E., 1921]

'And this,' said James Whistler, 'I've titled "Arrangement in Grey and Black".'

It was a strange painting of a seated woman in profile. I felt drawn to it for reasons I couldn't define. I was uneducated in art. Quietly, I said, 'It is most unusual.' I attempted to turn away but found my eyes locked on to the canvas.

'It is James's mother,' said Edward. 'I, too, have an attachment to it and have suggested to him that he change the title to "Portrait of My Mother".'

'No,' said Whistler, 'you continue to miss the point. Perhaps Miss Everleigh will understand.' He grasped my shoulder, turning me towards him. 'As I have been trying for years to explain to this royal dunderhead, the important factor in my work, Miss Everleigh, is not the subject, but rather the harmonious relationship of light, form and colour. My mother has little to do with this painting.'

'Whistler's Mother.' I spoke just above a whisper.

'What?'

'It should be titled "Whistler's Mother",' said I, repeating myself with more confidence now because of the delighted approval on Edward's royal countenance.

'Never!' cried Whistler. 'This woman is yet another of your pretty little Philistines!'

'Wrong!' said the Prince of Wales, laughing. 'She is actually our most beautiful and intelligent recruit and I welcome her to the Philistinian ranks.' With that, he put his arm around my waist and kissed me affectionately on the cheek.

I had arrived at the home of the American, James Whistler, at tea time, honouring the agreement made with Prince Edward at Tewfik Pasha's ball. I was surprised to find Mr Whistler himself present as I had understood the afternoon and evening would be a tête-à-tête – just His Majesty and I in 'borrowed' premises.

Also present was another woman, Lady Lititia Faversham, wife of one Colonel Harry Mandrake Faversham of the Royal Northumberland. She was pretty in an aquiline way, with thin lips and round eyes above which she sported a beautiful coif of red hair. Over tea, she had asked an assortment of pointed questions, mentioning this one and that one in an obvious effort to ferret out my place in society. I fended her off adroitly.

Then, an hour later, Mr Whistler was showing me some of his work. Despite his disapproval of my title suggestion, he still seemed intent on gaining my approval. It was an attitude I found even more flattering than Edward's insistent compliments.

'And this,' said Whistler, flinging a tarpaulin off a large canvas, 'I call "Nocturne in Black and Gold".' He stepped back.

At first I could make neither hide nor hair of the painting. It was like no other I'd ever seen. I searched for content, some hint as to the subject. In just a few moments I found myself mesmerized by colour, forms, and shapes I couldn't define. After a few more moments I found it unnecessary to define them. The painting seemed to go beyond a mere visual description of something. It affected a part of me I had hitherto been unfamiliar with. I stared, drinking it in, unaware of passing time.

Finally, when I turned, I found the three of them seated about the room staring at me curiously.

'Well?' asked the artist.

'I'm sure,' said I, 'that no matter how diligently I searched for them, I could find no words to describe your painting or to express my reaction to it. Such words do not exist.'

Whistler stood. 'Exactly!' He clapped his hands. 'All is forgiven! You, Miss Everleigh, are one of the few who understand the full meaning of art for art's sake, a phrase I coined that, along with some of my better paintings, has suffered derision from self-styled art experts and critics. Art – true art – defies description. The world of art is bogged down in meaningless jargon. Descriptive words applied to art are a pretence resorted to by those without the talent to see or feel.' He laid a hand on my shoulder. 'Where, Edward, did you find this wonderful woman?'

'At a ball.'

Whistler looked at me intently. 'Did she lose her glass slipper?'

His words startled me. Could he know that I was but a Cinderella, a mere scullery maid posing as a lady and that Madame Kooshay was my fairy godmother?

'Hardly,' said Edward. 'Though she started many tongues wagging.'

'I seem to be a woman of mystery,' said I.

'Ah then,' said Whistler. 'We will drink to you.'

He knew! I was certain of it. I could tell by the look in his eye, by the intense manner in which he stared at me.

We sat about drinking champagne. Whistler said, 'Jenny, I'm going to paint you.'

'And I will buy the painting,' said Edward.

'Nude,' said Whistler.

'In which case I will pay you double for it!'

I turned to Lady Lititia who had been quiet till now. 'Has he painted you in that manner?'

'No, thank heaven,' she said, raising her glass to her lips. 'Such would be the ruin of me.'

'But not you, Jenny,' said Whistler.

'No,' said I. 'But even if it were, I would be honoured to pose for you.'

'Bravo!' cried the Prince of Wales. 'Lititia and I will watch.'

'I'd love to watch,' said Lady Lititia.

'No,' said Whistler. I'm sorry, dear friends, but it must be a private sitting – no distractions.'

'When?' said I.

'Soon, very soon.'

'But I'm going abroad in just a few days.'

'Then tonight, tomorrow morning. . . .'

'Whenever you decide,' said I, speaking over the rim of my glass. 'But I thought that content was of no importance to you.'

'There are exceptions. I also paint portraits.'

'It would seem to me,' said Edward, 'that painting Jenny in the nude would be an erotic act unto itself.'

'Art transcends such pettiness.'

'And for you, Jenny?'

'I find exhibiting myself extremely erotic,' said I. 'But then, unlike Mr Whistler, I've experienced nothing that transcends the sexual . . . yet.'

'Ah,' said Lady Lititia, 'this conversation is becoming deliciously randy.'

'Indeed?' asked Whistler. He stepped behind her chair, reached over it and inserted a hand into her bodice.

Lady Lititia looked up at him. 'Petty, petty, petty, dear James.'

'There is a time for everything, dear lady.'

'Here or in the bedroom?'

Whistler looked up at me for a moment, then shifted his gaze to Edward. Smiling, he said, 'That depends, Lady Lititia, on whether or not you share Jenny's penchant for exhibition.'

'I would find an audience quite stimulating, particularly this one.' She, too, looked up for a moment, caught my eye and smiled. I smiled back. 'But,' she continued, 'wouldn't you, as you said before, find it distracting?'

'Painting yes, my dear. Fucking, no. They're two separate art forms, though, and I must reiterate, one is petty compared to the other.' While he spoke, he fumbled about with Lady Lititia's bodice, attempting to undo it.

'Truly spoken,' said Edward, who seated himself next to me on the settee. 'But which is which?'

Whistler laughed. 'To each his own, my Prince.' He was experiencing increasing difficulties with Lady Lititia's clothing.

I asked, 'May I help?'

'Ah, Miss Everleigh, would you please?' asked Lady Lititia. 'He is all thumbs.'

James stepped back, bowing graciously. 'My guest,' he said.

I helped Lady Lititia with her hooks and buttons. Beneath her dress were a few petticoats, a voluminous pair of bloomers and a tight corset. It took minutes to divest her of all but the corset. At one point in our labours, I glanced over my shoulder to see the two men seated side by side observing us as if we were on stage at a music hall. They were smoking cigars whose length and breadth were reminiscent of two long, fat cocks. I whispered this impression into Lady Lititia's ear and we both laughed.

As I removed her bloomers I glanced downward to see if her pubic tresses matched the reddish, auburn hue of her coiffure. I gasped in astonishment! Her mound of Venus was bare! Not a single hair obscured my view of the totally naked, V-shaped pube. I glanced up to find Lady Lititia grinning at me.

Our two men did not share my view of the strange cuntal configuration as it was blocked by the chair back. She placed a finger over her lips to hush me.

'What is it?' asked Edward.

'No doubt some hideous deformity of recent vintage,' said Whistler. 'Perhaps we should trade women.'

'How ungallant of you, James,' said the Prince of Wales, standing in an attempt to acquire a better view.

'Stay as you are, gentlemen,' said I. 'All will be revealed to you in due time.' Then to Lady Lititia, 'May I?'

'Oh, please do. . . .'

I knelt down to examine the strange sight. The plump 'V' was smoothly fleshed, somewhat more pale than the skin around it, as if it had just emerged from some hairy, primordial forest and was seeing the light of day for the first time. The slit was perfectly delineated, punctuated with a neatly hooded clitoris. The view excited me. Never had I seen female equipment in such clear detail. It seemed so utilitarian and yet, at the same time, strangely romantic.

I reached out with a tentative finger. The skin was smooth, like a baby's. Lady Lititia must have shaved quite recently as there was no hint of a stubble. I ran my finger up the length of the slit, allowing it to come to rest on the base of her clitoris.

'Do you like it, Miss Everleigh?'

'I'm fascinated,' said I. 'May I kiss it?'

'Oh yes, please do.' She moved her feet slightly, spreading her legs.

I grasped a buttock in each hand and pulled her forward. Then, tilting my head, I kissed her naked vagina as if it were a pair of lips. With my mouth pressed against the soft, yielding flesh, I probed gently with my tongue.

'What,' said the Prince of Wales, 'is going on down there?'

'Miss Everleigh is making my acquaintance,' said Lady

Lititia, her voice climbing the scale as my tongue fluttered up the length of her slit.

I, along with those parts of my new-found friend Lititia below the waist, was not visible to our male friends. The concealment added a piquant note to the proceedings. I felt a perverse desire to provide them a show that would consist entirely of Lady Lititia's reactions to the lascivious machinations of a phantom lover. She would be an orgasmic puppet, manipulated by invisible strings.

I moved away momentarily and looked up to whisper, 'Spread your lips for me, dear lady.'

Her fingers pressed against the gorged labia; they pulled gently. As I watched, her deliciously naked puss opened like the blooming of an exotic pink flower. I tongued lightly, teasingly, working my way upward. Lady Lititia groaned, quivered, as I made tentative contact with the tiny tip of her clitoris. Her long, graceful fingers pulled, stretching the succulent flesh even more, opening the gash to my questing fingers.

'Ah, Miss Everleigh,' said she, her voice trembling. 'You practice the art with such consummate skill!'

My tongue tweaked firmly, transmitting tactile shocks to the sensitive arrow of erectile cunt flesh.

'Jenny is sucking her!' James Whistler's voice was muffled as Lady Lititia had inadvertently covered my ears whilst grasping my head.

'Lovely,' said the future king.

'An artist . . .'

'Petty, dear fellow?'

'Perhaps she is the exception.'

I grinned into Lady Lititia's oozing pussy, grasping her bottom cheeks even tighter. Her gyrating hips were like those of a dervish, rotating her bald quim against my face. She moaned continuously now, a low-pitched tremolo, a counterpoint to the increasingly rapturous trembling of her buttocks.

It was my experience that female arse-trembling of a

certain kind was an erotic clue indicating impending orgasm. I thrilled to her reactions, aware of a twitching in my own nest. I had brought Lady Lititia halfway up the mountain. The peak was in view! I took her clitoris between my lips and suctioned it into my mouth where it was subjected to a tempestuous tongue-lashing.

'Heaven!' she shouted, her entire body jerking spasmodically. 'Ah, I'm going to spend! Suck me! Oh, suck me, Miss Everleigh!'

She grasped my head tightly, locking it into place as she rubbed her swollen, gushing cunt against my face. At the ideal moment, I managed to drop down less than an inch or so and with my nose pressed against her clit, insinuated my stiffened oral probe into her succulent tunnel. Delicious! Maddened with passion, I fucked Lady Lititia with a stiffened tongue. I felt carried away by her responses – uncontrollable twitchings, tremblings, gushing spasms!

Moments later she grasped my arms to pull me up next to her. We kissed, at first affectionately, then as she tasted her essence on my lips, passionately, sucking my tongue as if it were a long-lost penis home from the wars.

'Thank you,' she said, 'dearest Miss Everleigh.'

I turned to observe both our gentlemen seated next to each other, their trousers open, their rampant pricks firmly in hand. They were both masturbating slowly as though to some secret drummer.

TWENTY

There are long, thin rapiers and thick, blunt battering rams. As I became more sophisticated about such physiological matters, I grew to prefer breadth over length. With the latter, one takes the risk of not being truly aware of what is going on until the rapier strikes bottom. [J.E., 1903]

I came half awake in a strange room, curled on my side in a strange bed. A strange hand lay heavily on my naked breast and a strange, half-hard pego was stuffed part way up my poor, battered quim. It was still dark.

Moments passed before I realized that I was in James Whistler's bedroom. The hand and prick belonged to Edward, the future King of England, who lay, snoring, behind me.

It took just a few moments to realize that I had been awakened by yet another presence in the room – a man. He stood, silhouetted in the doorway. Vaguely, I wondered how long he had been there.

Edward's flaccid tool plopped out as soon as I rolled onto my back. I spoke quietly to the apparition in the doorway. 'Good morning.'

'It is not quite morning,' said James Whistler. 'And I want you. Now!'

Such words were not exactly the proper road to a lady's heart, nor for that matter to any other part of her anatomy. But it mattered not. 'Perhaps another time,' said I, still half asleep and very tired. 'Good night, dear Mr Whistler.' My muscles ached. Edward and I had copulated for hours. I could not have been sleeping for very long. My eyes closed. Breathing deeply, I began to drift off.

He was to the bed in seconds. He grasped my arm, pulled me up and off. Staggering from the shock of a rude and sudden awakening, I trailed behind him groggily as he pulled me from the room.

He half led, half dragged me to a raised platform in the centre of the studio. It was bathed in the warm glow of the half-dozen oil lamps surrounding it.

'Lie down,' said Whistler, 'on your side.'

'Please,' said I. 'Not now. I'm so tired . . .'

'You're young. You'll recover very quickly. Nothing you've ever done before is as important as this.'

'Perhaps, but let's do it later when I can enjoy it.' I curled up, longing for sleep.

'Now!'

I was jolted fully awake by a slap on my bare bottom! I shot upright, glaring at him. 'Beast!' I cried. 'You would take a half-conscious lady against her will?'

'Take? What in bloody hell do you mean by take?' He laughed. 'Do you think I intend to fuck you?'

I rubbed my arse hesitantly. It smarted. 'Well,' said I, confused, 'isn't that what . . .?'

'You silly girl! I want to paint you.' He stood, looming over me.

'You should have said so,' I said ruefully. 'And you could have been gentle with me.'

He spoke quickly, running his words together. 'You excite me and I want to get on with it . . . a seated nude. I have the painting in my head, right here.' He tapped his forehead. 'The entire painting. I've been thinking about it for hours. Now it is just a simple matter of execution.' He paused to stare at me as if, thought I, I were a bowl of fruit. 'In less than an hour 'twill be daylight.' He glanced up at the large overhead skylight. 'In the meantime I can start with what light there is.'

Whistler sat me in a large chair atop a few pillows so that my feet would be off the floor. The pose was not an uncomfortable one. I felt it would be a simple matter to drift off.

In the shadows at the opposite end of the large studio, splayed out on her back atop a colourful assortment of pillows was Lady Lititia. Clothed only in her corset, she lay in sleep, her hand tucked between her thighs, her hair spread out in a beautiful red fan. Vaguely, I wondered about her. What sort of man was her husband? Were there children? How often did she indulge herself thusly?

Whistler, clothed only in paint-spattered white trousers, was in the process of setting up his easel. His movements were nervously impatient as if his work was a matter of life or death. Watching him, I felt a sudden, overpowering desire for a cup of tea. Quietly, I expressed it.

'A cup of tea!' He glared at me. 'Now?'

'Yes, please.'

'No!'

'Without a nice cuppa,' said I, feeling a flush of anger, 'I am sure to expire and you will have to reconcile yourself to painting a seated corpse.'

'Good Lord, if it's not one thing, 'tis another!'

'Please.'

He growled impatiently. Picking up a pillow, he tossed it across the studio where it struck Lady Lititia's head. 'Litty,' he shouted. 'Wake up!'

The sleeping woman's dainty, ladylike snores continued unabated. Calling out again, the artist threw another pillow with a similar lack of results.

'Damn! Wake up, woman!' He set down his pallet and strode across the room. Grasping her under the arms, he attempted to raise her to her feet.

Angrily, I stood up. 'Beast!' I shouted. 'Unhand her! Leave her be! Never mind the tea!'

'Tea you want, tea you shall have, if I have to move heaven and earth.' He turned to me, dropping Lady Lititia back onto the pillows as if she were a rag doll. 'You broke the pose,' he said, his voice ragged with exasperation. Without another word, he bent to Lady Lititia's recumbent form to slap her bottom. It was as a pistol shot, momentarily startling. Lady Lititia jolted awake as much as I had under a similar stimulus just five minutes earlier. She sat up, a confused, disoriented expression on her face.

'Tea,' said Whistler.

'What?'

'Brew up,' said Whistler. 'And I think there are some scones.'

She stood, her lovely body slumped in exhaustion. 'Miss Everleigh,' she said. 'How pretty you are.'

'I'm sorry,' said I lamely. 'I didn't mean for the beast to wake you . . .'

Ten minutes later the three of us sat around the edge of the posing stand, sipping tea and eating stale scones spread heavily with dark orange marmalade. Whistler, though taciturn, seemed reconciled to waiting me out.

I posed throughout the day and into the night. It was mesmerizing; some of the hours passed speedily, others seemed to last forever. Edward departed. Lady Lititia left and returned. Whistler and I barely exchanged three words. The big studio clock ticked on and on as once again P.M. became A.M. He was totally immersed in his work, sometimes going for as long as a half hour before looking up at me. Thrice I fell asleep, slumping in the chair. Thrice he awakened me with impatient words. At one point, Lady Lititia halted the proceedings to serve us boiled eggs, kidneys and tea. Darkness descended and for a few hours, Whistler painted by lamplight. Finally, he stepped back, put down his palette and covered the canvas before I could see it.

'There,' said he, breathing deeply as if he had been running. 'I'll not need you again.'

'May I see it?'

'When I've finished,' he said.

'But I'm going abroad in just a few days,' said I.

'It is a work of art meant for posterity. A year, five, ten – what matters? Eventually you will see it.'

Lady Lititia asked, 'Where are you going?'

'Egypt.' Disconcerted, I draped myself in a large embroidered throw.

'My husband is there,' said she.

I begged Whistler to allow me a glimpse at the painting. He was adamant. Angered, I began to dress. As I did so, Lady Lititia proceeded to do the opposite. She smiled, winking at me conspiratorially. 'Could you help me once more, Miss Everleigh?'

Whistler said, 'What are you up to, Litty?'

'It is most imperative that I remove my clothing, dear James.'

'Why?'

'In order to be naked.'

'Toward what end, my dear?'

'My own.'

'Ah, you want me to fuck you again.'

'Precisely.'

'Surely you got enough last night.'

'I never get enough,' said Lady Lititia.

A truly noble woman, thought I.

He laughed, seating himself to watch while, once again, I helped her disrobe. She indicated with secret little eye motions that she was doing so in order to provide a diversion so that I might manage a peek at the painting. This time I removed her corset. She had lovely breasts of the kind that would fit perfectly into champagne glasses.

Lady Lititia approached Whistler in a slow walk, her full hips swaying with erotic suggestion. Her naked pubic triangle moved in counterrhythm, animated by the sympathetic motion of her thighs. Finally, she pressed her belly into Whistler's lustful face.

He put his arms about her, grasped her arse with powerful hands, squeezing it. She lowered her body slowly as his lips trailed upward to her breasts. I watched as he sucked a nipple into his mouth.

'You're going to fuck me,' she said, her voice trembling, her head thrown back. 'Aren't you?'

'*Mmmm.*'

It was my turn to be the seated observer. I watched, spellbound, as she helped him off with his trousers. In seconds through adroit use of her hands and fingertips, she had him cocked and ready. Unlike the fat, sausagelike protuberance attached to his friend Edward, Whistler's machine was extraordinarily long and lean. She held it for a moment, gently frigging just below the head. Then they stood, their bodies pressed together, their lips and tongues engaged in lascivious combat. His concupiscent lance was between them, pressed against the softly accommodating pillow of her belly.

Moving back slightly, he reached between her thighs, passing his hand through till he was able to reach around behind to grasp a rotund bottom cheek. She responded by rotating her hips in slow, voluptuous circles, riding the intrusive wrist.

'Give it to me now,' she said. 'I want you inside me. . . .'

I thrilled to the passion in her voice, fighting a desire to join their amorous twosome, to share in the joys of Whistler's long, muscular, fifth limb, which even now, as the lovers separated, stood straight out from his body as if pointing the way.

Lady Lititia turned away from him and stepped to the back of the chair in which I was sitting. I twisted about to find her face just inches from mine. She grasped hold of the chair and bent forward to present Whistler her arse.

'Fuck me, dear James. I adore it this way!'

I looked over her shoulder to observe as her lover, with his long prick leading the way, stepped behind her to grasp her hips.

'Miss Everleigh,' she whispered. 'Do you also like it thusly?'

'Yes,' said I, looking into her eyes. 'Sometimes 'tis best of all.'

'He's at the portal. . . .'

'Lovely,' said I, running my hand affectionately through her hair.

'Ah . . . the head has entered.'

Her eyes closed. Her lips parted. I thrilled to see her facial muscles tightening into what appeared to be a visage of pain but was actually an expression of intense pleasure.

'Oh, kiss me, Miss Everleigh!'

I held her face in two hands, pressed her lips to mine. 'Tell me.'

'I'm being fucked.' She whispered into my mouth. 'In and out of me . . . cock . . . cunt . . . fuck!'

The chair rocked with their amorous exertions. In a cadence matching the tempo of her lover's thrusting, Lady Lititia's tongue darted in and out of my suctioning mouth. I trembled, feeling my own quim spasm in lustful sympathy.

Then, quite suddenly, she pulled away from me. In a spasmodic pant, barely able to enunciate the words, she said, 'The painting. . . !'

Taken by surprise, I realized I had forgotten the motive behind Lady Lititia's lascivious sacrifice! The painting! With James Whistler's attentions focused elsewhere, I could now view it! By presenting him her arse, an erotically adroit Lady Lititia had managed to face the artist away from his work.

I breathed deeply, then stood to make my casual way across the room. The canvas was large. Carefully, I lifted a corner of the tarpaulin. In the dim light of a single oil lamp, the composition was obscure, a dark, indistinct mass against an even darker background.

I turned to check up on the lovers. From the rear, Whistler's naked, hulking form completely hid Lady Lititia from my view. She was, I assumed, controlling the pace of their activities in order to leave me sufficient time. I felt a rush of gratitude towards my new friend and vowed to repay her, somehow, at the first opportunity.

I fetched the lamp and held it close to the canvas while with the other hand I raised the tarpaulin once again. What I saw will forever live in my mind!

It was a study in a hundred shades and varieties of blue. The chair in which I had posed had been transformed into a massive, ornate, ancient blue throne. I was a blue queen, seated in erect and noble dignity, crowned with a royal tiara of priceless blue stones above which floated a ghostly blue halo. My face, as depicted, glowed with a beatific calm seeming to resemble not a queen but rather a haloed Virgin Mary. Yet it was, at the same time, very obviously, me – Jenny Everleigh. Blasphemy!

The only colour other than blue was a large, exotic, magenta orchid that grew out of my vagina. It was not, mind you, merely inserted, but was anatomical – flesh of my flesh! Tiny rootlike tendrils were as pubic hairs. The larger roots were one with the labia, the mons veneris, the oversized clitoris. My vaginal opening gaped beneath the main stem. The entire area glistened, as with dew.

The man was mad! 'Twas no wonder he forbid me to view the painting! I looked up. Across the studio, the mad artist's milk-white, thrusting arse remained at its labours.

I concentrated my attention on the painting. Would it ever see the light of day? Surely, I thought, if *I* found it shocking, wouldn't virtually everyone else? Who would hang such a bizarre grotesquery?

I dropped the tarpaulin and was about to return to the copulating duet on the other side of the studio when I felt a nagging compulsion to take one last look. Again I raised the tarpaulin. It was the same picture that had greeted me the first time, but inexplicably, my reaction to it now was totally different. It was as if my eyes were functioning for the very first time. I drew in a deep lungful of air, forgetting to release it as my startled heart palpitated out of control! Whistler's painting seemed now a shattering statement transmitted in a hundred mystic shades of blue. An instantaneous comprehension set my head to reeling! I was struck, as though by lightning, with an understanding of female eroticism not even dreamed of by the innocent girl I had been just moments earlier.

Transfixed, I stared, allowing the artist's subtle manipulations to lead my eyes from one detail to another, details that had eluded me the first time. The hands had seven long, graceful fingers. The feet were webbed. There was no navel. The nipples were tiny, Oriental faces, sporting antennae. The eyes reflected two different, highly detailed, miniature images, one of a beautiful winged woman, the other of a man dressed in a loincloth. Painted into the leaves and colourful petals of the orchid were many barely discernible nymphs and nymphettes in the act of pleasuring one another in twos, threes and fours of every gender combination. (Most of these were as yet unfinished, merely sketched in.)

Even now, I struggle to conjure words with which to explain both the significance of the content and my reaction to it. Suffice it to say that viewing the painting changed forever the way in which I thought of myself. Perhaps someday it will be explicable. . . .

Later, I was to wonder whether Whistler's masterpiece would have a similar effect on other women and men. It was a vain speculation as I was never to meet anyone who had seen it, nor in years to come had I ever heard of it being hung in a museum or gallery . . . nor was I myself ever to view it again.*

I'm not sure how long I stared at the masterpiece, but finally I found myself back in the chair with Lady Lititia's rapture-ridden face, once again, inches from my own. Behind her, his hands clutching gyrating female hips, the genius James Abbott McNeill Whistler was as a powerful

* Decades later, after his death, neither Pennell's biography of Whistler nor either of two published catalogues made any reference to this particular work. [J.E., 1920]

and precise fucking machine, driving into her with ever increasing fury.

I kissed her gaping mouth, whispering, 'Thank you, Lady Lititia.'

'I've spent thrice,' said she, 'perhaps more. . . .'

'And he?'

'I've little tricks to hold him off – do you know them too?'

'No, you must teach me.'

'Then we are to be friends?'

I kissed her deeply. 'Forever,' said I, my hands reaching under to cup her breasts.

'Ahhhh . . . Miss Everleigh. . . .'

'Please call me Jenny,' said I.

'And I am Litty,' said she.

'Litty,' said I, savouring the sound. 'Litty, dearest.'

She was silent for a moment, then, with her body heaving and twitching, she threw her arms around me, 'Ahhhh, Jenny . . . his balls are bouncing against my clit! Oh how I love being fucked!'

'Cum, my sweet little Litty,' said I, caught up in her lust, almost as if it were I who was being pleasured.

'Yes. Oh, God, yes!'

I sucked on her mouth. I pinched her nipples.

'Now. Now, Jenny . . . ahhhh!' She trembled, her body transmitting spasms of pleasure.

She tensed as the tremors increased, reached their peak and then slowly receded. Whistler slowed the pace as Litty's head slumped on my shoulder.

'Lovely,' said I.

'Yes,' said she, 'lovely.' She raised her head. 'Now,' she whispered, 'I'm going to cause him to spend.'

'How?'

'By milking his cock. There are secret muscles.'

'I think I know of them,' said I. 'But I have never succeeded. . . .'

'One must practise clutching,' said she. 'I will teach you.'

Litty was not to have the opportunity to 'milk' her lover.

With a squishing sound that seemed like a drawn-out, liquid sigh, Whistler pulled out of her.

He took both of us in his arms, his lips passing from Litty's to mine. I reached down to encircle his rampant organ. It was damp with Litty's honey.

'Ah, Litty,' he said. 'You are a fuck worthy of this blessed kingdom.'

'And you,' said she, her hand joining mine in its penile exploration, 'are a noble fucker, a man amongst men.'

''Tis Jenny's turn at the wicket,' said the mad artist.

'Lovely,' said Litty, her other hand seeking my eager quim.

Whistler took me in his arms, lifting me as if I were but a weightless rag doll. He carried me to the pillows, deposited me gently on my back.

Litty stretched out next to me, running her tongue around the sensitive encirclement of my aureole. The nipple, thus teased, was soon engorged and tingling for attention. Cupping my breast in a delicate hand, she took the swollen protuberance between her lips to nibble gently. She was joined in this vivacious activity by Whistler, who took my other breast in his mouth, sucking on it as if he were a babe, flicking the hardened nipple with his tongue, then gently nibbling, just as was Litty, on its twin.

I reached down to grasp his prick only to find another hand. It was Litty's, encircling just under the crown. She was frigging slowly, using a fluid wrist action. I reached lower to cup Whistler's lovely swollen bollocks, massaging them gently.

The suctioning lips, the tweaking tongues, the nipping teeth were having their way with my nipples. Shocks of delicious rapture transmitted themselves from my breasts to the craving nest between my thighs. Then, suddenly, there was a hand there. Whose? I knew not, nor did it matter. The three of us were rapidly becoming one – a single, powerful machine of mutual joy.

Strolling fingers wended their way through my sodden

love garden. I shivered with pleasure and reached under Whistler's balls to apply pressure to that wondrous, sensitive, secret area of flesh hidden away between gonads and rosebud.

'Ah,' said he in low-pitched tones. 'Lovely . . . lovely.'

Litty's mouth detached itself from my breast. She slithered up my body and inserted an insistent tongue in my ear. 'Jenny, darling,' said she in an amorous whisper, 'are you ready to take his cock?'

'Yes. . . .'

'It is a delight, quite the longest I've ever experienced. . . .'

'Oh yes, Litty, put it in me!'

I was rolled over on to my belly. Hands grasped my hips, raising them.

'Fuck her, James.'

I glanced between my thighs. Whistler knelt between them. Litty's hand was at my cunt, spreading the lips, opening me for what was to come. I watched as her other hand took hold of Whistler's distended rod, bringing it to bear at the very entrance.

I moaned, repeating her lascivious demand. 'Fuck me, James!'

Then, suddenly, he was in me! My cuntal lips grasped him fervently as I rotated my arse around the fulcrum of his plunging cock. I heard myself whimper in appreciation as, without hesitation, he gave me full measure. With a deep groan of pleasure that was octaves lower than mine, he echoed me. He withdrew slowly, till only the rotund head remained inserted. Then the delicious process was repeated. Looking back between my thighs, I was both thrilled and amazed by my ability to swallow with ease all of such a lengthy monster. It glistened along its entire length with the lubrication of my ambrosial juices.

Then my view was interrupted as Lady Lititia squirmed into position beneath me. Whistler shifted upward, his tool now entering at a higher angle in order to make room for her head. Seconds later, I felt the feathery touch of her tongue on my clit! I was being fucked and sucked simultaneously! Fingers, I knew not whose, were pinching both my nipples.

He increased the pace, battering the cushion of my bottom. 'Take my cock, Jenny,' he said, his voice husky with lust. 'Fuck! Fuck! Fuck!'

Litty moaned as she sucked furiously on my clit. I reached out, searching blindly for hers. Soon my fingers were gambolling in her luscious cuntal swamp. I felt her body quiver in appreciation.

'Finger-fuck me, Jenny,' she muttered.

I eased a single digit into her love tunnel, rotating the finger to open it further. Soon, it was joined by two more – a miniature cock. I fucked her in tempo to Whistler's now pounding tool. Litty reciprocated by sucking on my clitoris even more fervently. She grasped it between her lips, tongue-whipped it, nibbled on it.

I was being ravished! A wildfire of sensations raced madly through my body. My breasts, my fingertips, my buttocks, the back of my neck all vibrated in rapturous sympathy. From head to toe, my skin tingled.

Whistler, sensing an approaching climax, gave me my head. He ceased his rhythmic pistoning and plugging me to the hilt rode my wildly gyrating rump. I was in control – it was my fuck to do with what I would.

'Ah, Jenny . . . fuck it out of me. . . . Masturbate me with your cunt!'

'Spunk!' I cried, madly finger-fucking Lady Lititia, my thumb rubbing her swollen clit. The ecstatic pressure was building. I felt about to burst.

Lady Lititia was first. Her form stiffened under mine as she entered the maelstrom.

'Ohh . . . I'm cumming!' She called out into the sodden folds of my cock-stuffed puss. 'Now, Jenny! Now!'

I could sense Whistler's weapon vibrating, throbbing as I fucked it, rotating my arse in tight circles. Faster and faster – my body was racked with uncontrollable spasms. Then, suddenly, as if I were a bursting balloon, I spent! The orgasmic release was different than any I had yet experienced. It was much like a man's – an excruciating pressure, a sudden, intense, instantaneous explosion!

I felt Whistler withdraw. He groaned mightily. Between my thighs I thrilled to the sight of his spurting cock between Lady Lititia's lips. Creamy spunk dribbled from the corners of her mouth.

Then, a few moments later, she was beside me. 'I've brought you a gift,' she muttered, pressing her lips to mine. With her tongue she spooned the piquant jism into my mouth. Trembling, I felt I would swoon from the sheer lewdness of her act. We pulled Whistler down to us and kissed him fervently, in order to return to him, via lips and tongue, his own dulcet nectar.

Later, as the three of us reclined about the posing stand, Lady Lititia asked me about my Egyptian voyage. I told her of Tewfik Pasha. (I mentioned nothing of my current abode or of my association with Madame Kooshay.) She was intrigued and asked if she also might gain passage.

'As I mentioned,' she said, 'my husband's regiment is there. I've promised to join him but have been putting it off – ocean voyages are such a trial, you see. But this one sounds a treat. Perhaps you can arrange it. I can pay my way, of course.'

'I will try,' said I. 'I'm sure Tewfik Pasha will be delighted to have another young Englishwoman aboard. But as for paying your way, Litty, I presume he'll accept payment of a kind other than money. He seems to have more of that than he'll ever need – more, I suspect, than the Bank of England.'

'Oh, what a delight it will be to share such an exotic voyage with my dear, new-found friend!' She reached over to me, planting a kiss on my cheek.

'So,' said Whistler. 'My two fickle lovers are to sail off into the sunset with a greasy wog prince. What will I do?'

'Would you care to accompany us?' asked Lady Lititia.

'I would like to,' said he, 'but other matters detain me. I have commissions to fulfil and women whom I must periodically pleasure – a sworn responsibility. Such is the life of an artist.'

It was dawn when Whistler put me in a cab. On arrival at Madame Kooshay's, the hackman removed a large, flat, paper-wrapped package from the rack. 'This is yours, my lady,' he said. 'The gentleman asked me to help you in with it.'

With Madame Kooshay and a few of our late-sleeping ladies gathered round, I ripped the paper off. I was surprised to discover that it was not, as I had assumed, the unfinished painting of myself. Rather, it was 'Arrangements in Grey and Black'. A note was attached to the frame.

Dearest Miss Everleigh:

You have ruined this for me forever. Since you dubbed it 'Whistler's Mother', a most inane and inappropriate title, I will probably always think of it as such (much in the way that one sometimes finds it impossible to rid oneself of an offensive melody one has been humming for days and days).

There is another reason that I give it to you. As an artist I prefer my work, whenever possible, to fall into the hands of those I admire and respect. Such, of course, is a luxury afforded to us but rarely. One must earn what one can in order to live so that one may paint, and so on. People with the means to purchase art are seldom worthy of the privilege of owning it. (There exist, thank God, a few exceptions.)

So be it, dear Jenny.

I am aware, my love, that you peeked. I chanced to glance over my shoulder and saw you doing so. I was about to break my delightful connection with the ravishing Lady Lititia in order to reprimand you when, quite suddenly, I had second thoughts. First, it requires an act of will, of which I am barely capable, to remove oneself from the insistent clutch of such an exquisite shrine. And second, as I observed, you were standing, lost in the painting as if mesmerized by it. It seemed to me that you had been transported to a secret place deep within yourself. Despite myself, I am flattered.

Perhaps I overstate it. Suffice it to say that, though there are many definitions of the term 'art', there is one thing that most have in common: art causes us to see things anew. Few viewers of art (and certainly none of its jackal-like critics) are capable of this. You are. That, my pet, is one of the most complimentary things I am capable of saying to another human being – male or female.

I'm sure, as you unwrapped this, you expected to see the painting of which I speak. No, Jenny; that canvas is much too important to me. I can neither give it away nor sell it nor even, for the moment, expose it to public view. It is much easier for me to part with this one. In fact, I would sooner dispense with any one of my works rather than give up what I have titled 'Rhapsody in Blue' (except, perhaps, 'Falling Rocket' or 'Nocturne in Black and Gold').

And yet, I am unsure of what I have wrought. Perhaps I have attempted too much. The painting may never actually see the light of day. I may burn it – who knows? I have never had the experience of being unsuccessful. But nevertheless, for the moment, 'Rhapsody in Blue' stands as one of the three most important works of my career.

It is clear to me that you are a lady made, rather than born. This is to your credit. I know not how I came by this; perhaps something about you – a spoken phrase, a gesture – gave you away. But fear not, the secret is safe with me. As an American I believe strongly in hoisting oneself by one's bootstraps or, as in your case, by *whatever else comes to hand. As they say in my country, 'If you can't lick 'em, join 'em!'*

Your short presence in my life has been of more value to me than you can ever possibly know.

Bon Voyage—
James Abbott McNeill Whistler

Tewfik Pasha had agreed to postpone sailing for a few days on my behalf. He also agreed, through Madame Kooshay's request to Hassan, to consider an additional female passenger. After Hassan called on her and reported his findings to Tewfik Pasha, a formal invitation was handed to my new friend, Lady Lititia Faversham. Madame also agreed to store 'Whistler's Mother' until such time as I could retrieve it. It was hung in the main parlour, where, I was later told, it elicited many strong comments.

Finally, on the first of May, with my share of Tewfik Pasha's liberal payment safely deposited in my account in the Bank of England, I boarded the luxurious, 215-foot steam yacht, *Maratini*, along with my baggage – two steamer trunks and a host of hat boxes. Lady Lititia, having received, at my instigation, a formal invitation, was a few steps behind me on the gangplank. It was to be a most memorable voyage.

TWENTY ONE

The sea, when reasonably placid, is a medium not only for voyages to other lands, but is an equally ideal medium for extensive cruises into one's own mind. [J.E., 1889]

Less than a year had gone by since I, a virginal guttersnipe, penniless and ignorant in the ways of the world, had taken my first train ride. Now here I was on the private yacht of a future khedive of Egypt. In a short time I had become a sophisticated woman of the world. I had deposited the small fortune of fifteen hundred pounds sterling in the Bank of England and adopted the ways of my betters. I had hobnobbed with gentry and royalty and had been to bed with a few of the most glamorous and sought-after womanizers in London society. Now, sharing the rail with my friend Lady Lititia Faversham and a young gentleman named Freddy Harcourt (who described himself as an African explorer), I stood watching England disappear below the horizon and wondering what the next year would have in store. (If I had but known, I would have demanded the vessel turn about so that I might disembark safe and sound on Blighty's friendly and familiar shores. Or would I?)

The good ship *Maratini* was indeed luxurious. My quarters on the main deck consisted of a large cabin furnished with a four-poster bed, a bedside table, a chest, a dressing table, a chaise, an Oriental carpet, two curtained portholes and, wonder of wonders, a cunningly hidden water closet. The furnishings were new and of impeccable taste. There were three doors, one leading to the deck, a second to the corridor and a third, opening into Lady Lititia's cabin, which was just a trifle smaller than mine. Freddy Harcourt's quarters were just across the corridor on the port side.

The ship sported a dining salon complete with fireplace, wood-panelled walls and potted palms. The food was superb, more than worthy of its elegant setting. Quantity was the equal of quality and consisted of breakfast, lunch, high tea, dinner and a late supper. I had never before experienced the pleasures of French cuisine and stood in awe of its delicacy, its subtle nuance of flavour and texture. Responsible for this magnificence was ship's cook, a talented young chef named Auguste Escoffier – a genius – late of the Reine Blanche in Paris. Auguste took a fancy to me, allowing me the liberty whenever I chose to visit his large, well-equipped galley. By observing, listening and on a few occasions, actually preparing food under his tutelage, I became, myself, an accomplished practitioner of the culinary art.

There was also a cosy, well-stocked library and a comfortable public salon. Weather permitting, an awninged portion of the afterdeck served as an outdoor lounge and *al fresco* dining area. There were lounging chaises everywhere.

A small orchestra played for meals and for occasional evening entertainments or *dansants* on deck. On Sundays there were concerts, favouring the likes of Mozart and Corelli. Quite often, as we entered semi-tropical waters, these same musicians, varying their instruments and dress styles from formal black tie to jilaba and fez, would also play Arabian music, accompanying exotic Arabian female dancers from Tewfik Pasha's shipboard harem.

In addition to myself and my friend, Lady Lititia Faversham, and the aforementioned Freddy Harcourt, the passenger list included: Mademoiselle Gisselle Fondeaux, an enigmatic young Parisian of awesome beauty; Miss Lilly Roundtree, an American actress of indeterminate age, who, as her Christian name implied, was indeed a rounded individual (pleasantly so, in both personality and physiognomy); Dr Jordan Freemantle, a tall, hawklike surgeon in his mid-thirties, on his way to join Chinese Gordon's staff in Khartoum; Major Bertram Sedgewick, a portly gentleman well into his fifties who acted as Tewfik Pasha's military and political adviser-tutor; Mrs Sarah Sedgewick, the major's wife, a large-breasted bird of brilliant plumage, also in her fifties but much better preserved than her husband; and Eva and Gunther von Seydlitz, a perfectly matched pair of blond, blue-eyed, lean beings, who seemed Teutonic gods. (Gunther was a handsome, if somewhat severe-looking gentleman of about thirty-five years. Eva, roughly five years younger, was beautiful in a cold and stately fashion. Both, unlike the others aboard the *Maratini*, seemed to be totally lacking in humour.)

Each of the passengers was provided with a private steward. Mine was Haki, a Turkish boy about sixteen who dressed constantly in crisp white livery topped with an ever-present fez that I began to assume was somehow attached permanently to his skull. Haki was to serve me faithfully, night and day, as butler, waiter, messenger, launderer, lady's maid and devoted teacher of Arabic. He himself spoke passable, if somewhat humorously phrased English.

Ship's crew consisted of about twenty men headed by Captain DiCosta, a portly Spanish gentleman somewhat along in years who sported a large mustache and a flamboyant manner. Below deck, three large cabins housed the seagoing contingent of Tewfik Pasha's harem: nine Oriental ladies who were never seen without their veils, except on those festive ocasions when they were naked. (Have no fear, dear reader, I will deal with them, shortly.) Tewfik Pasha and his aide, Mr Hassan, occupied a luxurious suite housed in a separate cabin, amidships.

Mine host (or shoud I say, my client?) presented himself at

dinner on the first day out. He seemed a much younger and less formidable man than when I had first met him at the ball. (I guessed Tewfik Pasha to have a half-dozen years to live before he reached thirty.) Dark, somewhat vacant eyes peered questioningly out of a pleasant, if vacuous, face decorated with a prominent beak and black whiskers. It was an almost perfect oval of a face, topped with a jaunty red fez. His outer dress, even in the hottest climes, consisted of a peculiar black frock coat known throughout the Near East as a Stambouli. At times, particularly when seated crosslegged on a divan, he had the appearance of a shiny black crow. Despite this, he seemed to me now a young European gentleman, play-acting the role of an Oriental.

'Ah, Miss Everleigh.' He smiled broadly, coming awkwardly to his feet with the other gentlemen as Lady Lititia and I arrived at the table. 'You are even more beautiful than I remember.' He took my hand, pressing it to his lips.

'Thank you, Your Majesty,' said I. 'And may I present my companion, Lady Lititia Faversham?' I turned to Litty who curtsied charmingly, extending her hand.

'You are, madam, yet another jewel of that sceptred isle.' He kissed her hand.

Tewfik Pasha introduced us to our fellow passengers. When the wine had been poured, he stood with the other men for a toast. 'Gentlemen,' he said, in his lisping, French-accented English. 'To the ladies. We are fortunate indeed, to be surrounded by the most charming and beautiful of all the women of four nations: Britain, France, Prussia and America.'

As the toast was drunk, the small orchestra, tucked away in the midst of a forest of potted palms, broke into spirited renditions of all four national anthems. It was a most gracious and stirring gesture on the part of this strange young man, who would soon be ruling, with Ottoman acquiescence and British help, the most ancient of countries.

Finally seated, Tewfik Pasha said, 'As you know, the ceremony celebrating the opening of De Lessep's canal is to be held shortly. As some of you are aware, the *Maratini* is scheduled to arrive at Suez in time for us to participate in the grand flotilla. A French dreadnaught bearing the Empress Eugénie will lead the fleet. Next in line, aboard the royal yacht *Mahrousa*, will be my father, the Khedive. He will be followed by the Prince of Wales aboard HMS *Illustrious* and then the Crown Prince of Austria-Hungary aboard his imperial yacht. The *Maratini* will be fifth in line; following her will be at least fifty ships bearing a host of crowned heads and important dignitaries. You are, of course, all invited to take part in these ceremonies as the *Maratini* becomes the fifth ship to pass through the new Suez Canal.'

Distracted by the pleasant possibility of seeing Edward again, I sipped my wine, paying little attention to the appreciative comments flying back and forth across the table. The fact that the Prince of Wales was to be in Egypt I found an exciting prospect indeed. Perhaps, through Tewfik Pasha's good offices, I might get word to him of my presence.

Our dinner conversation consisted of small talk. Over a dessert course of petit fours and, wonder of wonders, iced glacé and fresh strawberries, the conversation became somewhat less tedious.

'And you, sir,' said Dr Freemantle, turning to Freddy Harcourt, 'what is your purpose in visiting the Near East?'

Young Freddy Harcourt who, up till now, had little to say seemed momentarily flustered. He was rescued by our gracious host.

'Mr Harcourt is displaying undue modesty,' said Tewfik Pasha. 'He has actually expressed a strong desire to devote his efforts to exposing our dark continent to the light of day.'

'An explorer,' said Sarah Sedgewick. 'How exciting!'

'Yes, quite,' said Harcourt brightly, suddenly pleased to be the object of female interest. 'Thank you, madam. . . .'

'I would just love to hear of some of your exploits!' Miss

Lilly Roundtree spoke in breathless tones, affecting the peculiar accent I was to find favoured, for reason beyond my understanding, by most Americans. 'Please tell us!'

'Well, I'm afraid there aren't any exploits to speak of at the moment,' said Freddy Harcourt, his tones tentative, hesitant, as if he were momentarily expecting news of a personal exploit he might pass on to us. 'You see,' he went on, 'I'm what you might call a new fellow at the game and I'm at a loss now that Speke's discovery of the Nile source has been confirmed by that chap Stanley.'

'Well,' said Freemantle, 'there is still much to discover.'

'There remains the River Congo,' said Major Sedgewick. 'A most important undertaking. Whoever explores it will fill in the remaining blank spaces on the map of Africa. And then, too, there are places other than Africa where many geographic mysteries wait to be resolved – the Amazon Basin, for example, and a good deal of the Pacific.'

'Perhaps, Mr Harcourt,' said Herr Gunther von Seydlitz. 'You might visit Mecca. Few Christians have done so.'

Tewfik Pasha smiled ruefully. 'It is my duty as a Moslem, dear Doctor, to tell you that such an intrusion would be considered blasphemy.'

'Then I would suggest that Mr Harcourt convert to Islam,' said Major Sedgewick, chuckling.

'Egad!' said an unthinking Freddy Harcourt. 'I'd jolly well rather be dead!'

'Ah,' said a most diplomatic Tewfik Pasha, 'but I do believe we bore the ladies.'

I was not the least bit bored. I found such talk stimulating, despite the fact that I had concluded Freddy Harcourt to be a bit of a ninny – unimaginative, uncreative and certainly not intellectual. One would assume an African explorer to require quite the opposite by way of attributes. Harcourt's calling would seem more properly to have been politics or the army.

Tewfik Pasha clapped his hands and, in seconds, a steward appeared with cigars. As proper ladies should, we females retired to the lounge, leaving the gentlemen to their cigars and 'boring' conversation.

Later that evening, Major and Mrs Sedgewick taught Litty and me a new card game. It was based on whist but was much more sophisticated. He called it 'auction bridge' and explained that it was originally a Near Eastern game but that it had become quite popular with the Indian Army in which he had served many years before. It had been a long day. Before going to bed, Litty and I spent an hour on the open deck lost in contemplation of the thousand blue-white diamonds that was the moon's fragmented reflection in our wake. Off to the east, we could see the wistful lights of the city of Brest.

We spoke of our fellow passengers, wondering as to the common denominator among us. We suspected that Tewfik Pasha had applied some specific criteria for assembling such an otherwise varied group. The puzzle, such as it was, defied our attempts at solution. We were, as it turned out, soon to have the answer.

In the morning, as the *Maratini* knifed its way through the choppy waters of the Bay of Biscay, I repaired to the library, where for a few hours I perused Tewfik Pasha's collection of French and English first editions. I found myself lost in *The Celebrated Jumping Frog of Calaveras County*, a book of humorous stories and sketches by an American calling himself Mark Twain. I was about to leave with the book under my arm, when, inadvertently, my shoulder brushed against a corner of one of the shelves. It must have released a hidden spring of some sort, as suddenly a portion of the bookcase began to revolve. Before my startled eyes, the magical transformation revealed a completely different set of volumes.

A strange collection of roughly a hundred titles presented themselves, among them: *The Vice* by Sir Richard Burton; *The Freelovers* by William Breedlove; *The Lustful*

Turk by Anonymous; *Pleasures and Follies* by Restif de la Bretonne; *The Merry Adventures of Lord Roxboro* by Sir Walter Bone; *The Autobiography of a Flea* by Anonymous; *Histoire de Juliette*, a six-volume boxed set in French by the Marquis de Sade; *Dark Hunger* by James A. Test; *Abandon* by Bernhardt von Soda; *Lust* by Count Palmiro Vicaron.

Fascinated, I chose a book at random as a companion to my previous choice. Then I set about searching for the secret mechanism that might revert the bookcase to its previous, more conventional aspect. Five minutes of effort proved to no avail. With a shrug, I gave up and left the library to choose a comfortable, sunlit lounging chaise on the port deck.

Stretched out under a light blanket provided by the faithful Haki, I thumbed through both volumes. In addition to the marvellous Mark Twain, I had chosen a book titled *Memoirs of a Russian Princess*. It was a small volume, exquisitely bound in gold-embossed Moroccan leather. There was no mention of the author. The introduction spoke of the book as having been edited from an actual diary kept by Princess Vavara and deposited, along with other family papers, into the keeping of the chief librarian of the Russian State Depository.

Fascinated by the quality of the prose and the seeming historical accuracy, I read:

The period when the events of which I write happened was after the close of the reign of Catherine II, and while her son, Paul, having succeeded that most dissolute of sovereigns, allowed his court, already contaminated by the open profligacy of his mother, to wallow in the unrestrained vices she had inculcated. The date was 1796–7.

If, reader, you wish a few words to summarize the manners of the court of Russia during the reign of Catherine II, read the following passage from an Imperial historian: 'We do not believe,' he writes, 'that the history of any other people presents in modern times, a more complete and more odious picture of immorality than that of the Russian people during the reign of the all-too-famous Catherine. The abominations of a Tiberius, the debaucheries of a Heliogabalus, all the impure traditions of degenerate and degraded Rome, do not strike the imagination with more astonishment. St Petersburg had become a second Babylon, aye, ten thousand times worse than Babylon in the unrestrained excesses in which each and every class of its inhabitants, court nobles and people, regardless of social status, plunged and indulged . . . instigated by the fatal example of this much flattered Czarina.'

Intrigued, I read on. Princess Vavara Sofia was the daughter and only child of Prince Demetri, one of the greatest and richest boyars of the empire. The author went on to remind his reader that as a Russian girl of fourteen, she was advanced as an Englishwoman five years her senior.

Delightful, thought I. Exciting adventures must lie ahead. I was not to be disappointed. The story developed quickly. Princess Vavara was beautiful, an accomplished linguist in four languages, a superior horsewoman and well versed in 'all the fashionable trivialities which go to complete a cultured finish for the *grande mode*.'

Comfortably ensconced in my lounge chair, warmed by the sun, I read of secret Russian history, of Princess Vavara's deflowering, her early liaisons, her increasing appetite for debauchery along with her maid and confidant, Proscovia.

I had never dreamed that such writings existed. The lewd, descriptive phrases, the lascivious action and tempestuous feelings were delineated in scarlet prose equal to the best of English literature. Breathless with anticipation, I turned page after page, growing more randy with each.

. . . A general calm succeeded the violence of the orgy. The little Olivette, attended to by Proscovia, who supplied all present with a liberal libation of wine and sweetmeats, revived under the attention she received. The Princess enjoyed the period of well-merited repose. The fair Georgette had so far escaped the salacious attention of the group. She could not hope long to continue so fortunate. The Princess herself ran wanton hands over all the charms of the pretty girl and finally insisted on placing her, naked, between the knees of Faddaye.

'My dear Faddaye,' she said. 'Here is food for thy lust and more to spare. See these exquisite breasts, how firm are the nipples, this belly white and rounded. Ah! Behold these loins, graceful and supple. The exquisite contour round these swelling hips, this moss-covered mound of Venus. Ah, how lovely, and 'tis yours.'

Meantime the wrestler had drawn the beautiful Georgette toward him and had impudently placed his redoubtable member in her delicate hands. Refreshed by the repose, warmed by the wine and the provoking nature of the young girl's charms, he gave the reins to his desire and commenced to run his hands freely over her body. As his huge limb regained its full dimension in Georgette's tentative grasp, its formidable character became apparent.

'Put both of your little hands upon it, Georgette,' cried the Princess. 'Do you not see that there is room on that purple gland for both your palms to play?'

Polskivitch, following the other's example, seized the trembling Olivette and, subjecting her to his lewd caresses, appeared equally inclined to renew his pleasures. But now, Faddaye was no longer content just to let Georgette continue her indecent touches. Notwithstanding her evident repugnance, he insisted on her taking the flaming crescent of his massive instrument between her red lips and then pushing as much of it into her mouth as he could without choking her. He allowed himself this wanton pleasure at his ease. Vavara only encouraged his conduct.

Indeed, it seemed as if the Princess took delight in further exciting the brutal moujik to the extreme of her ability. 'Place your hands on her buttocks, Faddaye, you dog; you have never felt such skin before; it is satin! The girl is made for an emperor and she is in your grip! Those thighs! Those legs!'

I glanced up from my reading, suddenly aware that, as if of its own volition, my hand had crept secretly to the core of my growing lust. Beneath the blanket, my fingers were pressing avidly into the juncture of my thighs. Despite layers of clothing, I was aware of a voluptuous lubrication. Sighing deeply, I closed my eyes.

Ah, thought I, Princess Vavara was really a woman after my own heart! I could visualize her encouraging the moujik, Faddaye, to have his way with Georgette. Those thighs! Those legs! That white, rounded belly! Those firm, pink nipples! And Polskivitch's massive cock about to enter the receptive quim of the passionate Olivette!

Rubbing even more vigorously, I provoked the tingling sensation into exquisite flutters and voluptuous quivers. I had to read on! Perhaps I could manage the book with one hand while with the other . . . I felt a presence nearby! I could hear heavy breathing, the rustling of clothing. My eyes opened abruptly. There before me stood Mrs Sedgewick! I stilled my hand abruptly.

'Good morning, Miss Everleigh.' She smiled sweetly. 'The sea air is most invigorating.'

'Good morning,' said I, wondering if she'd seen my hand moving about under the blanket.

'A most invigorating morning.'

'Indeed.' The obvious double-entendre brought a flush of mortification to my cheeks.

She asked, 'May I join you?' Before I could answer, she seated herself in the adjoining chaise. 'I assume you're enjoying the book.'

'Yes,' said I, wishing I were somewhere else. 'It's most

educational – about Russia a hundred years ago. I take keen pleasure in reading history.' I heard my voice trail off in embarrassment.

'One can see,' said Mrs Sedgewick, 'that you are a well-educated young lady.' She reached over to pat my hands, both of which were now above the blanket. 'The trials and triumphs of Princess Vavara come as a revelation to an intelligent woman privileged to read of them.'

'Ah, then, you've read it . . .'

'More than that, my dear; my husband, the major, wrote it.'

My astonishment must have been obvious. Mrs Sedgewick laughed, then in kindly, disarming tones, said, 'Perhaps I might tell you all about it over a nice cup of tea.' She squeezed my hand affectionately.

'That would be lovely,' said I, warming to the twinkle in her eye.

'It is best if we have it in my cabin,' said she. 'They're readying the dining salon for lunch at the moment and the gentlemen have taken over the lounge with their morning cigars.'

'Lovely,' I repeated. She seemed to be a most interesting woman.

TWENTY TWO

Consider that the average middle-class woman of my generation suffered, for her entire lifetime, a total ignorance of her intimate geography and plumbing. Poor dear. [J.E., 1919]

The cabin accommodations that Mrs Sedgewick shared with her husband were larger and more luxurious than my own, being second only, I was to discover, to Tewfik Pasha's. There was a sitting room, of respectable size, fitted out elegantly with French furniture and a modestly sized bed chamber. A small compartment accommodated a water closet, sink and a bathtub that could be filled with fresh water piped up from the *Maratini's* boiler. All of this on shipboard! Would there be no end to the wonders of science?

'Perhaps, Miss Everleigh,' said she, waving me into a comfortable settee, 'you might prefer something a trifle more stimulating than tea?'

Said I, 'Isn't it a bit early in the day . . .?'

'You'll find, dear Jenny . . . may I call you Jenny?'

'Please do.'

'And I am Sarah.' She smiled sweetly. 'As I was about to say – you will find that when at sea, such social inhibitions as relating to the consumption of *spiritus fermenti* – as my husband calls it – disappear on the second or third day. It is one of the joys of ocean-voyaging. But, if you prefer tea, I've naught but to ring for it.'

'Since it is now our second day at sea,' said I, happily entering into the spirit of things, 'it's in for a penny, in for a pound and may the nautical spirit prevail.'

Mrs Sedgewick laughed. 'You are not only beautiful beyond measure, but you possess a jolly disposition. And because I value both attributes highly, I am going to concoct a very special treat for us.' She crossed to the far corner of the cabin where stood a small commode graced with bottles of various shapes and sizes. 'Gin,' she said. 'It's important it be British, not Dutch, otherwise the magic elixir will taste like fish.' Taking one of the bottles in hand, she uncorked it to pour a good-sized portion into an ornate crock. 'One must always use glass or crockery, never silver or base metal such as would impart a foreign flavour. This is a drink easily subject to contamination.'

A second, larger bottle was uncorked. She turned to me, a serious expression replacing her smile. 'French wine, dear Jenny, in this case quite dry – as opposed to sweet.' Intently, as if she were an alchemist mixing a secret potion, she held both crock and wine bottle at eye level where, with great care, she poured a small amount. 'The perfect mixture is about one part in five. It takes some skill, but in a little while one can become quite adept at getting it just right.' She swirled the crock thrice one way and then thrice the other, in an effort, I assumed, to blend the two liquids. Quietly, as if fearing to awaken someone, she whispered, 'One must not bruise the gin.' I found myself fascinated by the studied intensity of the ritual. It was, after all, just a drink.

'Never mix it any other way and never for longer than three turns in each direction. Above the equator one must begin with a clockwise motion; below the equator, counter-clockwise.'

Smiling at the idea, I asked, 'If one does otherwise, will it explode?'

Mrs Sedgewick, echoing my smile, looked up at me. 'Hardly, Jenny. But it has a like effect when one drinks it, as you shall soon see.' She filled two glasses and handed me one.

'This libation,' said she, 'is a serious discovery of my husband's. He maintains, and I agree, that it is the equal of any invention of this century or the last, including the steam engine of James Watt, the cotton gin of Eli Whitney and even the Polonaise tunis of Frederick Worth.' She raised her glass. 'To the Queen.'

'To the Queen,' I echoed.

Mrs Sedgewick watched closely as I took an initial sip. It was unlike anything that had ever passed my lips, causing a perceivable shudder to pass through my body.

'Courage, Jenny,' said Mrs Sedgewick. 'Like all things unusual and worthwhile, it is an acquired taste.'

'I'm sure,' said I, grimacing. 'What is it called?'

'Sedgewick's ambrosia,' said she, sipping happily. 'The major deciphered its formula from an ancient Babylonian tablet. It is, we have found, a specific for melancholia and gout. It may even have some therapeutic value as a cure for plague. But most important is its ability to instil in one a sense of well-being. In modest quantities, it has also been known to inflame the carnal passions.'

Once more I raised the glass to my lips. The concoction seemed to improve somewhat with the second swallow – even more so with the third, which soon followed. I sipped, beginning actually to savour the taste.

'I have,' said Mrs Sedgewick, 'suggested to my husband that he bottle it. It could be our fortune, but he nevertheless resists the idea. He insists that both the gentry and common people of the world are undeserving of the gift. Perhaps in the next century . . .'

'Twas true, as my hostess had pointed out, that Sedgewick's ambrosia contributed to well-being. Mine was improving, in quick measure, with each sip. I said, 'One grows accustomed.'

'Indeed,' said Mrs Sedgewick.

We emptied the crock. My hostess sat across from me in

a high-back chair and spoke of the sea. This was, she explained, her third cruise aboard the *Maratini*. I studied her carefully, aware of her tone of voice, her charming manner. She was at least twice my age, older than my mother would have been had she lived. Yet she didn't seem so. She possessed a vitality and optimistic point of view that gave the lie to chronology. Would I be so at her age?

I soon found that my usual, proper posture had somehow transformed itself into a sprawl. Mrs Sedgewick smiled sweetly. She knelt by the settee and reached up to remove my shoes. 'You might be more comfortable without these my dear . . . and perhaps a pillow.'

Soon I was reclining more gracefully, a comfortable pillow under my head. 'Ah, thank you, Mrs Sedgewick,' said I, amused by the fact that the cabin was revolving slowly about its axis. Another invention of the Major's?

Mrs Sedgewick asked, 'Would you like me to read aloud to you?'

'Oh, yes,' said I. 'I love being read to.' Reggie had read to me . . . Milton, Keats, Wordsworth, Poe . . . She seated herself on the floor next to the chaise. 'I see you have marked your place.'

'My place?'

'In *Memoirs of a Russian Princess*.'

I had forgotten. Once again I flushed under Mrs Sedgewick's eyes. Before I could demur out of embarrassment, she began to read in a warm and liquid voice:

The face of the wrestler grew scarlet with lewd desire, his immense parts at their full distention. Raising the head of the young Georgette, he joined his thick lips to hers and thrust his tongue into her mouth. The whole time, he kept his eye on his mistress, Princess Vavara, as if demanding permission to go further. His belly rubbed Georgette's as his stiff limb was inserted between her thighs.

The Princess held in either hand a member. That of the

young Alaska throbbed once again in her left whilst the weapon of Moditzki filled her right. In this position, Vavara looked on the proceedings between Faddaye and Georgette. She knew Faddaye was seething with desire to enjoy Georgette but that he was loathe to give offense to herself, the giver of largesse. Princess Vavara hastened to reasure him.

'You will enjoy her, Faddaye; you shall lie with her and enter her body. Your parts shall know the innermost recesses of her hidden charms. Take her, strong one! Spread her white thighs! The lewd road to paradise is open to you. Enter and find joy!'

Mrs Sedgewick had ceased reading. I glanced down, my heart fluttering, to find her eyes on mine.

'What are your thoughts, Jenny?'

'It is so true to life,' said I.

'Does it make you randy?'

'Indeed,' said I, feeling the heat of her hand on my naked ankle.

I closed my eyes, seeing before me the torrid scene taking place in the St Petersburg palace. Mrs Sedgewick read on:

. . . her naked form. The maid, Proscovia, assisted him, opening Georgette's thighs, placing his huge limb in position.

Georgette, although not quite a virgin, quailed before the attack. With desperate lunges, the wrestler attempted to overcome her delicate resistance. Fortunately, Dame Nature herself had conspired to assist him, as the salacious, though unacknowledged, preliminaries in which she had been engaged had caused a creamy moisture to pervade her parts. Taking advantage of this lubrication, the assailant was soon buried to its full length.

A sigh, half of agony, half of ecstasy, arose from Georgette as she felt herself pierced by the fierce weapon. The wrestler, relishing the tight conjunction of their bodies, now commenced the luxurious game of love.

Mrs Sedgewick's hand made its way under my skirt, advancing slowly from ankle to calf. Delicate fingers massaged the sensitive flesh. It was most pleasant, though I wondered briefly how she was turning the pages.

The sight was too much for Princess Vavara. She put her tongue into Moditzki's mouth and, sucking kisses in this fashion, bade him enjoy her.

Seating him upon the couch, she straddled him and received to her womb the sturdy limb. Whispering to Alaska, she directed him to occupy himself with her bottom. He, not altogether a novice at such joys, nor for the first time to sound this forbidden route, hastened to comply.

'Enter only the portal, loved one,' murmured the Princess. She turned her head to speak more intimately to the excited boy whose weapon, ever ready, now pressed against the narrow entrance. 'Let but the glans go through.'

'I am there, but I can scarcely restrain myself from pushing right up.'

'Feel now, my darling. I work for you – I can hardly support two such champions. I do my best – there – feel – Heavens! What sensations!'

'Ah, you clutch me and I can feel him on the other side!'

My body warmed to Mrs Sedgewick's reading. A voluptuous craving had established itself at the juncture of my thighs, the tips of my breasts, the back of my neck. I opened my eyes to glance down at her. Though she read on, her eyes were closed, as was the book which lay at her feet! She knew Vavara's story by rote! Her hands, unoccupied in the literary sense, were busy elsewhere. One was beneath her skirt. I could see lewd movements under the fabric. The other was busy climbing my leg and had reached the bare flesh of my thigh. I was moist, open like a dew-drenched flower to whatever was to come. I stretched my body in languid anticipation as her voice, now husky and breathy, continued with the salacious adventures of the long-ago princess.

'I feel your pressures now, my Queen,' cried Alaska. 'I feel your muscles back here gripping me with delicious spasms. Ah! My Vavara, what pleasure! The head, the shoulders are within – in the secret sheath – the rest is without. But it matters not, the delight is communicated throughout all.'

Mrs Sedgewick's strolling fingers had reached the silken garden that was their destination. She broke off the story in mid-sentence. 'You wear nothing beneath your skirt,' she whispered. 'Naked under your clothes . . . how charming.'

'The better to be ventilated by cool sea air,' said I.

'You are indeed a naughty nautical,' said she, flitting happily through my grotto with prancing digits. 'You have a lovely puss.'

'And you, Sarah, have lovely fingers.' I spread my legs to allow her easier access. A quick glance confirmed she was diddling both of us. 'But pray,' I said, closing my eyes and attempting to control my breathing, 'continue . . .'

The young Princess was thus between the two and they were neither of them mean champions. The moujik Moditzki had never known such pleasure as provided by the beautiful body that rose and fell upon him. He met each movement halfway as the close, tight pressure excited him into a furious mania of pleasure. He was fast approaching the point of madness!

It was too soon for the wanton Princess. She attempted to still her movements, but in seconds the moujik, with a low wail of rapture, discharged deep within her.

At this very moment the amorous conflict of Faddaye with the beautiful Georgette reached its crisis and . . .

Mrs Sedgewick was applying light thumb pressure to the base of my love button while her fingers ran the length of my quivering pussy. I sighed with pleasure as she inserted a fingertip and moved it about as if stirring sugar in a tiny teacup.

She let off the story of Vavara to say in dulcet tones, 'Ah, Jenny, you like that, don't you?'

'Heaven,' said I.

The finger was replaced by two in tandem. She thrust them in to their full length. 'And this?'

'Ohhh yes . . . fuck me, dearest Sarah . . .'

Sarah Sedgewick hooked her fingers upward to find the secret spot. She moved them in a slow, delicious orbit. 'Tell me, Jenny . . .'

'As if I have to pee,' said I, gasping ecstatically. 'But more than that, much more. I feel I have a second clit – inside.' I shuddered. 'Ah, 'tis lovely . . . lovely . . .'

'Mmm, lovely, indeed.'

. . .Faddaye and the beautiful Georgette reached their crisis together. She lay, only half conscious, deluged with the evidence of his vigorous manhood. Meanwhile, Polskivitch laboured with all the frenzy of complete possession to finish the business for the pretty Olivette.

The Princess, her senses gratified, heard all, saw all. The cries of the ravished Georgette were music to her ears and now the groans and sobs of ecstasy from little Olivette were no less sweet.

Alaska held his place. Careful to comply with the desires of his mistress, he abstained from exerting force and remained as he had declared, lodged within the portals. Soon though, the frantic movements made by his mistress whilst receiving the hot injection of Moditzki in the adjacent sheath, produced so much excitement upon his sensitive parts that he felt his discharge about to come forth. Finally, unable to control himself, he buried his weapon with one determined lunge into the bowels of the Princess, inundating them with the proofs of his vigour.

The couple, now detached from their amorous embraces, gathered round to witness the completion of Polskivich's ravishment of Olivette. He was at the height of . . .

Sarah Sedgewick's voice trailed off in a sob. With lascivious intensity, she masturbated both of us. I squirmed in rapture as the older woman's machinations beneath our skirts grew more heated. Our clothing did little to conceal the rhythmic squishing sounds. Finally, our spending was joyously simultaneous.

I lay back, allowing a calm to pervade my heated loins as Sarah, her right hand from under her skirt, presented me with her wet fingers. I licked, then sucked avidly, intoxicated with a spicy bouquet. Then, with three fingers bunched together as a miniature cock, she fucked my mouth as I opened my eyes to stare amorously into hers. I noted with lewd pleasure that she, in turn, was sucking on the fingers of her left hand, fingers sodden with my own cuntal syrup.

She asked in languished tones, 'Did you enjoy the story?'

'Oh, yes. 'Twas a lovely tale. I must read on.'

She stood. 'I have a marvellous toy to show you.'

I watched as she crossed the cabin to return with a small hand-carved wooden box. She slid the top back to reveal, lying cosily on a bed of blue velvet, an exquisite reproduction of a fully erect penis. She removed it and laid it in my hand. Had my eyes been closed I would not have suspected it to be anything but authentic! An amazing replica! It was cunningly perfect in every detail: the fine tracery of veins, the swollen aspect of its bulbous helmet, the fleshy creases gone taut with erection. Of healthy size, it seemed to have been constructed of a kind of India rubber.

I toyed with it for a few moments as Sarah, beaming, looked on. Then, removing a key from a separate compartment in the box, she inserted it into an opening on the blunt end. As I held the instrument steady, she wound the key.

Said she, 'This is yet another invention from the major's fertile brain.' She finished winding, then pulled the metal key from its socket.

'Good Lord,' said I, intrigued, yet naive of its function. 'What does it do?'

'Ah, dearest Jenny, you shall soon know. Lie back and close your eyes.'

I did as told. Once again she reached under my skirt. I spread my legs to ease the access. Suddenly, I was startled by a buzzing sound and an instant later was subjected to a wildfire of cuntal sensations I had never dreamed could be! The lewd machine, in contact with the sensitive flesh of my quim, was vibrating at a furious rate! Each fervent pulse was transmitting itself to suddenly tempestuous parts! In just seconds I was close to spending again! Then, quickly, Sarah manipulated the weird dildoe, inserting it with a single thrust into my gushing cunt! My body palpitated wildly – shook uncontrollably – almost tossing me from the settee! I was being ravished by a miraculous fucking machine!

The sound of a male voice caused me to open my eyes. Sarah was gone from the settee. She was at the door greeting her husband. Major Sedgewick stood there, his eyes on me, his face alight with what I took to be a most lustful grin. Under my skirt, the lewd machine, buried to the hilt, buzzed on.

The major's voice boomed. 'Aha! Surely, what I hear must be the amorous buzz of mechanical fuckery!'

As the major and his wife looked on, I once again approached orgasm. I cared neither for modesty nor for any other demure emotion. My only thoughts were of the uncanny vibrations, throbbings and palpitations that were racing madly from the tempestuous core to every part of my body! I was fast approaching the pinnacle!

Dimly, I heard Sarah Sedgewick's voice. 'Will she cum before the spring runs down?'

'If not,' said the major, 'we will simply rewind it so that

she may continue. Soon I will have perfected my steam-powered dildoe – 'twill run continuously for hours . . . but for now . . .'

With an explosive series of groans and squeals, I spent gloriously. Moments later the machine died as if it, too, had climaxed.

'Good morning, Miss Everleigh', said the major. I opened my eyes to find him looming over me. 'Good morning, sir,' I said breathlessly.

'I'm pleased that you've made such excellent use of my little toy.'

'You should be knighted for it!'

'Indeed, I should,' said the major. 'I have wrought a miracle in a century of miracles. Steamships, iron bridges, rifled canon, railways, Bessemer steel and the Sedgewick Patented Clockwork Vibracock!' He watched intently as his wife reached under my skirt to retrieve his marvellous device. It made a squishing sound punctuated with a barely perceptible 'pop' as, redolent with my juices, it was withdrawn. Sarah held it aloft, under the major's nose.

'Ambrosia,' he said, sniffing. 'A rare vintage.'

'Thank you,' said I.

'I am driven, my dear Miss Everleigh,' said he, 'to seek the source!'

With that, the major grasped both my ankles, lifting so that his wife might raise my skirt. This she did, folding it over my head. My legs were spread and suddenly the major's eager face was between them, his immense tongue lapping the full length of my labia. Blindly, I wrapped my thighs around his neck, locking his head deliciously in my gushing love-grotto. Snakelike, his tongue entered me.

'Suck her!' cried Sarah.

'*Mmmphhh*!' answered the major.

After minutes, during which I felt I might spend again, he fought his way loose from my grappling legs. He pulled the skirt from my face, then kissed me, greeting my tongue with his. 'Fuck,' he said into my open mouth. He stood abruptly, allowing Mrs Sedgewick to open his trousers.

He pego was enormous: a fat sausage capped with a monstrous purple rotundity. Sarah had hold of the intrepid shaft at its base; I grasped the upper part. The bulbous mushroom remained free, growing out of my clasping hand. Monstrous!

'I want it,' said I. 'I want it inside me!'

'And you shall have it, my dear,' said Sarah. 'Never fear.'

Once again my ankles were grasped, this time by Sarah, who pulled my legs back till the knees rested on my shoulders.

'Fuck!' she said, watching the major grasp his prick as if it were a club.

Almost overwhelmed by the sight, I stared, unblinking, as he inserted the bulbous head into my oozing orifice. Doubled up as I was, my eyes were less than a foot from the swell of my groin.

'Fuck her!' cried Mrs Sedgewick.

'Fuck me!' I attempted to lunge upward, to swallow him in one lustful thrust. But I was immobile, doubled over, locked in place, my cunt a gaping offering! I watched mesmerized as just inches away his corpulent cock sunk, inch by inch, into my body.

Soon I had him to the hilt, his heavy bollocks resting on my nether cheeks. Sarah Sedgewick released my legs, allowing me to wrap them over the major's shoulders. With no preliminaries, he began, with brute force, to thrust his awful machine in and out. Like the crack of a pistol, each downward plunge slapped his thighs against my buttocks; he pounded me, stretched me, filled me with surging, rockhard, male flesh!

I managed now to move my bottom in sensuous orbit about his pistoning tool. The pressure built; I was filled to bursting.

Mrs Sedgewick, with her skirt raised, stood just inches away. She had wound up the patented Clockwork Vibracock and was masturbating with it.

'Cunt!' groaned Major Sedgewick.

'Cock!' I gasped.

'Fuck!' cried Mrs Sedgewick.

The three of us spent within seconds of one another. I gloried in the feel of the major's cock when, after a series of tempestuous spasms, it exploded, spurting spunk deep within me.

Twenty minutes later I was in my cabin, taking my first lesson in Arabic from Haki. It was a language, he assured me, that despite (or perhaps because of) its imprecision, was more than any other a language for lovers.

I took my lunch in my cabin, then napped till tea time. It had been a most exhilarating morning.

That evening I described my adventure with the Sedgewicks to my friend Lady Lititia. Litty was delighted with my good fortune. She asked many questions, particularly about the major's invention, the Clockwork Vibracock.

She, too, had been involved in an adventure – a tête-à-tête with Captain DiCosta in his cabin. 'A most invigorating afternoon,' said Litty. 'The captain is indeed a mad Spaniard. Bedding him is much like doing a music-hall turn with a contortionist!'

'Sounds a delight,' said I.

'Indeed. But if you should try him, beware; your body will ache long afterwards.' She winced at the thought.

I placed my hand on her shoulder. 'Perhaps I should ask Haki to give you a nice massage.'

'Ah, your boy gives massages?'

'Well, not yet, but surely we can teach him.'

We both laughed. We were leaning on the rail, amidships, gazing at a beautiful sunset. Lititia turned to me, a serious look on her face. 'I have been meaning to ask you a question, Jenny,' said she.

'Yes?' asked I, curiously.

'What do you intend to do when you get to Egypt?'

It was a question I hadn't yet asked myself. I replied, 'I've not given it much thought. I'll probably book return passage immediately.'

'You mean, you'll have come all that way just for the ocean voyage?'

I looked away from her at the spectacular sunset colours reflected in a long pathway on the calm surface of the sea: a thousand variants of scarlet, russet and gold. To answer her question truthfully would require an explanation of my background – Madame Kooshay, Reggie, all of it. Dare I expose myself to my new friend?

She said, 'Perhaps you might want to stay with us – my husband, Harry, and me – in Cairo for a few months.'

'I would like that, Litty,' said I. 'But first, since you are my good friend, I think it is proper that you know my secret.'

'Capital. I love secrets almost as much as I love you.'

I turned to her, taking her hand in mine. 'I'm not who I seem to be.'

'What do you mean?'

'I'm not quite the lady you think I am. . . .'

'Certainly you are!'

'I was paid to take this voyage.'

She blinked perceptibly. 'Tewfik Pasha?'

'Yes.'

'Bully! I wish he had offered me money.'

I took a deep breath and released her hand. 'Litty . . . a year ago I was living in Liverpool with my father and my brother. I was an ignorant little guttersnipe. Daddy was a blacksmith.'

She stared at me, speechless.

'I came to London to live with my aunt – a little too late, I'm afraid.'

'But your accent . . .'

'Fortunately, I was befriended by a lovely woman – Madame Kooshay. She is the proprietress of a house of assignation.'

'Good Lord! A whorehouse?'

'Precisely,' said I, certain I had lost a friend.

'And you. . . ?'

'Yes.'

Silently, she surveyed me head to foot as if she had never seen me before. Finally, in quiet, perfectly modulated tones, she said, 'Please tell me everything, Jenny.'

'You are still my friend?'

'Of course.'

'But . . .'

'Jenny, I'm not judging you.' She took my hand once more. 'How could I dare? We are, both of us, despite the differing nature of our birth, sisters under the skin – bawds, harlots, ladies of pleasure. I realize the only reason I have never accepted money for my favours is that no one has thought to offer.'

I threw my arms about her. 'We are,' I said, near to sobbing, 'friends to the death!'

'Friends to the death!' She laughed as we hugged each other. Then, holding me at arm's length, her voice grew conspiratorial. 'But, nevertheless, I want to hear everything! It seems, Jenny Everleigh, that you have hoisted yourself by your own bootstraps, a singular achievement. I envy you – as a friend, of course. But tell me everything, when you have mastered yourself, of your life since you left your home in Liverpool!'

Quietly and in great detail, I proceeded to do so.

TWENTY THREE

I know of no feeling of pleasure quite like that of the initial penetration of a cocked and loaded penis. It is indeed the most voluptuous of sensations. Withdrawal, on the other hand, is the most poignant. [J.E., 1902]

On our third night out from Plymouth, the Spanish coast was a dim outline off the port side and the temperature a balmy eighty degrees. Tewfik Pasha invited all of us out to the afterdeck for an evening's entertainment. We assembled under the blue-striped awning for champagne and petit fours from Escoffier's galley. The men in formal waistcoasts seemed strikingly handsome and the women, perfectly coiffed and gorgeously gowned, looked beautiful in the warm light of a dozen Japanese lanterns. The ship's small orchestra, wearing their Near Eastern costumes for the first time, played for us.

Their music at first seemed hardly music at all, but rather a kind of discordant noise executed on strange instruments. As the evening wore on, however, my ear grew more accustomed to the unusual melodies and sensuous rhythms. Soon I found my body reacting, my hips and shoulders swaying of their own accord.

Tewfik Pasha introduced the first dancer as Fatima. She was dressed biblically in seven diaphanous white veils, which contrasted beautifully with her coffee-coloured skin, her mysterious, kohl-lined, black eyes and long, flowing ebony hair. With slow, exquisite movements, she removed the veils one by one till she was naked but for a bangled girdle barely covering her loins and a pair of ornate breast cups. She danced barefoot, her voluptuous belly and rotund hips rotating to the surging rhythms. Her movements were those of a passionate female in the heat of tempestuous lovemaking.

I found myself mesmerized by the flashing brilliance of a ruby inserted in Fatima's navel. As the tempo increased, her movements seemed centred even more on the bejewelled triangle between her thighs. It seemed to be the source of an uncontrollable ardour that animated the rest of her body.

After the entertainment, as still more champagne bottles were being uncorked, I took Tewfik Pasha aside to ask him if Fatima or one of the other dancers who had followed her could teach me to dance as they did.

'Yes,' said he, 'with but one provision: when you have mastered the rudiments, you must dance for us.'

'With a ruby in my navel?'

'I shall personally implant it, Miss Everleigh.'

'Ah, 'twill be my pleasure,' said I.

As we rejoined the others, Miss Lilly Roundtree laid her hand on my arm, saying, 'I was absolutely thrilled with the dancing, weren't you, Miss Everleigh?'

'Yes,' said I, smiling.

'Left me all a-tizzy.'

'That is an American expression?' Tewfik Pasha asked politely.

'Uh-huh, it means it left me excited.'

'Perhaps you need something to calm you?'

'What do you have in mind, Your Highness?'

'Perhaps a bit more of Herr von Seydlitz's services. . . .'

Miss Roundtree's eyes went wide with astonishment. 'He told you about our little party?' She turned to von Seydlitz. 'I took for granted, sir, you were a gentleman.'

'Your assumption, Fräulein Roundtree, was correct,' said Gunther von Seydlitz. 'I spoke of it to no one but Frau Seydlitz.'

'And rightly so,' said Frau Seydlitz.

'Then how in the world,' said Lilly Roundtree, returning her attention to Tewfik Pasha, 'could he know of it?'

'I know of everything.' He turned to me. 'For example, I also know of your little adventure, Miss Everleigh, with Major and Mrs Sedgewick.'

I flushed. 'Everything?' I asked.

'Everything,' said Tewfik Pasha. 'A most imaginative flight of erotic fancy.'

'Bravo!' said the major, his voice booming. 'I must say, you have it right, old chap.'

Tewfik Pasha turned to Litty. 'And you, Lady Lititia; I hope you found our captain satisfactory as a love partner?'

Litty's smile was free of the surprise she must have felt. 'Surely, my Prince, if you know of everything, as you say, you would know the answer to that.'

'I can only surmise, Lady Lititia. I suspect the answer is in the affirmative since you kept referring to Captain DiCosta as "my well-hung Spanish bull".'

'Touché,' said Litty. 'He is indeed that.' She looked over at the subject of their little discussion. He was grinning in obvious pride.

'Such a compliment, madame,' said Captain DiCosta in Spanish-accented English, 'is most gratifying when pronounced by you. You are a most accomplished and sophisticated connoisseur and I value highly both your judgement and your taste.'

'Thank you, dear Captain,' said she. 'And if you are as good a seaman as you are a lover, I would feel confident sailing with you, even into the maelstrom.'

'Hip, hip, hooray!' shouted the major.

'Ah, Major,' said Tewfik Pasha. 'I hope Frau Seydlitz's talents lived up to your expectations?'

'Most certainly, you devil,' said Major Sedgewick. 'In fact, she exceeded them, most particularly in the oral department.'

'Thank you, Major,' said Eva von Seydlitz.

'My pleasure, madam.'

'And you, Mademoiselle Fondeaux?' asked Tewfik Pasha. 'Do you wish to enter into the spirit of things?'

'I doubt I have the choice,' said she.

'Then tell us of your evening with Dr Freemantle.'

'It was most educational, *chérie*.'

'I say, Tewfik,' said Freddy Harcourt. 'You peeking at keyholes?'

'No,' said Tewfik Pasha. 'That would be quite undignified.'

'By jove!' said Harcourt. 'Then you must be some sort of magician, a swami or whatever you Arabian chaps call it.'

'Quite so, Mr Harcourt. And it leaves me certain that you, too, must have some comment as to the amorous abilities of both the Mademoiselle Gisselle and the good doctor.'

'Well, old shoe, if you must know,' said Freddy Harcourt. 'Both were more than satisfactory.'

'Indeed,' said Dr Freemantle dryly.

'Aha!' said the major. 'Buggery aboard the *Maratini*!'

'Quite,' said Dr Freemantle, sipping his champagne.

'Tell us, please,' said Lilly Roundtree in her musical voice. 'Who did what to whom?'

'The three of us did everything to each other,' said Freddy.

'It was quite educational,' repeated Gisselle Fondeaux, her eyes staring off into the dark sea.

Lady Lititia stood, placing a caressing hand on Tewfik Pasha's cheek. 'We are indeed a cosy little group. You have accounted for each of us here, but one.'

'And who may that be, Lady Lititia?'

'Yourself.'

'Up till now, I have restricted such activities to my small, seaborne harem.'

'And to one another,' said Mrs Sedgewick in a loud tone.

'And how could you know of that, madam?'

'What goes in must come out,' she said cryptically.

I glanced over at Litty who shrugged, indicating that she, too, was puzzled by the older woman's statement.

Mrs Sedgewick, a triumphant grin lighting her face, turned to Gisselle Foneaux. 'And what, Mademoiselle, have you to say of your tea-time endeavour in Tewfik Pasha's cabin? Did you find him to be as educational as were the two gentlemen of your earlier adventure?'

'There was little I did with Tewfik Pasha,' said Mademoiselle Fondeaux, 'of which I had not previously been educated.'

Miss Roundtree, her face flushed, asked, 'Did you spend?'

'Thrice, *ma chérie*.'

'Bully!' said the major.

I sipped my champagne, thinking that Sarah Sedgewick's knowledge of our host's tête-à-tête with Gisselle Fondeaux could have been arrived at by the older woman having observed her entering or leaving Tewfik Pasha's cabin. But, I wondered, how could Tewfik Pasha know, in such intimate detail, the lusty peccadillos committed by the rest of us? It was a mystery I felt determined to solve.

'It should be clear now,' said Tewfik Pasha, 'that you are all here because of a common addiction.' His eyes shifted quickly to each of us in turn. 'I speak of lust. It is an attribute to which I, too, am addicted. Before inviting you aboard, I took pains to affirm that each of you shared that attitude and that neither fear nor moral pretence would inhibit your passage on this lustful voyage. Indeed, for each of us now aboard the *Maratini*, pleasures of the flesh are the ultimate pleasures. No one here can deny that. In three days at sea, each of my guests has already indulged, at least once, in an enthusiastic sampling of carnal joy. It pleases me that my judgement of you was correct. May I extend a belated welcome aboard.'

Major Sedgewick stood and raised his glass. 'I propose a toast to our gracious commodore. May each of us live up to his most lascivious expectations!'

We all stood, raised our glasses and chorused, 'Hear, hear!'

I looked over at Litty who winked at me mischievously.

The small orchestra had removed their fezzes and were once again playing a 'civilized' waltz. Freddy Harcourt stood before me. 'Miss Everleigh,' said he, 'would you give me the honour of this dance?'

I gave him my hand and, in the warm glow of Japanese lanterns, we twirled about on the teak deck. The champagne had accomplished its purpose. I felt giddy, joyful at being at sea, dancing to Strauss under a blanket of twinkling stars.

'Permit me to say, Miss Everleigh, that you are the most beautiful woman I have ever seen.'

'Ah, you flatterer,' said I in mock seriousness. 'You said the very same thing to my friend Lady Lititia.'

'No, dear lady, I did not. I told her that she was the most beautiful woman aboard the *Maratini*.'

'Forgive me,' said I, laughing at the contradiction. He pulled me a bit closer, allowing his hand to stray from my narrow waist to the swell of my hip.

We danced on. Freddy moved stiffly as if by rote. I sensed he was counting the cadence under his breath. Soon we were joined by Captain DiCosta and Mrs Sedgewick. The brawny captain, unlike my partner, led his lady with a secure, effortless grace. I found myself wondering if individual waltzing styles echoed the manner in which men made love.

A high-pitched squeal interrupted my conjecture. I twisted about to determine its source. With her gown pulled up over her hips, Miss Lilly Roundtree was bent forward over the shipside rail. Her naked bottom, thus exposed, was raised high. The major, his trousers down about his ankles, stood behind her, his hands gripping her waist. He was fucking Miss Roundtree with long, regular strokes timed to the flowing music of Strauss. The others, champagne glasses in hand, were seated about as if they were spectators at a sporting event. Freddy Harcourt and I joined them.

Mademoiselle Fondeaux sat at the feet of the lovers, her skirt spread in a circle around her. She spoke over the rim of her glass. 'Ah, *chérie*, how does it feel?'

'Wonderful!' Lilly Roundtree raised her backside even higher as her amorous assailant increased his tempo to doubtle-time. 'His balls are bouncing against my clit!'

From where I sat, there was a clear view of the major's magnificent machine pumping in and out of Miss Roundtree's pretty pink quim. I felt a sudden flush as if the heat of their activities had invaded my body.

Freddy Harcourt stood and reached out to lay a caressing hand on Lilly's joyously gyrating bottom. 'Miss Roundtree,' said he, 'seems most enthusiastic.'

'Indeed she is!' said Major Sedgewick, breathing heavily. 'She's bloody marvellous and tight as a glove into the bargain!' The major thrust mightily as if to accent his words. Once again the lustful American actress emitted an ecstatic squeal as his thighs slapped against her pneumatic derrière.

I glanced about. My friend Lititia Faversham was deep in conversation with Tewfik Pasha. I was curious but the music drowned out their words. Behind them in the darkness appeared, as if by magic, the six exotic young women of his harem. They were costumed in diaphanous, loose-fitting trousers and beaded breast cups. Two cabin boys appeared with mattresses which they distributed about the deck.

Dr Freemantle was seated just behind me, his eyes locked on the lewd scene at the rail. Through his gaping trousers protruded a long, rapierlike prick. He was frigging slowly with his left hand whilst his right searched in the open trousers of Tewfik Pasha. He fumbled about, having difficulty, but finally his hand emerged, grasping the distended organ of our host.

Till then, I had never seen a gentleman handle the affair of another gentleman. The sight was an erotic shock! I stared for moments, attempting to organize my thoughts.

It was an act that seemed to me to be somehow less natural than one of women toying with each other (but somehow no less fetching). Did men do more than just masturbate each other? Were the tales I had heard indeed true?

I glanced about to find that Mrs Sedgewick and Captain DiCosta were no longer dancing. They stood facing each other as two of the harem girls undressed them. Each garment, as it was removed, was folded carefully and laid out on a small table.

At the rail, Lilly Roundtree had collapsed on to her knees. With her head resting on the deck and her rotund bottom raised, she was being pounded mercilessly by Major Sedgewick. As I watched, her squeals grew more fervent. Then, suddenly, her rhythmic arse movements grew uneven, erratic, as if she had lost control of her body.

Mademoiselle Fondeaux, still seated on the deck next to them, leaned close, bringing her face just inches from Miss Roundtree's. 'Ah, Miss Lilly,' said she, 'you're spending.'

'Yes. . . !'

'Spunk!' cried the major. 'Cunt! Fuck!'

'Squeeze it out of him, *chérie*.'

Suddenly, the major, too, was still – frozen in place, his cock fully implanted. A series of spasms rocked his body.

Mademoiselle Fondeaux spoke quietly, 'Cum, my dear Major, cum.' Reaching out, she slapped his arse sharply. 'Shoot your spunk into her!'

As a mere observer, I could sense his ejaculation. My vivacious puss throbbed. It clutched at an imaginary intruder spurting imaginary jism deep within me. I placed my hand between my legs, pressing hard through the heavy material of my gown, rubbing my thighs one against the other.

Groaning, the major collapsed on to the back of his panting partner. They lay still, breathing heavily as the orchestra finished its selection. For the moment, all was quiet except the distant rumble of the *Maratini*'s steam engine.

Then from behind me, accented by the silence, I became aware of the familiar, juicy, squishing sounds of sexual congress. Someone, I realized, was doing something to someone. I turned to observe Dr Freemantle, on his knees, his mouth bulging with Tewfik Pasha's considerable pego! I was astonished! I had, of course, heard of such things but had never quite been able to visualize them!

The harem girls were busy removing the last garments from Captain DiCosta and Mrs Sedgewick. One of the girls who had danced earlier was helping Mademoiselle Fondeaux to her feet. As I watched, she began to unfasten hooks and buttons. Others were in the process of disrobing Freddy Harcourt and Lady Lititia.

I stood as, I, too, was approached by one of the harem girls. It required but a few minutes for her to divest me of my gown. Prepared well for the evening, I wore nothing beneath it. Naked, I thanked her with a brief embrace. Her body, pressed momentarily against mine, seemed marvellously supple. Despite the veil that covered the lower part of her face, she seemed a pretty little thing, coffee-coloured with large eyes darkened with kohl. Her breasts were massive, challenging the integrity of the jewelled cups that barely contained them. With smiling eyes, she said, 'My name is Mefik Habad.'

I responded by introducing myself, using an Arabic phrase I had learned that very morning during a tutoring session with young Haki. In surprise, she placed her hand to her cheek. In Arabic she said, 'Your accent is very good for a foreigner.'

'Thank you,' said I in Arabic. 'You are most gracious and very beautiful.'

Despite the veil, I was certain she blushed and I was pleased with the realization that she had understood the short phrases I had spoken. Equally exciting – I had also understood her. After just a few two-hour lessons with Haki, I felt well on my way to conversational Arabic.

I had a sudden desire to be off by myself. Crossing to the

port side, away from the increasing activity of my fellow passengers, I stretched languidly, pressed against the rail. I stared out over the indigo sea, luxuriating in the euphoric tonic of cool salt air on my naked body. The Japanese lanterns had been extinguished and the striped awning rolled back. As my eyes accustomed themselves to the dark, I could make out the dimlights of a Spanish town in the distance.

Suddenly, despite the darkness, I realized there was someone next to me on the rail. It was a naked Tewfik Pasha.

'The town of Vigo,' he said. 'North of it is Spain; to the south, Portugal.'

As he spoke, the moon emerged swiftly from behind a cloud. It drew a pathway of phosphorescence across the water; a glowing finger that pointed out the dark land the moon itself had revealed. It was as if Tewfik Pasha had ordered the clouds to part so that he might have sufficient light to illustrate his geography lesson.

'And you are enjoying the voyage?' he asked.

'Immensely, Your Royal Highness.'

'I am pleased,' said he. 'And you may call me Tewfik.'

He laid a light hand on my arm. We were quiet as the orchestra began to play 'Tales from the Vienna Woods'. Its sweet, flowing melody seemed orchestrated to the rhythmic vibrations of the *Maratini*'s engines and to the sound of the sea rushing past her hull.

'I asked, 'How did you know?'

'Ah, Jenny. What a lovely-sounding name you have.'

'How,' I continued, 'do you know of the intimate activities of your passengers?'

'A secret, Miss Jenny.'

'Some of us, I believe, think it might be magic . . . clairvoyance, perhaps.'

'And you?'

'I feel there is a simpler, more practical explanation.'

'Such as?'

He was teasing me. 'Spying,' said I. 'But how?'
'Your curiosity does you justice.'
'Thank you, Tewfik.' It was the first time I had used his given name. I liked the feel of it on my lips. 'Tewfik,' I repeated.
His arm snaked around the bare flesh of my waist. Once again we were quiet, staring out over the moonlit sea. The town of Vigo now lay to our stern, its lights but a pinprick on the dark mass of the coast. Behind us, one of the female guests, I knew not which, cried out in passion. There followed a series of masculine grunts, then a general vocal hubbub obscured in the rising swell of Strauss.
'My guests seem to be enjoying themselves,' said Tewfik Pasha.
I turned to him. With his thick black beard and dark flashing eyes, he was, if not actually handsome, quite striking. My eyes strolled down his body, past his wide shoulders and muscular chest. He displayed a very slight paunch beneath which a flaccid penis lay at rest. It was a male member unlike any I had ever seen. I reached down to take its soft bulk in the palm of my hand. It was still damp with Dr Freemantle's saliva. The bulbous head was naked, lacking the protection of loose skin common to all the other unerect organs of my experience.
'The lack of foreskin puzzles you?'
'Indeed,' said I. 'Though I must admit my acquaintance with male organs in their soft state is limited, I've seen none like it.'
'Then you've known no Moslems before myself?'
'No,' said I, puzzled. 'Are Moslems born thus?'
'Hardly. It is a rite called circumcision in your language. The foreskin is removed when one is a child. Many share the custom with Islam: the Copts, the Jews and others.'
I ran the fingers of my other hand down the length of his relaxed member. The skin was soft, its texture reminiscent of a flower petal. The organ itself was prettier than the dangling, formless shards of more conventional, British

penises. I looked up at him, saying, ''Tis lovely . . . but why?'

'Rite of passage into Islam – a covenant between God and man. And there is also the advantage of cleanliness.'

I closed my fingers, encasing the lovely thing in my hand. 'And women,' said I. 'Is there also a rite of passage?'

'Female circumcision has been banned in Egypt by my father. It is a horrid, deforming custom. The labia are removed, but worse, so is the clitoris.'

'Good Lord!' I felt a sudden shock of sympathy in my loins. 'How positively awful!'

'The reason for it is even more awful. The clitoris, as a centre of female passion, is a woman's main source of joy; its removal discourages her from seeking pleasure where none, or very little, can exist. Thus she has no reason to stray and will remain solely the property of her husband or master.'

'Your harem girls. . . ?'

'They are complete. I have no interest in half women who, for whatever reason, are incapable of taking pleasure from me. Be she Islamic or infidel, English lady or huriyah, a woman's capacity for joy is sacred.'

Despite his strange religious faith, Tewfik Pasha seemed far from the savage I had suspected him of being. He was, thought I, a most sensitive and civilized man.

From the group aft came sounds of passion. A chorus of feminine squeals and masculine groans formed a counterpoint to the lilting music of Strauss.

Retaining my grip on Tewfik's exotic penis, I turned to face him. 'You are, Tewfik Pasha,' said I, 'a lovely gentleman.'

'And you, Jenny Everleigh, are a most lovely woman.'

Tentatively, as if to test my response, his lips touched mine. I greeted them with the tip of my tongue. He drew it into his mouth, sucked on it passionately as, thought I, Dr Freemantle had been sucking on his cock just minutes before. It was an aberrant thought, strangely exciting but quickly displaced by another as I became aware that the exotic boodle in my hand was expanding, forcing my fingers apart in order to accommodate its increased breadth.

Speaking into his parted lips, I said, 'Dance with me, Tewfik.'

He pulled me to him, crushing my breasts against his chest. Then, with his body pressed tightly to mine, he swung me out in waltz time. I thrilled to the feel of a now fully erect pego snugly between us, against my belly.

With my lips caressing his ear, I whispered, 'The waltz, dear Tewfik, was meant to be danced at arm's length. Surely, no couple has ever before waltzed this close.'

'Shocking,' said he.

'No,' said I, "twould be shocking only if we were fully clothed.'

'Ah,' said he, laughing softly as, with skilful grace, he swung me about. 'Then how would you characterize this innovation?'

I buried my face in his neck and pressed my avid body even closer to his. 'I would characterize it,' said I, 'as a delight.'

'Truly. And perhaps it will become the fashion. Visualize, if you will, an embassy ball, such as the one at which we met, filled with naked dancers.'

'Some,' said I, 'would be incapable of dancing close – the Serbian ambassador, for example, minus his corset!'

Twirling about, we laughed. It was as if Tewfik Pasha and I were one, perfectly coordinated. Would we, I wondered, make love with equal humour and grace?

As one waltz ended and another, 'The Merry Widow', began, my charming partner pulled away momentarily. I smiled into his eyes, then glanced downward at his rampant penis. Like a giant finger, it pointed upward at my navel.

'It occurs to me, Jenny,' said Tewfik Pasha, 'that you possess the perfect sanctuary for it.'

Without a word, I spread my legs just enough to give him access. Then, with his corpulent cock nestled snugly in the dewy folds of my passion garden, we danced on.

Never, I'm sure, had anyone taken more pleasure than I from a gay waltz of Vienna. The swollen knob of his gigantic staff was lodged against my love button. Every lilting movement of our bodies was a separate joy! Each step, each swaying motion, each graceful, swirling turn was a voluptuous exercise in waltz time! Soon, combined with the more traditional steps, I was rotating my hips, even as he pistoned his. Our passion built slowly, lovingly. Then, as the music ascended to its climax, so did we. Tewfik Pasha's hands grasped my swaying buttocks as his loaded weapon spasmed within the soft folds of my seething pussy. I thrilled as a copious ejaculation burst forth, greasing my nether lips with a warm and creamy essence that overflowed to the inside of my thighs. Then, along with the final, tempestuous chord of 'The Merry Widow', I spent. It was not a ravishing orgasm of the kind that usually transports me but rather a sweet one, orchestrated in a minor key – piquant and exquisitely loving.

TWENTY FOUR

Disease protection and what is now spoken of as birth control was indeed a problem in days gone by. It still is, of course, except that women are a bit better informed nowadays. There was then, as there is now, the concept of coitus interruptus, an unreliable means that accomplished just what its term implied – it interrupted the smooth, aesthetic 'flow' of events. There was also the familiar condom. It was called a 'French letter' and was reasonably effective. I and many other sensualists, however, objected to its use as it constituted an artificial barrier between male and female. (Condoms have since become thinner – a single one will no longer suffice to vulcanize an automobile tyre.) During my early days in London, Madame Kooshay introduced me to the use of mercuric cyanide. Taken as a douche after intercourse, it served the double purpose of a spermaticide and a prophylactic. Unfortunately we little realized its potential danger as a corrosive poison. [J.E., 1921]

Tewfik Pasha carried me bodily to his quarters. There he laid me naked in a nest of colourful pillows. The large cabin, hardly resembling anything one might expect to find aboard a ship, was dominated by a large Oriental booth dressed in gossamer chiffon. Persian rugs lined the walls and floor. Above, the striped fabric of a desert seraglio formed a tentlike canopy.

I stared up at him as he loomed above me in the warm

glow of a dozen filigreed brass lamps. I thrilled to his broad, enigmatic grin, the sight of his strange but beautiful penis.

Afloat on a sea of euphoria, I extended eager arms. 'Kiss me, my prince.'

'Soon, my princess,' he said and stepped back. 'But first you must be made ready.'

Before I could digest his strange words, he brought his hands together in a single clap. Almost immediately, two of the harem ladies appeared. Though I was seeing them for the first time without their distinctive veils, I was nevertheless able to recognize them as the dancers, Fatima and Mefik. One bore a graceful silver flagon, the other an ornate ceramic pot.

Tewfik Pasha was seated at a distance on a stool that was actually an unusually shaped wooden saddle. He spoke softly. 'You are, darling Jenny, about to be anointed with rare oils and unguents of the East. It is a custom practised by Turkish sultans to prepare only the most voluptuous and desirable of their harems for the rigours of love.'

Silently, I lay back in the pillows. I breathed deeply, relaxing, in an attempt to ready myself for what I was certain was to be a most unusual experience.

Fatima and Mefik knelt beside me. They smiled briefly, then each assumed the serious mien of women dedicated to their art. I willed myself limp as they rolled me over on to my belly.

Seconds passed. Hot oil saturated my back and was smoothed and massaged into my skin by skilful hands. I became aware of a scent like none I had ever experienced. Sweet, ambrosial, redolent of unknown, exotic blossoms, its liquid heat ascended my spine. My shoulders were kneaded, my calves and buttocks stroked and pummelled. Sensuous hands caressed my feet, pressing, massaging, stretching my toes. The world outside myself retreated.

Then the hands were gone as another scent – strangely

aromatic, heady, intoxicating – invaded my senses. Only a single contact remained: a fingertip pressing my coccyx. It inserted itself in the deep cleft and was followed by a sharp, stinging slap on my plump rump, which I interpreted correctly as a demand to spread my legs. As I complied, the single digit was replaced with many. Gently, they massaged a cooling salve deep between my buttock cheeks. In seconds the sensitive flesh grew warm and began to tingle. My secret rosebud seemed exquisitely afire. For the first time, I uttered a sound – a long, fluttering sigh of pleasure. My body and I, no longer separate entities, became one.

Once again I was rolled over. This time my breasts, my belly and my legs were anointed with hot, scented oil. The massage was more subtle now, more gentle – rather a series of sensuous caresses.

As I watched expectantly through hooded eyes, the erotically beautiful Fatima set aside the flagon of oil. She reached out with a graceful hand to scoop up from the ceramic pot another serving of thick, aromatic unguent. The full-breasted Mefik emulated her. I closed my eyes, breathing deeply the musky scent, as magic grease was rubbed gently into the tender flesh of my breasts.

Feathery fingers played ring-a-rosy about my aureole, grasped my nipples between them, squeezing and pinching. My breasts tingled from the marvellous ointment and soon my nipples, extended into fat, slippery little fingers, burned as with an inner fire.

My hips, of their own accord, began a slow but restive rotation. Fatima scooped up another helping of the enchanted salve. My legs parted expectantly as she reached out to apply the stuff between my thighs.

With lascivious expertise, Fatima greased my labia, the inner lips, the clitoris. I trembled. In seconds my vagina was ablaze, twitching and tingling!

Then, once again, Tewfik Pasha loomed over me. I stared upward in rapturous torment, craving beyond reason the noble rod now extending gloriously from his loins. Hail – the princely prick! (How much more worthy of its station than that common member of my other prince – Edward!) Here indeed was a priapus worthy of a potentate: corpulent, straight as an arrow, a precise tool of Bessemer steel and finest velvet. Neither too big nor too small, it was a concupiscence based on a set of perfect spheres; its cap, a bulbous, ideally proportioned mushroom. Perfect! 'Twas indeed a beauteous and joyful tool that could well have been fashioned by a convocation of the most worldly and truly sensuous women for their own use! In short: a masterpiece!

As I watched, Mefik transferred her attention from my seething breast to the object of my fanatical desire. Putting the magic unguent to different use, she used her palm to anoint the head of Tewfik Pasha's organ. Then, with both hands, she massaged the musky stuff into the shaft, frigging him, sliding her grasping hand up and down along its length. He threw his head back to groan ecstatically as the tingling heat made itself known.

I lay, twitching with lustful craving. Only Tewfik Pasha could cool the fire that was now consuming me. Only he could soothe the prickling in my loins, quiet the fluttering, fill the vacuum! My desire knew no bounds!

The two harem girls had stepped aside. Soon, my lover's lips were consuming mine. We lay in slippery embrace, his body pressing me deep into the pillows. His leg slithered back and forth between my thighs, pressing against my burning pussy. The effect was almost immediate! What would ordinarily have been tentative play transported me instantaneously up the mountain to within sight of its peak. 'I'm going to spend,' said I, moaning into his open mouth.

'Yes, cum, my sweet Jenny!' He reached down between us, grasped my cunt in his hand and squeezed.

'Now . . .' Delicious waves of pleasure spread outward like ripples on a lake. I lay still, luxuriating in the rapturous palpitations. It was a climax much like the one preceding it, lacking a crashing crescendo but soul-stirring nonetheless.

Tewfik Pasha stood over me, straddling my rapture-ridden body. Gazing down into my eyes, he masturbated. As I thrilled to the sight of his hand sliding easily up and down the handsome shaft, Fatima grasped one of my ankles, Mefik the other. They lifted my legs skyward, then spread them outward to their limit. I was thus spread-eagled, an offering to my lover. He lay atop me, slipping and sliding on my oiled body. I reached down for his tool. It was plump and heavy in my hand as I inserted its rotund knob into the voluptuous space that nature had fashioned for it. With no effort it slipped in to the hilt, its passage facilitated by greasy musk so recently applied.

With legs held akimbo, I was filled with Tewfik Pasha's exquisite organ. Positioned thus, locked in place by the firm grips of Fatima and Mefik, I was, though spread open for him, incapable of moving my hips. My body – all of me – was but a willing receptacle. The very thought thrilled me. He could do with me what he would . . . anything. . . .

'Ah, Tewfik, my love, my champion. I'm an open cunt . . . I exist only for your pleasure! Fuck me! Fill me! Use me!'

He groaned, calling out to me in Arabic. The few lessons I'd had with Haki enabled me to understand three of his words: *cush, zubrik, zigazig* – cunt, prick, fuck.

Thrust after powerful thrust, Tewfik Pasha pistoned into me, pounding my spread-eagled groin! I was alternately emptied and stuffed filled to brimming with his fat, enthusiastic cock!

Again, with no warning, I felt myself transported. I was suddenly racked with deep orgasmic shocks, radiating outward from my seething pussy! It seemed neverending! Despite the restraining hands of the harem ladies, my body, out of control, slithered, twisted and humped upward to meet his in a mad attempt to swallow even more of him . . . his balls . . . everything! In seconds I wrenched my legs free from their lascivious captors to lock them about his thrusting hips.

Free now to pump from him the essence of his manhood, I twisted about and, powered with the energy of continuing orgasm, turned him on to his back, facing rearward. I sat astride, impaled on his *zubrik*.

'Jenny, my love,' he cried breathlessly. 'I can see it all! Your arse! Your cunt! Fuck . . . fuck! My cock . . . in you! Cunt! Fuck . . .'

He thrust upward with increasing fury. I leaned forward, grasping his ankles, posting like a steeplechase jockey riding to the finish.

Tewfik Pasha burst within me, drowning my cuntal fire in a gush of creamy spunk! I called out in lewd and loving encouragement as he twitched and fluttered deep inside me.

Finally, we lay still, allowing me to milk him with newly discovered muscles. His spasms continued for several minutes, ejaculating little afterspurts of jism that added to my internal reservoir.

Afterwards, Fatima and Mefik bathed us in hot, scented water. Then, as the harem ladies graciously bowed their exit, both Tewfik and I donned silken robes. A steward served a repast of olives, dates and figs, goose-liver pâté and a platter of strawberries, plums and grapes nested in a bed of ice. I expressed surprise.

'The ice?' asked Tewfik.

'Yes. How do you keep it aboard ship? Surely an ice house is impossible. . . .'

'We make it.'

'You make ice?'

'Yes. We have an American device – a Perkins Patented Ice Maker. It was explained to me that the principle has something to do with compression and expansion. I'm not too clear on it, except that the device is somehow driven by the *Maratini*'s engine. It was Escoffier's idea that it be installed. With ice, he was convinced we could provide the ship with provisions like no other. I was sceptical at first, but now I'm overjoyed. Imagine eating at sea as well as one can eat on land! Without it, we would be like every other ship after a few days underway – filled with salted meats and hardtack.'

We feasted. The strawberries seemed as fresh as if they had just been picked. The pâté, unlike most I had eaten, had not even begun to go bad. Of course, the same could be said for all the marvellous food served to us aboard the *Maratini*. But until now, though I was appreciative, it had not occurred to me to wonder at its variety and the novelty of its freshness.

Tewfik Pasha asked, 'Would you, Miss Everleigh, care for a libation?'

'Please.'

'Perhaps something of an alcoholic nature, wine?' He stood. 'I'm a good Moslem in most other ways, but I'm afraid that strong drink is one of my many western appreciations.'

'Have you any gin?' I asked.

'Gin?'

'There is a drink I would like to mix – Sedgewick's ambrosia.'

'Aha,' said he. 'You speak of our Major Sedgewick's delightful concoction.' He clapped his hands twice. The steward appeared as if by magic and was ordered to fetch the gin and an assortment of white wines so that I might choose.

He returned in minutes. There was English gin and three French wines that I sampled for dryness. Having little experience in that sort of thing, I was nevertheless intrigued by one, which was labelled 'dry vermouth'. In a glass bowl that came to hand, I mixed the ingredients according to Sedgewick's formula: one part white wine (in this case, vermouth) and four parts English gin. I twirled it about, two turns clockwise, two turns counter-clockwise.

As I did so, a second innovation occurred to me. Perhaps, thought I, chilling the concoction might further improve it. Impulsively, I grasped a handful of ice from the fruit platter and unceremoniously dropped it into the bowl. I waited a moment, then, straining out the ice, poured the result into two glasses.

'Marvellous,' said Tewfik Pasha, sipping slowly. 'A decided improvement on Sedgewick's ambrosia.'

'Wait. One more thing,' said I. Bowing to yet another impulse, I was about to drop a fig into each glass – but no, the colour was wrong – inharmonious. Instead I chose olives.

We sipped in silence. Finally, Tewfik Pasha spoke over the rim of his glass. 'Ingenious. I don't believe I have ever experienced an iced drink, nor probably, till now, has anyone else. I believe this to be the most civilized of libations.' He sipped again. 'But more than that.' He closed his eyes and tilted his head in conjecture. 'It's as if we drink liquid pearls. You must give it a name.'

'It has a name,' said I. 'Sedgewick's ambrosia. This is but an improvement on the original.'

'No, Jenny, 'tis different in kind. A new name would be in order.'

I thought for a moment, consuming half the drink before a name occurred to me. Raising my glass in mock salute, I said, 'In honour of this great yacht, I dub thee – *Maratini*!'

Before dawn broke we consumed six maratinis between us, stopping only to make love, just once, in the massive Oriental booth. Afterwards, I fell asleep certain in the knowledge that the maratini (the drink, not the ship) was my first major contribution to the glory of Britain. Nay, more than that, thought I, savouring the wondrous effects of what Tewfik Pasha had characterized as *liquid pearls*. The maratini was a contribution to the glory of all mankind!

I awoke alone on silken sheets in the Oriental booth.

Tewfik Pasha was nowhere present. I dressed, then pulled a drape back to determine the time of day through a porthole. The sun was high in the sky.

As I was about to slide the drapes back, I noted to the left a glint of brass. Curiosity aroused, I pulled the heavy brocade even further. My action revealed seven brass tubes ascending from the deck. Their ends, at approximately eye level, were bent gracefully at right angles from the bulkhead and were fluted at the end like trumpet bells. They were capped with snug-fitting brass discs.

At random, I removed one of the caps, allowing it to hang by the small chain attaching it to the tube. The result caused me to recoil halfway across the cabin!

'*. . . Ahhh, chérie . . . yes . . . fuck me with your tongue . . .*'

The voice was that of Mademoiselle Gisselle Fondeaux! It was coming from the open end of the glass tube! Surely, I thought, some kind of diabolical magic was at hand!

'*You like this?*'

'*Mmmmm!*'

'*And this?*'

'*Ahhh . . . marvellous! It sends chills through my body . . .*'

'*And this?*'

'*Oh yes! Yes.*'

The other woman was Lady Lititia! Impulsively, I replaced the cap, breathing deeply to restore my equilibrium. After a moment or two I was calm enough to consider the phenomenon in a rational manner. 'Twas surely, thought I, an incredible device that carried voices much in the way a pipe carries water. Most ingenious! The eavesdropping tubes were obviously routed through the ship, each terminating in a specific cabin. Here surely was the explanation for Tewfik Pasha's intimate knowledge of our recent tête-à-têtes!

At random, I uncapped another tube to be greeted with silence. I recapped it and tried yet another. This time I was pleased to hear the sounds of heavy breathing and much fumbling about. There followed an increasing crescendo of male groans and female squeals, then silence, broken only by breathless sighs. Since there were no words spoken, I found it impossible to determine the partners of this particular erotic coupling.

With growing eagerness I tried two more of the ingenious tubes. The first was silent; the second, resulting in heavy snoring, indicating that someone, probably male, was indulging himself with a late-morning nap. The third painted a tableau I felt tempted to join!

'*... Miss Roundtree, you must raise your bottom, so ... And you, Dr Freemantle, onto your knees ... Ach, good. You will mount her thusly – from behind.*'

'Twas Eva von Seydlitz. There was no mistaking the Teutonic accent and the Prussian bent for leadership!

'Herr Freddy, you will kneel behind him ... thusly.'

'I'm to bugger old Freemantle again?'

'Yah.'

'Jolly good!'

'But easy, old chap. You were a bit forceful the last time.'

'Have no fear. I'll take care.'

'No talking! We must all concentrate!'

'Where will you be, Frau von Seydlitz?'

'I am going to insert myself beneath you ... thusly ... You will suck my cunt while I diddle your clitoris.'

'Oh golly! I'm to be fucked and licked at the same time!'

'Silence!'

'Sorry ...'

'We must be precise! Our movements must be as one so that all four of us will spend simultaneously. And you, Doctor, at that very instant you must pull your schanzy out of Miss Roundtree so that I might suck it.'

'I'm to spend in your mouth?'

'Precisely.'

'Bully!'

'And I'm to spend in Freemantle's bum?'

'Yah. And you will time your movements with his. As he withdraws from Miss Roundtree, you will plunge home and as he thrusts, you will withdraw and move onward. Timing is everything.'

'Quite so.'

'Are you all ready to begin?'

'Yes.'

'Rather.'

'All set.'

'Then we begin . . . now!'

'Ah, that's lovely . . .'

'Steady on, old shoe.'

'Oh fuck . . . fuck!'

'No talking! We must concentrate! One – two – one – two – one – two . . .'

There followed the juicy sounds of love, the sounds of flesh impacting on flesh: a chorus of ecstatic, but incoherent sighs, groans, grunts and squeals. The tumult grew more frantic with each passing minute. I found myself in admiration of Frau von Seydlitz's perseverence. A simultaneous, quadruple spending was indeed an ambitious undertaking. Unfortunately, I was unable to listen further as I became suddenly aware of Tewfik Pasha's return. I quickly replaced the brass cap, pulled the drapes and turned just in time to greet him with an innocent smile.

TWENTY FIVE

There is no finer educational experience than that imparted in bed by an experienced and sensitive older woman upon an inexperienced and naive younger man. [J.E., 1890]

In confidence, I told Lady Lititia about the secret tubes for listening. Together we searched our cabins and found them: circular brass openings that looked like ventilators, high up on the bulkheads over our beds.

'He can eavesdrop at his leisure on any of the guest cabins! I counted seven tubes.'

'Aha!' said Litty. 'That accounts also for Mrs Sedgewick's knowledge of Gisselle Fondeaux and Tewfik himself! Remember, if you will, that Mrs Sedgewick said, "What goes in, must come out."'

'Very interesting,' said I. 'The tubes must be capable of carrying voices in either direction. When he was pleasuring Mademoiselle Fondeaux, Tewfik must have inadvertently left the cap off the tube leading to the Sedgewick's cabin.'

'We can do the same,' said Litty, a mischievous edge to her voice. 'It's just a matter of getting into Tewfik's quarters to remove the proper cap. I simply love to eavesdrop.'

'A marvellous idea,' said I.

'I would have found it most intriguing to have eavesdropped on you and Tewfik last night.'

'Ah, Litty,' said I. 'Next time you can be there with us in the flesh.'

'Lovely,' said she, running her fingers up my arm. 'But to

watch or listen secretly is nonetheless delicious.' Litty brought her lips within an inch of mine: 'Don't you think so?'

'Indeed,' said I. 'It makes me feel randy.' I halved the distance between us. 'And you?'

'Ah, yes.'

'Are you randy now . . . this minute?'

'Yes, Jenny. And you?'

I answered by blending my lips with hers in a tender kiss. She whispered into my mouth, 'Do you think he is listening now?'

I glanced up at the glass tube. 'Perhaps.'

'That makes me even randier!'

We removed all our clothing and fell naked together onto my narrow bed. Our lips were one, our tongues engaged in an amorous game. Then, slowly, Litty licked and kissed her way down my neck and onward to my breast where she circumnavigated the sensitive aurole with a fluttering tongue. I turned her about so that I might do likewise. Her nipple was a tender nub that grew turgid between my lips. In turn, she nibbled delicately on mine. Our fervent sighs were a rapturous counterpoint.

There was a knock on the door. It deterred Litty not at all from my turgid tit. I looked up nervously to call out, 'Who's there?'

'Haki, my Lady.'

Litty, sporting a sly grin, raised her head. 'Ask him in,' she whispered.

There was no mistaking the lewd suggestion of her tone. For just an instant I was taken aback. 'He's only fifteen,' said I under my breath.

'Not quite ripe,' said she, 'but probably delicious nevertheless.'

Concerned more for Haki's welfare than for Litty's lewd desire (or for that matter, my own), it occurred to me that if young Haki were a virgin, he would indeed be fortunate to have fallen into our hands. Who else could provide him a more edifying initial experience? If he were not a virgin, then our gift, though less dramatic, would still be one of great value. Feeling a sudden affection, I called out for him to enter.

He stood in the open doorway, his mouth gaping, his eyes bulging with shock. He seemed rooted to the spot – half in, half out – unable to exit or enter.

'Come in,' said I.

'Yes, dear boy,' said Litty, standing erect in exquisite nakedness. 'And please close the door behind you.'

Haki stumbled forth and turned bodily to close the door. 'Perhaps,' said he, his back to us. 'I should return later when . . .'

'No, Haki,' said Lititia. 'You may stay.'

'We'd like you to,' said I, approaching him to lay a hand on his shoulder. 'Turn around.'

'Oh, Miss Everleigh . . .'

I felt him tremble as Litty asked, 'Have you ever seen a naked woman before, Haki?'

'No, Lady Faversham, never. I swear on the Koran.'

'Then, if you turn about, you may see one – two actually.'

'Be brave, dear Haki,' said I. 'You are a man.'

He turned slowly, his eyes glued on his ornate sandals. I stood directly in front of him. We were silent as, slowly, he raised his eyes. I could feel the heat of his scrutiny on my ankles, my calves, my knees, my thighs and finally my mossy groin. He looked away sharply, then back again, finally expelling the breath he had held for almost a full minute.

'Take all the time you need, Haki,' said I.

'Yes, Miss Everleigh.' His face was flushed scarlet, his breathing now erratic.

'You know what it's called; you taught me the word.'

'Madam insisted . . .'

'Say it.'

He spoke softly, '*Cush*.'

'Lovely,' said I.

Litty said, 'You knew that, even though you had never seen one?'

'Yes,' said the young Haki, continuing to stare at my silken triangle as if mesmerized.

Litty stood next to me, her arm around my waist. Haki's eyes darted back and forth.

'Mine is different than Miss Jenny's,' said she. 'Would you like to feel the difference?'

Once again, Haki stopped breathing, his hand flexing, seemingly of its own accord. Gently, I took it, placing the fingertips on Litty's hairless *cush*.

'I promise it won't bite,' she said. 'You may move your hand about in order to get acquainted.'

Tentatively, his fingers explored. After a moment, Litty took his hand as if it were an inanimate object and transferred it to my more conventionally bearded quim. His delicate fingers entangled themselves in the soft brush. Then, barely touching the sensitive flesh, they moved nervously about between my legs.

'Which do you prefer?' asked Litty.

In a choked voice, Haki answered, 'Either . . . both . . .'

'You are a true gentleman.'

He nodded dumbly, his fingertips still engaged in awkward cuntal research. He glanced up at Lititia's breasts. He seemed dazed, staring fixedly from bulging eyes that had lost their ability to blink.

'I think, young man,' said Litty, 'that perhaps it is time you removed your clothing.'

His fingers disengaged from my nest as if it were a hot coal stove. 'Must I?' he asked plaintively.

'Yes, dear boy,' she said, getting to her knees. 'It is most improper for a gentleman to remain clothed in the presence of naked ladies.' She untied the cord holding up his baggy, Islamic pantaloons.

He bit his lip and shut his eyes as I reached out to unbutton his shirt. I was touched by his innocence but nevertheless felt a growing excitement. Beneath the rough fabric, I felt his heart beating rapidly. A band of perspiration glistened on his forehead. The poor boy was terror-stricken,but as Litty pulled the pantaloons down to his ankles, a full erection indicated that fear was at war with an abject lust.

The innocent organ lacked the roundity of a fully developed, man-sized member, but it was long and graceful, pointing upward in youthful exuberance. Fetched by this combination of innocence and concupiscence, I felt a delicious stab of desire. As Lititia reached up to touch the lovely thing, it twitched as if possessed with a life of its own.

Reaching out, I cupped his tight little gonads.

'You are,' I said, 'a most beautiful boy.'

'And we are going to make a beautiful man of you,' said Lady Lititia.

She took one of his hands, I, the other. Together we led him to the bed. With his bobbing pego leading the way, he walked the few paces as if sleepwalking.

Haki lay on his back, one arm across his eyes. His body was lean and well-muscled. Litty ran her fingers down the length of it, finally grasping his youthful prick at its base. She smiled up at me lasciviously as if presenting a gift. Overwhelmed by her lewd offering, I opened my mouth and engulfed it.

Seconds later, I was in full possession. Lady Lititia moved to the head of the bed and removed Haki's arm from across his face.

'Ah, Haki,' she said, her voice husky with lustful promise, 'how does it feel?'

'Oh, it's good . . . very good, Lady Faversham . . . good . . .'

I flicked my tongue under the swelling helmet. Then, bobbing my head in a deliberately slow tempo, I began to fuck him with my suctioning mouth.

'My breast,' said Litty. 'Would you like to suck it?'

'Oh yes, Lady Faversham!' Haki's breath was heavy, erratic.

Out of the corner of my eye, I watched as the young boy took half her breast into his mouth. Carried away, he suckled it with a rhythm matching my own. His exuberance was such that I feared for its safety. Cupping his buttocks, I could feel him trembling.

'The nipple, Haki,' said Litty. 'You must learn to concentrate on the nipple . . . mmmmm, that's better . . . there's a good lad. Flick it with your tongue . . . just so . . . ah, what an excellent pupil you are!'

He groaned deeply in his throat as I felt the telltale spasms begin. No longer passive, his hips began to move, at first tentatively but then faster, thrusting, pumping his iron-hard rod in and out of my mouth as with tightly compressed lips I held my head still to accommodate him.

Then, with a drawn-out whimper, Haki experienced his first orgasm with a woman! His young, inexperienced cock swelled from an irrestistible pressure. Three seconds later he detonated! An immense gusher of thick, bittersweet spunk filled my mouth! It dribbled out of the corners down my chin.

My lips held him tightly. I refrained from swallowing, knowing that my dear friend Litty would want her share of the lovely cream. She was beside me in a trice. I grasped Haki's still twitching *zubrik*, offering it to her. As it touched her lips it spit a tiny, final measure of jism. She licked it clean, running her pink tongue across the tip to scoop up what remained. I watched with amorous approval, then, grasping the back of her head, I brought my lips to hers in order to deposit, on her demanding tongue, the portion I had saved for her.

'A lovely, unassuming bouquet,' said Litty. 'Quite pleasant, sweet with a slightly tart aftertaste.'

'It will gain character with age,' said I.

Haki remained soft for a few minutes, just long enough for Lititia to observe, for the first time, a circumcised penis at rest. Her fascination and delight with the unusual novelty was equal to what my own had been with Tewfik Pasha. Soon the precocious young man was hard again, his beautiful prick standing much like a soldier on parade.

This time he was less fearful, less shy, though not actually forward: an eager, attentive student of female geography. We began our lesson with a delineation of the sensitive areas: earlobes, neck, breasts, buttocks, spine, belly, insides of the thighs, feet. We taught our young pupil the advantages of a light and tender touch, of the voluptuous kiss and fluttering tongue. He learned also of stroking and kneading, love bites and titillation. We made him aware of the sensitivity of his own nipples and of the secret place near the base of his scrotum.

Because of its naked state, Lady Lititia's hairless quim served well as a model. Haki learned to use his fingers and tongue to manipulate the labia and clitoris. Fascinated, he watched as the little organ emerged from its protective sheath, increasing in size like a diminutive penis. We taught him the exquisite, secret spot that one can only reach with a hooked finger.

To demonstrate the female orgasm, we had Haki mouth both Litty and myself to a climax. He was well taught and we agreed that only a little more in the way of cunnilingal experience would make him into a true virtuoso. He was gaining confidence quickly. His youthful face no longer flushed with embarrassment, beamed with obvious pride at his accomplishments.

There followed his first experience with fucking. I lay on my back at the edge of the bed, my bottom elevated on a few pillows. Haki stood between my legs as Lady Lititia 'set the pin.' The position was chosen because of the clear, unobstructed view it afforded our pupil. We had Haki experiment with various movements as I demonstrated their counterpoints. With proper instruction he was also made to understand the control inherent in riding low or high, of thrusting deep or shallow, fast or slow.

Finally, after he spent in me, it was Litty's turn. She got on her knees, presenting him with her full, shapely bottom. Haki knelt behind her as I lay underneath, my head between her legs, my face close to her sodden, pink pussy. Grasping Hakii's impudent pego, I introduced it into the outer folds.

'Thrust home,' said I.

'Ah, you devil!' cried Lititia as he entered her delicious cunt to the bollocks.

She raised her plump arse even higher, dropping her head between my thighs. Then, as Haki fucked on with ever increasing fervour, she brought her mouth to my seething quim.

'Haki,' said I, my voice husky with passion. 'Slow your movements. You must learn to pace yourself . . . and your lady. As with all sport, timing is of great import.'

'Yes, Miss Everleigh,' said he, complying.

'Now enter her fully, as far as you can go. Then hold still.'

'Yes, Miss Everleigh.'

'Further, dear boy . . . all the way!'

'Yes, Miss Everleigh.'

Just inches from my enraptured eyes, his balls rested against her twitching puss. 'Tiny movements now,' said I. 'Round and about.'

As he rotated his hips clockwise, Lady Lititia rotated hers counterclockwise. 'Twas a lovely dance of the spheres. I thrilled to the view while at the other end, Litty ravaged my clit.

'How does it feel, Haki?'

'I have no words, Miss Everleigh, not even in Arabic . . .'

'Your bollocks are stroking her clitoris.'

'That is good?'

'Very good.'

Their movements grew faster. Litty raised her head from my soaking quim.

'Fuck!' she cried.

'Now thrust, Haki,' said I. 'All the way out – all the way in. Drive it home with all your might!'

He did as he was told, his thighs beating mercilessly against her whirling derrière. I ran my thumb up and down her clit as, frantically, she tongued mine.

'Ohhhh, I'm going to spend!' cried Lititia. 'I'm going to cum! Fuck me, you little devil!'

'Slap her arse, Haki!'

'Yes, Miss Everleigh . . . yesss!'

THWACK! The slap was like a pistol shot.

'Again, Haki!'

THWACK!

'Now,' said Litty. 'I'm cumming! Ahhh, how lovely . . .'

'And I, too, Lady Faversham!' Fully inserted, Haki trembled.

I could see the base of his cock spasm, his bullocks twitch. 'Go all the way!' I cried.

'Yes, Miss Jenny!'

Lititia's face was buried in my seething garden of lust. A wildfire of sensations raced through my body, throbbing, pulsing, palpitating! My orgasm, though short, was indeed intense – the third since awakening. And 'twas not yet tea time.

Afterwards, as she was dressing to go on deck, Lady Lititia lay an affectionate hand on Haki's arm. 'Today you have become a man,' she said quietly. 'Miss Everleigh and I are responsible for a transition in your life at least as momentous as any yet to come. No matter how long you live and what wondrous adventures you experience, you will never forget us.'

'Forever, Lady Lititia, Miss Jenny. A thousand thankyous would not suffice.' He bowed graciously, making the Moslem sign.

'You are gifted, Haki,' said Lititia. 'With our teaching, your gift will serve you well. Always remember that pleasure is equally for giving and receiving. One without the other constitutes the only true perversion.'

I stared at the door for seconds after Litty had left. I'd had no idea she possessed such a keen eloquence.

Fully clothed, Haki and I spent the remainder of the day together. Just has he had studied under my tutelage, I now studied under his. The subject was, as usual, Arabic. Despite our recent lewd adventures, his attitude toward me remained formal. There was, however, a difference; he no longer called me Miss Everleigh. As a kind of celebration of our intimacy, I was now *Miss Jenny*.

TWENTY SIX

I have been in love many times. Truly. Quite often it has been more than one man at a time – occasionally, more than two or even three. I have never understood the concept of exclusivity or 'fidelity' as it applies to love. Such has always seemed to me to be self-defeating and perhaps hypocritical. Love is neither owning nor being owned. Love is simply love. [J.E., 1980]

The days passed in lazy progression. After steaming through Gibraltar and into the limpid waters of the Mediterranean, we docked at Algeciras for a single day to take on fresh water and provisions. It was there we heard that HMS *Illustrious* (carrying the Prince of Wales), after having spent a few days at nearby Gibraltar, had steamed on just ten or twelve hours earlier.

Thanks to Haki's tutelage, I was becoming conversant in Arabic. By the time Tunis lay off our starboard side, I had reached a level of proficiency that enabled me to use that poetic language while making love to Tewfik Pasha. He was both surprised and delighted.

I spent considerable time visiting the harem in its large, forward compartment. There, for an hour a day, Fatima taught me belly dancing (a term, I learned, used only by Europeans). The other five ladies were most gracious. They introduced me to kohl as it is used to enhance the beauty of one's eyes, and I, in turn, intoduced them to mercuric cyanide as it is used to protect one from pregnancy.

From time to time, I would join Lititia and the Sedgewicks in the salon for a tea-time game of auction bridge. But early in the voyage there was another game that sparked my interest even more. Dr Freemantle, responding reluctantly to my polite insistence, taught me chess. At first he muttered objections to a woman attempting mastery of a traditional man's game, but as I began to show progress these comments were replaced with a grudging respect.

I spent my morning hours at these educational pursuits. My afternoons were usually devoted to relaxing in a deck chair, basking in the warmth of the Mediterranean sun and reading books from the *Maratini*'s extensive library. I also developed a propensity for what I came to call 'sunbathing.' There were sunny afternoons when I would recline totally nude on a mattress, thoughtfully provided by Haki. Turning front to back periodically and following the sun and the idiosyncrasies of the ship's course, I would move my mattress about the deck, much to the consternation of my fellow passengers. Exposure to the sun was thought by many to be responsible for brain fever and yellow fever; even more important, European fashion had always favoured a pale complexion. I felt otherwise, seeking successfully to emulate the lovely golden skin of the Arabian harem ladies.

After dinner, the setting sun in all its brilliant colour proclaimed the nightly *soirée*. There were *dansants*, treasure hunts, blind man's bluff and the other games. In one of them, the ladies, blindfolded, were required to identify the gentlemen's pegos by touch. (Of course, everyone recognized Tewfik Pasha's unusual instrument.) The consistent victor in this contest was Miss Lily Roundtree. She was seldom wrong. I held her substantial talent in high esteem.

In yet another game, the gentlemen, also blindfolded, were required to identify vaginas. The lady in question presented her bottom. With his hands clasped behind his back, the gentleman's prick was guided by one of us to its target. Each was limited to a minute. The best at this particular contest was Major Sedgewick; the worst was Freddy Harcourt, who was always wrong.

On one occasion, Dr Freemantle's bum, well lubricated with harem oil, was presented to a blindfolded Freddy. In obvious ecstasy, the young explorer buggered the good doctor for the full allotted minute. We waited expectantly for his decision.

'There can be no doubt,' said Freddy Harcourt, his tone strident, though assured. ''Tis most assuredly the well-ploughed cunt of the charming Frau Eva von Seydlitz!'

We all responded with great hilarity – all, that is, except Frau and Herr von Seydlitz.

'Poor Freddy,' said I, laughing.

''Tis a natural mistake,' whispered a delighted Lady Lititia.

Both she and I had developed a dislike for the German woman and her husband. The couple were sour notes in an otherwise pleasantly harmonic congregation.

Frau Eva von Seydlitz and Herr Gunther von Seydlitz seemed mirror images of each other. She possessed a severe, austere beauty and a personality to match. He was rigidly handsome and rigid of manner.

After an evening of orgiastic activity, neither of them would appear to have been engaged in anything more strenuous than a few hands of Major Sedgewick's auction bridge. They would emerge from a log pile of writhing bodies with neither a hair displaced nor a drop of perspiration.

Frau and Herr von Seydlitz derived great pleasure from precisely organized activities, be they attempts at orgies or group calisthenics at dawn (an undertaking that failed at the outset when not a single participant materialized on deck). In a manner typically Germanic, they insisted that our voluptuous activities were perverse and decadent unless organized into a kind of Prussian military drill. Thus transformed, they became 'acts of noble and high purpose,' dedicated to 'joy through discipline.'

For the first three days at sea, this was admittedly helpful. But as we all began to know each other and to feel comfortable together, we disregarded their attempts at leadership and their constant Teutonic harping on discipline. Eventually, as their calls for order were met with lighthearted derision and humoured catcalls, the proselytizing ceased, albeit, I sensed, reluctantly.

The von Seydlitzs lacked the single quality that was a common factor amongst the rest of us: a sense of humour. I sensed an evil and menacing presence. The *Maratini* was, except for them, a most relaxed and happy ship. When I spoke to Lititia about it, she insisted that they were little more than a pair of Germanic bores. She pooh-poohed my strangely ominous foreboding but did little to dispel my irrational fears. I felt strongly, for reasons I couldn't justify, that the two were up to no good.

But despite the efforts of the two Germans, the *Maratini* provided a most relaxed atmosphere. My shipmates were indeed a congenial lot and in less than a week on the high seas, I had experienced each of them – men and women – both singly and in varied and exciting combinations. All were equally randy though they differed in taste and propensity.

For myself, the most desirable was mine host. Tewfik Pasha. He sometimes enjoyed merely holding me in his arms for hours and was the only one with whom I spent entire nights. As the *Maratini* steamed serenely through moonlit waters toward the ancient land of the Pharaohs, we would sleep in his romantic Oriental booth, spooned together like proper lovers. We would awake in the morning amidst rumpled silk sheets to a sumptuous breakfast and an hour or two of languid lovemaking. Lying naked in his arms, I realized that, till now, in such circumstances only Reggie had aroused in me feelings that transcended mere lust. But it was hardly an exclusive relationship as Tewfik Pasha spent entire nights, alternately, with each of the ladies. Still, there were more nights with me than any of the others and he insisted that I was his favourite. I hardly believed the dear man, but he meant well. I felt I was falling in love with him . . . but I already loved Reggie. Could one love two? I asked my friend Lititia. She maintained that it was possible to love two men at the same time, and perhaps even three, but more than that the number was liable to become complicated. One would have a devil of a time keeping track.

TWENTY SEVEN

I have never understood why, in the eyes of contemporary Christianity, pleasures of the flesh and sin are one and the same. It is reasonable to assume that if our creator had agreed with this, he would not have placed certain nerve endings so strategically. Obviously, He created this gift for us to make use of them. It follows then, that contrary to contemporary religious belief, it is abstinence that is the true perversion. In that light, I am indeed a good Christian – perhaps a bit better than most. [J.E., 1888]

When the Empress Eugénie, on board the *Aigle*, reaches Port Said,' said Tewfik Pasha, 'Africa will be officially an island!'

'Hear, hear!' shouted the major.

'And the *Maratini* will be only three ships behind her in the grand flotilla!'

'By George!' said Freddy Harcourt. 'We'll make history!'

'The new canal is a marvel!' said Tewfik Pasha. 'It is one hundred miles long with a depth of eighteen metres and a minimum width, at the bottom, of twenty-two metres. It will accommodate any ship in the world – a miracle of man's endeavour!'

'And it is the French who deserve the credit,' said Mademoiselle Fondeaux. 'The Suez is our canal. We built it!'

'Ah, but it is also Egyptian,' said Tewfik Pasha. 'Without my father there would be no canal . . .'

Dr Freemantle stood, raising his maratini glass. 'A toast to the great engineer, Ferdinand de Lesseps, to Ismail Pasha and to the empire of France!'

We drank the toast as the *Maratini's* orchestra struck up the *Marseillaise*. We were, as usual, gathered under the striped awning on the afterdeck for an evening's entertainment. Tomorrow our ship would be docked on Egyptian soil.

'Think of it, ladies and gentlemen,' said Dr Freemantle. 'We will be sailing from the Mediterranean to the Red Sea in just one day; a voyage that until now would have required more than a month. The time from Southampton to Bombay will be cut in half.'

'The world,' said I, 'is to be a much smaller place.'

'From a melon to an apple.'

'Up the French!' said an exuberant Freddy Harcourt.

Gunther von Seydlitz stood, gesturing dramatically with his hands. 'The French are fools!'

'I say – why is that?'

'The French have not yet realized that they built the Suez Canal for the convenience and purpose of John Bull. The Indian Ocean is about to become an Englischer lake!'

'*British lake*, old chap,' said Major Sedgewick, smiling at me as if extending an invitation to join in baiting von Seydlitz. The major turned again to the angry Prussian, a note of condescension colouring his discourse. 'We will happily pay the tolls.'

'Only until you take over the canal,' said von Seydlitz.

'You think we shall?'

'Never!' said Mademoiselle Fondeaux.

'Not only will the Suez Canal be British,' said von Seydlitz, ignoring her, 'but it will enable you people to colonize most of West Africa, to steal from the historic destinies of Italy, Holland and Germany!'

'White man's burden and all that, you know,' said the major, smiling. 'Seems we're the best at that sort of thing.'

'Precisely,' said Dr Freemantle. 'The empire will most certainly absorb West Africa. It is the only way we can end the dastardly slave trade.'

'And you, Tewfik Pasha?' said the major. 'What is your opinion?'

'The canal is on Egyptian land and my father has signed an agreement with France. There is a matter of sovereignty . . .'

'Sovereignty be damned!' said von Seydlitz. 'There is no such thing as an Egyptian nation. Your father rules as an Ottoman. He is their sultan, their khedive. Though many treat him as such, Ismail is not a king; his true status is little more than that of a governor for the Turkish masters!' Gunther von Seydlitz stood, his fingers clasping and unclasping in agitation under his chin. 'Egypt has assumed a new importance and both the French and the British covet it. A pox on both their houses!'

'Jenny . . .?'

I was half asleep. I opened my eyes to stare fixedly at the ceiling. I had been dreaming . . .

'Jenny?' It was the ghostly voice of Lady Lititia.

'Litty?' I asked groggily, coming awake now but wondering if I were still dreaming.

'Thank God, its you!' Her voice was coming from overhead.

Aha! thought I, the speaking tube! I said aloud, 'You're in Tewfik's cabin . . .'

'Yes, but he left for a while. I decided to uncap the tubes one by one until I found yours. This is my third attempt. I was lucky – the first didn't respond and from the second I heard Captain DiCosta and the major pleasuring Lilly Roundtree. They were hard at it – poor Lilly will, as usual, be sore in the morning.'

'Poor Lilly,' said I vaguely.

'Then I uncapped this one and thank heaven 'twas your cabin. Were you sleeping?'

'I think I still am.'

'I felt 'twould be a delight if we could chat. I found the tubes just where you said they'd be. Marvellous! Imagine, you're a hundred feet away in another cabin and it's as if you were here next to me!'

'Yes,' said I, beginning to share her excitement. 'It's magical.'

'Come join us, Jenny. Tewfik would love having both of us together. Think of his surprise and delight when he returns to find you naked beside me in his bed.'

'Not tonight, Litty dear,' said I. 'But there will be other opportunities before we finally dock in Cairo.'

'Are you unwell? It's unlike you to go to bed so early . . . alone.'

'I want to be on deck at dawn for the landfall. Haki is going to awaken me.' A wave of nausea passed over me.

'In his usual manner?'

'His tongue improves daily – but not tomorrow morning, my dear.'

'Aha, the curse is upon you.'

'For another two days.'

'They will go quickly.'

'I pray they do,' said I, yawning.

'I must go. I hear Tewfik approaching. I'll leave the tube uncapped so you might listen.'

'Please do.'

I fell asleep, unaffected by the familiar, though still exciting, music of Lititia's ecstatic feminine squeals and Tewfik Pasha's hearty masculine groans.

At dawn, the new city of Port Said, three or four miles away, seemed a brightly polished jewel set in a flat, mysterious land of tawny sand. The view, at first fascinating, changed for the worst as the *Maratini* turned south and we got closer.

Finally, I stood at the rail, gazing out on a handful of new, white buildings glaring in the early sun. The promise of the town's earlier aspect when viewed from the sea remained unfulfilled. There was no variety in the architecture, no flavour of time or place. Despite the people shuffling hither and yon in Arab robes and fezzes, the place seemed lifeless. And no wonder; Port Said had been built all of a piece less than ten years earlier to function as the northern terminus for the future canal. Its character had as yet no chance to develop. Cities require centuries to come of age, to acquire the patina of an individual culture and enterprise that makes each a unique place. What I could see of Port Said was raw and artless – ugly, depressingly undistinguished and tasteless. I expressed a silent wish that we could leave soon.

There were ships everywhere about the harbour: warships, yachts, merchantmen. Some were wood, some ironclad; some powered by sail, others by steam. Tied up in the berth behind ours was a yacht even larger and more ornate than the *Maratini*. The sharply pointed bow was decorated with a winged, Pharaonic figurehead. Aft of it in gilt letters was the name *Mahrousa*. 'Twas, I realized, the khedive's yacht – Tewfik's father.

My Arabic was advanced enough for me to understand some of the phrases used by the nearby dockworkers. I amused myself by listening, trying to decipher as much as I could. I was so intent on this educational amusement that I remained unaware, until he appeared on the dock beneath me, of Tewfik Pasha leaving the *Maratini*.

He called up to me. 'I'm off to the *Mahrousa* to see my father. Would you care to lunch with us?'

'I'd be delighted,' said I.

'And Lady Lititia?'

'I shall extend your invitation, Tewfik Pasha.'

'I look forward to your enchanting presence then, and that of the Lady Lititia, shall we say at noon?'

I watched him stride down the dock, an armed attendant, like a grey shadow, three steps behind him. How fortunate I had been to have met this generous man. It occurred to me that wit, culture, graciousness and civilized behaviour were not the exclusive province of Christians.

Lititia and I mounted the *Mahrousa*'s gangway a few

minutes after twelve. We were shown into an ornate salon, furnished in the French style and half again as spacious as that aboard the *Maratini*. Ismail Pasha, the khedive of Egypt, was a more imposing figure than his heir. Whereas Tewfik dressed plainly, but elegantly, his rotund father was bejewelled, gowned in a brightly brocade robe and shod with golden slippers that formed a curlicue at the toes.

'Ah, my son does me proud,' said the khedive in French-accented English. 'His taste in women is renowned.'

'And your own taste in women, Your Majesty,' said Lititia in her usual brash fashion, 'is it not also renowned?'

'Like father like son, as you English say.' He smiled broadly, exhibiting a gold tooth studded with a single diamond. 'Welcome to the *Mahrousa*.' He kissed our hands, then motioned us to a pair of large pillows on the floor. They and the others scattered about seemed quite incongruous with the delicately civilized French furniture.

Facing us, Ismail Pasha lowered himself with some difficulty onto a pillow. When he was finally seated, Tewfik joined us. Servants materialized, bearing trays of dates and figs, flat bread, roasted lamb, stuffed grape leaves. There were no utensils. 'Twas obviously an Arabian custom to eat with one's fingers.

'I have just informed my son that tomorrow is the day,' said the khedive. 'Had the *Maratini* docked a day later, you would all have missed a good many of the festivities. Tonight is the official banquet. I have caused to be built three giant pavilions in the desert south of the city.' He spoke as if by rote in a dull, laconic voice. 'There are to be six thousand guests from every nation of the world. We have imported five hundred cooks from France and Italy to prepare the most expensive foods available and a thousand servants to serve it along with thousands of gallons of the best French wine. Afterwards will occur a gigantic fireworks display, the most magnificent ever seen.'

Lititia and I stared at him, fascinated, attempting to digest it all. We had expected a lavish celebration but this was beyond anything we could have imagined.

'Then tomorrow the armada will sail through the canal. It will consist of seventy-two ships. They will assemble at dawn to proceed, line astern, to the midpoint at Ismailia where we will be met by a smaller flotilla sailing north from the Red Sea. At that moment, the Suez Canal will be officially opened to the navies and merchant fleets of all the nations of the world.'

'A world,' said I, suddenly awed by it all, 'that will never again be the same.'

He stared at me for a moment, as if my words were an unwelcome interruption. After a moment, he glanced away, his vague, liquid eyes seeming to search for his place. Finally, in the same dispassionate singsong voice, he continued, 'It will all be repeated in Ismailia two nights hence – the banquet, the fireworks, a concert, everything. Then, next week in Cairo, my new state opera house will open with a performance of *Aïda*. The Italian Giuseppe Verdi has composed it especially for this occasion. I wish the two of you to join me in the royal box.'

Lititia and I thanked him. He beamed at us like a performer accepting applause, the small diamond in his mouth flashing brilliantly in the gaslight.

'My father,' said Tewfik Pasha, 'has never been known to do things halfway.'

I smiled lovingly at Tewfik. 'Like father like son,' said I facetiously. I reached forward to place a fig into the young man's mouth.

It was then that I noticed the khedive of Egypt had his hand up Lititia's skirt. Unperturbed, she bit into yet another stuffed grape leaf.

At this point our sanctum was invaded by a tall, harried-looking man. Topped with a fez, he was dressed in the European style. He transferred a sheaf of papers to his left hand and with his right, executed the Moslem sign of greeting and respect. 'Ah, affairs of state,' said the khedive, smiling apologetically. Gleaming with at least eight finger rings, his free hand motioned the man forward. In Arabic, pitched an octave above his previous English, he said, 'What have we here?'

'An execution order, Blessed One.' Magically, an attendant materialized bearing a writing tray. Ismail Pasha groaned with impatience. He withdrew his hand from beneath Lititia's skirt to wipe it fastidiously on a damask napkin. It was, I thought, a gross and most ungallant gesture.

Without bothering to read the document, Ismail Pasha signed it with an agitated flourish of a plumed pen. Then, rocking back and forth impatiently, he glowered as the attendant readied the hot wax. Finally, with a simultaneous gesture of dismissal, the khedive pressed one of the many rings on his left hand into the wax seal.

We were all quiet as the two men backed their way out of the salon. Tewfik Pasha looked my way, apologetically, as though he sensed my growing distaste for his father.

With his round face once again sporting a fixed smile, the khedive reverted to English. 'Affairs of state, my darlings, are a necessary evil, a bore I am forced to suffer.'

'Who is to be executed?' I asked.

'I have no idea, dear lady. Probably some thieving fellaheen – certainly no one of importance.'

'How do you know?'

'Pardon? How do I know what?'

'That 'tis no one of importance?'

Ismail's smile grew even more wooden. 'These are not the affairs of women.'

I felt a disgust bordering on nausea. This pig of a man, demonstrating no more concern than one feels after treading on an ant, had just condemned another human being to death. I glanced forlornly at Litty to find anger flashing in her eyes.

'Your Majesty,' said she, her voice like gentle ripples in a placid lake. 'We are Englishwomen and therefore unaware of your customs. Would you tell us why it is not our affair?'

Ismail's eyes went to the ceiling as if seeking help from Allah.

'Perhaps,' said I, feeling my gorge rising to even greater heights, 'unbeknownst to you, the one to be executed is your prime minister or your chief of staff or, for that matter, your favourite concubine . . .'

Tewfik Pasha spoke in Arabic. 'It is the British manner, father. They mean no insult.'

The khedive's face was a rotund blank. 'They exhibit the manners of female camels!'

'They mean only the best, my father, and there is some sense in what Miss Everleigh has said . . . a palace coup could take place under your very nose.'

Ismail disregarded the import of his son's remark. Continuing in Arabic, he said, 'These strange, meddling, infidel women – I wish it were *their* execution orders I had just signed!'

'Ah yes, father,' said Tewfik in an obvious attempt to mollify the older man, 'but such would be a sad waste of beauty.'

The older man turned and surveyed Lititia and I from head to foot. 'If only they wouldn't speak . . . I desire merely to fuck them.'

Tewfik again glanced my way, his eyes sadly questioning – an unspoken inquiry as to how much Arabic I had understood. I smiled grimly in response. Then, with as much charm as I could muster, I said, 'Perhaps it is time for us to take our leave.'

Without a word, Ismail Pasha rose painfully to his feet. He stood for a moment, then turned on his heel and, like a petulant little boy denied a new toy, strode from the salon.

I arose and turned to Litty to find her reaching under her skirt, fumbling about. Surprised at her action, I was about to suggest that it was neither the time nor place for such things. Before I could speak, she withdrew her hand. I was shocked to see that it clutched a finger-ring sporting a large blood-red ruby!

'Good Lord!' said I.

'Ah, Lady Lititia, I see my father has bestowed a gift upon you.'

'Not *upon* me, dear Tewfik – *inside* me.'

Tewfik Pasha looked pained. 'I must apologise for him,' said he, stumbling on the words as he uttered them.

'No need to,' said Lititia, caressing his cheek. ''Twas indeed a most handsome gesture. Had it been made by a true gentleman, such as yourself, I would have responded.'

'I would have swooned!' said I. 'It must have a great value.'

'Would you like it?' asked Lititia, holding it up to me.

I stared into the deep, red, hypnotic glow. It seemed evil. 'No, I have no need of it, nor have I earned it . . . thank heaven.'

'Well put, dearest Jenny,' said Litty. 'I feel the same way about it.' She deposited the ring in the centre of the large pillow still marked with the concavity of her lovely derrière.

A few minutes later, as we ascended the gangway of the nearby *Maratini*, Tewfik Pasha, a grim undertone defining his voice said, 'I, too, have little liking for my father.'

That evening, I was ill with an headache and stomach cramps. It was a malady that often accompanied my monthly, leaving me dreary and limp. Sadly, I decided it would be best for me to forego the giant banquet and other festivities of the evening. I would rest miserably in my cabin and later, if I could summon the strength, perhaps I might watch the fireworks from the deck. Lititia touchingly insisted on staying on board with me, but I convinced her that such a sacrifice was unnecessary as Haki would attend to all my needs.

Tewfik Pasha was another who expressed concern. I convinced him, however, that my ailment was not serious, merely troublesome and inconvenient. At sunset I heard, through my open porthole, the guests and crew disembark in small groups to board carriages that would transport them to the desert pavilions.

Sometime later, Haki brought my dinner – a bowl of what he described, in colourful Arabic, as being a healing chicken broth, compliments of Monsieur Escoffier. He went on in English to inform me that the *Maratini* was deserted except for a standby watch consisting of three crewmembers. But fear not, he would station himself on the deck, just outside my cabin. If I needed him for anything, he would hear my summons through the open porthole.

The cabin was hot and uncomfortable. I was unable to deal with more than a spoonful of the broth. Perspiring profusely in a rumpled silk dressing gown, my hair a mass of tangled strands, my head thudding, I sprawled fitfully onto the bunk bed.

I awoke in a miserable sweat. I had slept . . . how long? There was someone in the cabin – voices! No . . . not in the cabin . . . the speaking tube! Voices . . .

Groggily, trying to decipher the words, I sat up. The voices were those of Herr and Frau von Seydlitz! The language I now recognized as incomprehensible German. But I had heard them earlier – how much earlier? I had recognized their voices as they disembarked, arranging at dockside to share a carriage with others. Were the festivities now over, the guests returning? Had I slept through it all – even the fireworks? A vague apprehension gripped me. With some difficulty I came to my feet. My head was swimming as I made my way to the porthole. Haki sat in a deck chair just below it, snoozing, with his chin on his chest. I reached out and tapped his head, which brought him immediately awake. I placed a finger to my lips, shushing him. With startled eyes, he looked up at me.

A few moments later, he stood in my open doorway, the disembodied voices eliciting a startled expression on his face. Again I signalled for him to be quiet, pointing to the brass tube above my bed.

I fumbled about in my trunk, searching out my writing portfolio. In a hurried scrawl, on a sheet of scented notepaper, I wrote the words: *What are they talking about?*

With his face a fearful mask, Haki took the portfolio. I watched, my heart beating faster with each letter, as he printed a single word – *murder*.

TWENTY EIGHT

It is said, by some old wives and by many naive younger ones, that a man's sexual prowess has much to do with the size of his accoutrements. This I have found to be nonsense. A clod bearing a ten-inch blunderbuss is still a clod, whereas a gentleman is a gentleman no matter what his size. I would be willing to trade all such 'superlovers' for just one gentleman of wit, charm and caring grace, no matter what his measurements. With the former, one is restricted to but a single, uninspired action while with the latter, creativity and imagination have no bounds. [J.E., 1891]

Young Haki, my writing portfolio in his lap, was seated on the edge of the bunk bed, transcribing German into rapidly scrawled Arabic. For a few minutes it sounded as if the von Seydlitzes were in the throes of a violent argument, with Herr Gunther ascendant. After a few moments of silence, Frau von Seydlitz, her voice tearful, seemed to be pleading, Herr von Seydlitz went on, his voice calm but relentless, placing great emphasis on almost every other word.

Finally, Haki stood, his face ashen. Notepaper in hand, he motioned for me to follow him. Quietly, staying in the shadows, we made our way across the deck to the stern, then down a hatch into the deserted crew quarters. There, in a hoarse whisper sharply edged with anxiety, Haki said, 'They plan to blow up one of the ships.'

'Good God!' My legs suddenly weakened, and I sat on the edge of one of the bunks. 'When? Which ship?'

Haki turned up an oil lamp. Smooth[illegible] notepaper, he read aloud, translating his Arabic [illegible] singsong English. '*. . . we will lay in wait in the da*[illegible] *Then, when I am certain I'll light the fuse and as we r*[illegible] *by, I will hurl the bomb. You have seen me practise. My arm is strong – at ten metres my accuracy is proven. You must row with all your might so that we will be twice that distance when it explodes. The bomb contains lyddite, a new explosive that is the most powerful known to man. The wooden hut will be crushed as if it were match wood. The concussion and iron splinters will do the rest. No one will survive. If any do, I will finish them off in the water with my pistol.*' Haki lowered the paper. 'And then,' he said, his voice cracking, 'Frau von Seydlitz went on about the killing – she said sabotage was one thing, murder another. Herr von Seydlitz told her they had nothing to fear. Many people saw them leave the *Maratini* – the carriage driver himself and others. They were seen at the banquet before they returned here in secret. No one will suspect them.'

'But why?'

Haki leafed through his notes. He read: '*The French are certain to blame the British . . . It will mean war. That will leave a vacuum to be filled by us and the Hapsburgs and our new friends the Turks. The Suez Canal will be open only to those who meet our terms and it will be us who control East Africa and the Indian Ocean. Ismail, that fool, can be manipulated simply by providing him with women. It is, my dear, a carefully thought-out plan with no room for deviation.*'

Haki looked up at me with wide, unblinking eyes. 'What are we to do, my lady?'

I felt close to panic. 'I don't know . . .'

'Do you think it is the *Mahrousa* they plan to sink?'

'No,' said I, fighting to organize my wits. 'They spoke of controlling Ismail after the incident.'

'We must go to the authorities . . .'

ıey are all at the banquet,' said I. 'By the time we got there and found someone, it would be too late.'

'Then what can we do?'

I was silent, breathing deeply, fighting back the panic. I forced my brain to function as Haki stared at me, awaiting an answer.

Measuring my words carefully, I said, 'The bomb is to go off after the festivities when everyone has returned to their ships. But which ship is it to be? There are over seventy! There is hardly enough time to investigate even a tenth of them.' I clamped my eyes shut in an attempt to further clear my brain. 'We know it is not one of those tied to the dock – that includes the *Mahrousa*. It must be a ship that is anchored in the harbour because Herr von Seydlitz spoke of rowing to it.'

Haki stood, his face flushed now. 'Then we must stop the villains before they leave the *Maratini* with their diabolical bomb!'

I grasped Haki's arm. 'Yes . . . our only hope! Quick, we must get help from the men still on board!'

'There are three,' said Haki breathlessly, as we raced back on deck.

A dark figure stood, slumped over the rail at the gangway. As we ran toward him, Haki called out in a hoarse whisper, 'Abdullah!'

There was no response. Abdullah's mouth was twisted in a grimace of abject terror, his eyes locked open, unblinking. The ugly black handle of a knife protruded from his back! Horrified, I stepped back, my feet sliding from under me on the slippery deck. I found myself down, wallowing in a pool of blood!

Haki's swift hand covered my mouth, stilling the scream that welled up in my throat. 'No, Miss Jenny,' he said with a surprising calm. 'They will hear you . . .'

Terrified, I stared up at him. It all happened too quickly. I had been safe in my cabin and now, just minutes later, I was covered in the blood of a dead man!

Surely, it was all a nightmare brought on by my monthly malady!

'Please, Miss Jenny.' Haki hovered over me, whispering. 'The fate of my country – of the world, depends on you – on us. Please!'

I shut my eyes, praying that when I opened them I would be back in my cabin. Seconds later I looked up to find him hovering above me, his eyes pleading with mine. I nodded. 'Twas indeed reality. The hand lifted tentatively, freeing my mouth.

'I'm all right now, Haki,' I croaked. 'Help me to my feet.' I leaned against the rail for a moment, breathing deeply as if I had been running from death.

'Abdullah was my friend,' said Haki quietly. 'Herr von Seydlitz murdered him because he witnessed their return to the *Maratini*. I will avenge him.'

I placed my hand affectionately on his cheek. He was still a boy. But was I, in truth, yet a woman?

At that moment, to the south, a comet arched into the sky. Dazed, my eyes followed it till it burst into a hundred colourful fragments. Fireworks!

'Quickly,' said I, galvanized. We raced to the starboard side. In the dim light of yet another exploding rocket I could make out a single rowboat – the shadow of two oarsmen – moving slowly across the dark water of the harbour. 'It must be them!' said I. 'We must follow; it is the only way.'

'Yes!' said Haki. 'I will try to lower one of the dinghies. Go to the wheel house to get help.'

We raced off in different directions. I clambered up the ladder leading to the wheel house. Inside, two men lay sprawled against the aft bulkhead. A sickeningly sweet stench was present. The low light of a solitary oil lamp cast grotesque shadows. One of the men was drawing on a long pipe.

Breathlessly, I called out, 'We need your help!'

Showing vague curiosity, they turned to me for a

moment, then looked away as if a half-naked woman in a blood-stained kimono was a sight that bored them. I watched impatiently as the man with the pipe allowed his compatriot to take it. Both looked up at the ceiling as if an event of some importance had just occurred there. Their mouths gaped drunkenly. Their eyes seemed glazed over as if fevered. Was this opium, I wondered? I had heard of it but had never seen its effects. Opium or not, there would be no help from these two.

I raced aft to find Haki struggling to lower a small dinghy off the stern. A quick search of the bay revealed a dim, flickering image of the small rowboat, now about halfway across the harbour. It seemed headed toward a group of four ships anchored there. I turned my attention to the matter at hand. In the light of the distant fireworks, we managed somehow to get the dinghy into the water.

We had progressed less than fifty feet from the *Maratini* when, with a blinding suddenness, the southern sky exploded into shattering brilliance! I squinted painfully, aghast at a rising, multicoloured fireball that seemed brighter than a dozen suns! Seconds later my startled senses were struck by a muted roar, much like a distant thunderclap.

Haki, his face glowing from the light of the inferno, shouted. 'The fireworks! They've exploded!'

'Von Seydlitz!' said I.

'Perhaps,' said Haki. 'They spoke of sabotage. Something . . .'

It took a full minute for the pyrotechnic calamity to die, leaving a red glow. Haki resumed rowing.

Had it been just an accident, or had the explosion been an act committed by the villain von Seydlitz? But why? Perhaps, thought I, a madman needs no logical rationale for his actions. Destruction and murder for its own sake is surely sufficient!

The light in the sky behind us dimmed, leaving only blackness ahead of us. The four tiny lights of the ships were our only beacons. I stared at them for what must have been twenty minutes as, slowly, they grew from starlike points into glowing spots.

Aware that sound travels easily across water, I spoke softly, 'We must be almost halfway.'

'Good,' said Haki. 'But have you any idea what we are to do when we get there?'

'One of the four ships must be the one von Seydlitz intends to blow up. We must circle about quietly till we find him.'

'And then, Miss Everleigh?'

I had no idea how to answer. I was inexperienced in matters of this sort. Would the dark and forbidding harbour prove to be my watery grave before this night was out? Whispering now, I said, 'We'll know what to do when the time comes.'

'They must not see us before we see them,' said Haki. 'I think it best if we circle around behind the ships.'

I nodded and muttered something about it being the most prudent course. I screwed up my courage, and as navigator, directed the rearward-facing Haki to bear to the right.

We rowed on across the dark, placid water, the only sounds being the rhythmic squeak of our oarlocks and the vague, barely audible gurgles and splashes all about us. One of the lights seemed to pass around to our left, an illusion created by our own movement. We turned and glided softly toward it. Soon a dark hulk blotted out the dim glow of the town.

Haki shipped his oars as we passed under the stern. He was about to speak, but I shushed him. There were barely discernible voices, which seemed to drift across the water from no particular direction. The dinghy, seeking its own course, passed under the stern. As it did so, the voices grew loud enough to hear without straining one's senses.

Haki whispered, 'There . . . to our right.'

'Slowly,' said I, straining my eyes.

We moved cautiously toward the voices, which seemed to come from the direction of yet another anchored ship marked with a single light. As we did so a new sound made itself known: the distant chugging of an engine. Both Haki and I glanced toward the shoreline to see a tiny, bright pinpoint detach itself from the quay.

Haki whispered, ''Tis a steam launch, one of the lighters returning people to the ships.'

Our dinghy glided silently over the black water, steering unerringly toward the voices. They grew clearer – German words!

Then, quite suddenly, all was silent. Had they heard us? I sat stiffly in the bow seat, chilled, as an icy wind of fear caressed my body. Haki propelled us slowly but inevitably forward.

Moments later, the dark mass of a second ship loomed over us. Releasing the oars, Haki guided the dinghy along the side of the hull. As we approached the bow, our vociferous prey resumed their conversation. They were much louder now. Nearby! There was no mistaking the hushed, though arrogant tones of Herr von Seydlitz, the subdued, nervous chatter of his wife.

The steam launch was closer, its engines louder, its running lights circles of yellow reflecting in the dark waters. I noted three more lighters leaving the shore: more guests returning to their ships from the festivities. I wondered if any of them had been casualties of the fireworks explosion.

But now was not the time for such conjecture. We sat close to the hull. Should our enemy happen to glance in our direction we would be one with its shadowy mass.

Once again they ceased talking. We strained our eyes, our ears, hunting the blackness for them. Then, suddenly, other voices shattered the dark silence! Startled, we froze in place. It was moments before we realized that the voices came from overhead. 'Twas, I realized with relief, crew members, speaking French on the deck just above us.

Like a burst of heavenly light, the villainous plot was clear to me! *French*! The target of von Seydlitz's heinous plot could be none other than the Empress Eugénie! The ship we huddled against must be the French Imperial yacht *Aigle*. But, thought I, von Seydlitz's target 'twas not the ship itself. 'Twas instead the sleek steam launch returning even now with its royal party!

With no warning, there was suddenly light where an instant before there had been blackness! The crew, I realized, was lighting the oil lamps on deck. Haki gasped softly. And no wonder! There, less than fifty feet from us, was the rowboat we had been searching for! Gunther von Seydlitz sat at the oars; Frau von Seydlitz was just coming to her feet, her arm thrown across her eyes!

As we watched, Herr von Seydlitz quickly guided his boat into the shadow of the *Aigle*'s hull to escape detection from the deck. Haki, with equal speed, pulled us around to the blind side of the bow. As he did so, I considered raising the hue and cry, warning the crew above us to take action. I discarded the thought immediately. 'Twould be a confused and dangerous undertaking in the little time remaining. Von Seydlitz possessed both pistol and bomb. He would use either or both with no compunction!

Quickly, I got to my feet to scramble into the front of our dinghy. From the sound of its engine, the steam launch was almost upon us. I whispered my plan to Haki. With great care we moved our little boat forward till I could just manage to see around the *Aigle*'s prow.

The crew had lowered the boarding ladder. Von Seydlitz, still unaware of our presence, bobbed gently in the shadows, just thirty feet from us. The steam launch was less than a hundred yards off the *Aigle*'s bow and moving closer by the second.

We waited. Despite a pounding heart, I felt surprisingly calm, ready – indeed eager – to do battle! Finally, the launch, now well within the circle of light from the Imperial yacht, slowed to come about onto the boarding ramp. Von Seydlitz attacked! With Frau von Seydlitz at the oars, they shot out from the shadow of the *Aigle* like a racing scull with a bone in its teeth!

At that instant, I called out to Haki and we, too, launched ourselves into the fray. In seconds we were half the distance and bearing at right angles to the launch. The von Seydlitz boat was directly in its path. At the last second, both the launch and the rowboat swerved to avoid a collision. Herr von Seydlitz stood in the bow, his legs spread for balance. In his right hand was a menacing black ball the size of a melon. I could make out a short fuse throwing sparks as we closed the distance!

Von Seydlitz was less than twenty feet from the sleek hull of the launch. With the bomb clutched in his evil hand, he cocked his arm. For just an instant, I was sure we were too late. Then, suddenly, we were upon him! With a sickening impact, our brave little dinghy struck the larger rowboat amidships! In the sudden confusion, von Seydlitz turned his head. His startled eyes locked on mine as he lurched to his knees, screaming obscenities in German. I shot forward, propelled by the impact. I was aware of my head striking his shoulder, then something much harder, and suddenly the world was dark again.

TWENTY NINE

Cunnilingus, when executed with dedication, passion and expertise, is capable of producing the most subtle of sensations, more so than any other erotic activity. (Note that I use the word 'subtle,' not the word 'intense.') Certainly, no other pleasurable pursuit can bring to bear a more varied spectrum of nuance. All of this is transmitted via the buttocks into the sensitive palms and fingertips of a knowledgeable and creative artist. It is a most sensuous communication, enabling one to play his or her love partner like a violin – allegro, largo, adagio – to create a concerto of amourous sensations. [J.E., 1919]

'Where am I?'

I had awakened under the gaze of a beautiful woman. She smiled at me and spoke with a lovely, lilting French accent, reminiscent of dear Madame Kooshay's.

'Ah, Miss Everleigh, you are with us, finally.'

I stared up at her dumbly. My mind was a vacuum, absorbing images and recollections faster than I could deal with them.

'You are safe aboard the *Aigle*. I am Eugénie – Empress Eugénie.'

'Oh . . . I'm sorry, Your Majesty . . . I must have . . .'

'Please. Just lie back and rest. You are amongst friends and everything is all right now, dear Miss Everleigh.'

I attempted to sit up. She placed a firm hand on my shoulder, and then quite suddenly it all came back: our dinghy smashing into von Seydlitz's boat . . . the bomb . . . I heard myself say, 'Haki . . .?'

'Ah, the young Arab,' said the empress. 'He fares well. His wound should heal quickly.' She sat on the edge of the bed.

'Wound?' I felt a growing panic. 'Where? How bad? I must see him!'

'In due time.' She ran a tender hand across my cheek in an effort to calm me. 'He is not hurt badly. A bomb fragment struck his . . . his . . . that part of him that enters a room last.'

'His bottom?'

'Precisely, Miss Everleigh. But fear not. The ship's physician has treated his wound. It is slight, but nonetheless a hero's wound. Haki will be left with little more than a small scar on the left cheek. He is in good spirits and is concerned about you. A most devoted servant.'

His beautiful left cheek, I thought, scarred for life. But, thank God, he was alive and except for that, undamaged. (And he could always turn the other.) I breathed easier. Surely, she was telling the truth. An empress of France would not lie. Then, still dazed, I realized belatedly that she had spoke of a bomb fragment. I said, 'The bomb – it went off?'

'Yes. We saw it all from the launch. You knocked it from that villain's hand. It fell to the bottom of his boat just as you and the young Arab went overboard. You were fortunate to be under the water when it exploded.' She took my hand. 'Haki, too, was underwater – well, at least most of him was. That's what saved your lives. The two evil Prussians – they must have been mad – were killed outright. 'Twas indeed a horrid sight. Both they and their boat were reduced to shards. You and Haki were pulled out of the water in the nick of time; both of you were unconscious and near drowning. You suffered a blow on the head, but it has ended well. 'Twas very confusing till your Haki regained consciousness and explained it. Amazing! Such courage is rare indeed.' She smiled prettily, revealing perfect, pearl-white teeth. 'You are both heroes of France. You saved my life and perhaps a dozen others and you have forestalled an otherwise inevitable crisis, perhaps even a war! You are both heroes of France and shall be rewarded.' She squeezed my hand.

'Thank you,' said I quietly. 'Could you please inform Tewfik Pasha aboard the *Mahrousa* that Haki and I are safe and well?'

'We have already done so. But now you must sleep. When you awaken, we will be leading the flotilla into the canal.'

'Oh please, Your Majesty, don't let me sleep through that . . .'

'Have no fear. If it hadn't been for you and young Haki, we would not be alive to participate in this historic event. You, not I, are the guest of honour.'

Empress Eugénie took her leave. The memory of all that had occurred within the past few hours seemed a mad dream. I felt a delicious calm that bordered on euphoria. Within seconds a deep and well-deserved sleep overcame me.

The following morning, seated next to the empress in the bow of the *Aigle*, we entered the Suez Canal, the first vessel to do so officially. With Haki, aided by a cane, on one side of the empress and I on the other, we took the salute from the gorgeously uniformed troops standing under a hundred flags, while a military band of three hundred pieces played the *Marseillaise*. Moving slowly down the narrow channel, I thrilled as civilians and soldiers on both banks cheered us wildly! They called out my name and Haki's; we responded by standing and waving to the crowd. It was all quite breathtaking!

As we proceeded, I marvelled at the magical fête – nay – the incredible genius and labour that must have been expended on such an undertaking. Straight as an arrow, the canal cut its way through forbidding desert: Africa on one side, Asia on the other. It was a new, man-made addition to the geography of our globe, a line of blue between the Mediterranean and the Red Sea that would appear on all the world maps printed from now till the end of time! And I, Jenny Everleigh, only slightly more than a year removed from her father's smithy in Liverpool, was amongst the first few to voyage on its portentous waters!

That evening, at anchor in Ismailia, Haki and I were reunited with our companions aboard the *Maratini*. There were a million questions that I somehow managed to answer with the help of three or four or perhaps five ice-cold maratinis. My last memory of the day was being tucked into bed by my dear friend Litty. It was like being home.

On noon of the following day, a French military contingent came aboard the *Maratini* to escort all of us to the *Aigle*. I was under the impression that the Empress Eugénie, to show her gratitude, was giving us luncheon. The surprise that awaited me was probably the greatest I will ever experience!

As we boarded, Haki and I were separated from the others. There seemed to be some confusion and by the time everyone was sorted out, I found myself on the afterdeck, standing before the empress. She was wearing her crown and seemed very serious. Next to her stood an elderly French naval officer weighted down gloriously with a chest full of decorations. Seated behind them in four or five rows of chairs was a large group including my friends from the *Maratini*. Then, lo and behold, one of the gentlemen in the front row caught my eye. Dressed in a British naval uniform, he was moustached and handsome. As my dazed eyes locked with his, a wide smile lit his face. Then, suddenly, my confused brain accepted the evidence of my eyes!

'Edward!'

The Prince of Wales stood, removed his hat and bowed. The empress pinned me with a stern glance, as if somehow I had blasphemed a solemn occasion. I glanced down at my toes and wondered what it was all in aid of.

Empress Eugénie, referring from time to time to a rather ornate document, spoke interminably in French. As she went on, all eyes focused on me. I fidgeted nervously, wishing I were somewhere else, or was at least as knowledgeable as to the meaning of the mysterious event as were the spectators. After less than a minute, she concluded, lowering the paper; with her eyes on mine she spoke the English words that were obviously a brief résumé of the French.

'Miss Everleigh, you have by your extraordinary courage brought immense credit to yourself, your country and your sex. The empire of France salutes you!' She paused and turned to the admiral, who held an open case. It was book-sized and lined with purple silk. The empress withdrew a beautiful medallion, dangling from a long tricoloured ribbon. My heart skipped a beat, as she raised it up to eye level, saying, 'In the name of the empire of France and its emperor, Napoleon the Third, I confer upon you knighthood in the Legion of Honour.'

With that, the Empress Eugénie placed the ribbon around my neck, stepped back and kissed me first on one cheek, then on the other. The strange ceremony was repeated by the admiral.

There were shouts of 'Viva Jenny!' 'Viva la France!' Then as the band struck up the *Marseillaise* . . . I fainted!

Once again we were congregated under the awning on the afterdeck of the *Maratini*. Both Haki and I, formally dressed, wore our new decorations. We had all just returned from a huge banquet in Ismailia. This time the fireworks had refrained from exploding.

As I proceeded to mix maratinis for all, Haki, leaning on his cane, bowed politely, saying, 'Good night, Miss Jenny, ladies, gentlemen.'

'Haki,' said I. 'Please stay . . .'

'I have my duties.'

'You have no more duties, Haki,' said Tewfik Pasha, placing his arm about the young man's shoulders. 'It is inconceivable that a mere cabin boy would wear the decoration of the Legion of Honour. Therefore you are no longer a cabin boy.'

Haki seemed thunderstruck. 'I'm to be discharged?'

Tewfik Pasha grinned widely. 'No, Haki, your status has been raised from cabin boy to that of distinguished and honoured guest aboard the *Maratini*!' He turned to me. 'And you, too, my dear Jenny, have yet another exciting surprise awaiting you. My father has chosen to confer the highest decoration Egypt can bestow: the Order of the Golden Crescent! The ceremony is to take place in Cairo three days hence. How say you to that?'

'I'm flattered, Tewfik Pasha, and most grateful.' I smiled at him, then at Haki. 'I know I speak for Haki when I say we will both endeavour to live up to . . .'

'I'm afraid, Jenny, that this particular ceremony will not include our young friend. The khedive – my father – intends that only you shall receive the award.'

'Why is that?' I asked. 'Since Haki and I shared equally in the endeavour, do we not qualify equally for its rewards?'

'I'm sorry. 'Tis my father's wish.'

'Then I refuse to accept it!'

'Good girl!' said Major Sedgewick. 'That'll show the old reprobate what Britons are made of!'

'Jolly good show!' said Dr Freemantle.

'Stick to your guns, Jenny, old girl!' said Sarah Sedgewick.

There was a general hubbub of approval, then Haki, his hand on my arm, said, 'Ah, Miss Jenny, please change your mind and accept it. I appreciate such a noble gesture, but I have already been honoured beyond my wildest dreams.'

'As have I.'

'I am just a boy of lowly birth. If nothing more occurs in my life, this will be enough.'

'I, too, am of lowly birth,' said I. 'The khedive's attitude is an insult to both of us!'

'Perhaps, Jenny, I might help matters a bit,' said Tewfik Pasha. 'I have decided to send Haki to England to be educated. In the light of that, will you change your mind?'

I looked into his eyes long and hard. 'Does one thing depend on the other?'

'Of course not!' said he with some indignance.

'Then I thank you, dear Tewfik, but still refuse the Golden Crescent unless it be also awarded to Haki.'

Tewfik Pasha stepped forward and placed both arms about me. 'Your attitude impresses me immensely, Miss Everleigh. I was only the messenger carrying this news, not its perpetrator.' He looked deeply into my eyes. 'Ah, Jenny, you are a most noble woman! When I am khedive, and it may be soon, the Order of the Golden Crescent will be awarded to both of you. But for now, I want to state before those present that I respect you beyond all others. I have fallen in love with you!'

His words thrilled me. I whispered, 'And I, too, dearest Tewfik.'

I melted in his embrace. 'Twas wonderful to be in love! It suffused my body with a delicious warmth – a piquant sense of wanting and being wanted. And now, thought I, my mind afloat on a giddy white cloud, there were two men I loved. No woman could ask for more. I gazed into Tewfik's beautiful dark eyes and for just an instant his face was Reggie's. We bestowed upon each other a tender kiss as the congregation toasted us.

The second toast was to Haki, the third to the queen, the fourth to the *Maratini*. The fifth was to France, but remained unconsummated, as by that time we were, all of us, naked, divested as usual by the lovely harem girls.

Once again, to the heady strains of Strauss, I was dancing with my beloved Tewfik, his lovely, stiffened pego tucked between my thighs. We twirled about gaily, blind to all that was going on about us. A tide of tender passion engulfed me, and before the 'Merry Widow' reached its climax, I had reached two.

I glanced about. Captain DiCosta was on his back. My dearest Lititia sat astride, a rapturous jockey riding an unbroken steed. Her white body glowed golden in the dim light of Japanese lanterns as she rose and fell, impaling herself on the captain's mighty organ. Her buttocks slapped against DiCosta's thighs, her breasts, heavenly melons, heaved with lascivious exertions.

She caught my eye, communicating a rapture so intense that at once I felt I were riding with her! Surely, it was my *cush* playing hostess to the DiCosta's surging *zubrik*, my breasts that even now were being caressed, the nipples pinched between his powerful fingers!

Mesmerized, I freed myself from Tewfik's embrace. In three short steps, I was with her, my lips open to hers. With a fluttering tongue, she caressed mine. I reached down and ran my fingers up the length of the deep crevice between her plump, plunging buttocks.

'Jenny,' she moaned into my mouth. 'I love cock!'

'Hard cock!' said I.

'Fat cock!' said she.

'Fucking cock!' said I.

Beneath her, our captain drove upward to meet her downward plunge, driving his stout prick even deeper into her – to the hilt. She gasped as my finger, growing bolder, encircled the secret rosebud nestled deep between her cheeks. I caressed her breast and buried my face in her neck.

'Ah, your finger,' she moaned. 'Put it in me!'

With great delicacy I palmed her buttock, worming my way in to the first knuckle. I moved it about slowly.

'Oh, Jenny, your sweet finger,' said Litty breathlessly. She rotated her derrière even as it drove up and down, counter to DiCosta's energetic thrustings. 'Fuck . . . cunt . . . arsehole! Aren't we lewd!'

We were indeed – all of us – lewd. At one point I glanced to my left to see Mademoiselle Gisselle on her back, panting heavily. She was doubled over, her shapely legs about Haki's neck as he fucked her with slow but determined strokes. I felt a sudden pride in my handsome young protégé and reached out to caress his one good, unbandaged buttock.

There followed an orgy even more extensive than those that had proceeded it. The deck of the Good Ship *Maratini* resounded for hours with the liquid sounds of joy, punctuated by the rhythmic slapping of flesh on flesh – moans, groans, whimpers, squeals. Soon, the slightest touch was enough to transport me into shattering orgasm. I lost count! I was cunt! All of me! In just a few hours, as The Good Ship *Maratini* floated serenely on the moonlit waters of the Mediterranean, I fucked each of the men, at least once – eight or nine doses of luscious spunk combining in my seething pussy.

All about me others were doing likewise. Sarah Sedgewick gushed to Lilly Roundtree's educated tonguing; Freddy deposited his seed into Dr Freemantle's bum; Major Sedgewick spasmed into Lilly Roundtree; our good captain shot into Sarah Sedgewick's talented quim; Haki spent into an orgasm-racked Mademoiselle Fondeaux.

We rested, drank ice-cold maratinis and spoke of *cabbages and kings*. Then, insatiable, we were at it again. In every possible combination, the games continued, till dawn.

Finally, as the hot sun climbed the desert sky, we retired, happily exhausted, each to his own bed. Our last night aboard the *Maratini* had been the most exciting and fulfilling of all. I slept for eleven hours, waking to the sounds of a busy metropolis. From my porthole, Cairo gleamed in the warm light of a setting sun.

I mused on my life since boarding the train in Liverpool just over a year ago. How young I had been; how naive, innocent and tender! A century had passed since then. The poor, ignorant daughter of a smithy was now a sophisticated woman of the world. What would the next year bring for Jenny Everleigh?

I turned to find a note had been passed under my door. The envelope bore the crest of the House of Windsor. It was an invitation from the Prince of Wales – Edward – for a late tête-à-tête supper. Perhaps, I thought, smiling to myself, this was the start of the next year.